Unkempt

Unkempt

COURTNEY ELDRIDGE

Harcourt, Inc.

Orlando Austin New York San Diego Toronto London

Requests for permission to make copies of any part of
the work should be mailed to the following address:
Permissions Department, Harcourt, Inc.,
6277 Sea Harbor Drive, Orlando, Florida 32887-6777.

www.HarcourtBooks.com

"Majoring in Business Administration, with Graduate
Studies in the Theory and Practice of Booty Shaking"
reprinted by permission of Marshall Sella.

Library of Congress Cataloging-in-Publication Data
Eldridge, Courtney.
Unkempt/Courtney Eldridge.
p.   cm.
ISBN 0-15-101084-6
1. Psychological fiction, American.   I. Title.
PS3605.L37U55 2004
813'.6—dc22   2003023234

Text set in Garamond MT
Designed by Cathy Riggs

Printed in the United States of America

First edition
K J I H G F E D C B A

Contents

Acknowledgments

The following people have fed, clothed, housed, and loaned me large sums of money, little of which I have yet repaid. In short, their support, encouragement, generosity, and guidance made this book possible. Heartfelt thanks to: my parents, Mitch and Cathy Uttech, for believing in me all these years; my husband, Dan Lerner, for being crazy and/or stupid enough to marry a struggling writer—the jury's still out on that one; my mother-in-law, Dallia Penn Lerner; the Lerner family; my best friends—sisters, really—Vanessa and Piper Nilsson; the brilliant and talented pair known as Amy Goldwasser and Peter Arkle; Keyin Choi; Enid Nilsson; Rebecca Bauer; Deanne Koehn; Jill Stoddard; Bentley A. Wood; Laura ("Lovely") Wehrman; Drew Souza; Roger Hirsch and Brenna Schlitt; Catharine Dill; A.T. Timpson; Dan Ferrara; Fiona Maazel; Dave Eggers; David Ryan; Maile Chapman; Julia Slavin; Frederick Barthelme; Tim Hohmann; Susan Swenson; my agent, Nat Sobel, who has the patience of a saint—and don't we know it!;

the fabulous Jenni Lapidus; and everyone at SobelWeber Associates. To André Bernard, Julie Marshall, David Hough, Erin DeWitt, Amanda Erickson, and everyone at Harcourt who I don't have the space to name, I'm damn lucky to have you all behind me and I know it. Last, but certainly not least, special thanks to Rick Moody for his faith.

"Fits & Starts" appeared in *McSweeney's #5,* © 2000; "Young Professionals" appeared in *McSweeney's #1,* © 1998; "Becky" appeared in *Post Road,* © 2001; "Summer of Mopeds" appeared in *The Mississippi Review,* © 2002; "Thieves" appeared in *Salt Hill Journal,* © 2001; "Sharks" appeared in *The Mississippi Review,* © 2001; "The Former World Record Holder Settles Down" appeared in *McSweeney's #8,* © 2002.

Unkempt

Fits & Starts

What happens is I write a first sentence, then I read the sentence that I've just written, and then I immediately erase that sentence; then I begin anew by writing another first sentence for a completely different story; then another first sentence for another story, so on and so forth. Though I might not immediately write, read, and erase: a week or two or more might pass before the sentence (paragraph, page, or twenty pages) begins to bother me. At first, I usually think the sentence is fine, good even. And at those times, feeling okay about the sentence, I read and reread, as I continue working on the story, moving forward, making progress. Then, occasionally, I'll feel good about what I'm writing. I'll actually feel excited and hopeful, and life seems good. But of course it never lasts.

Because eventually, somewhere along the line, I begin to hear something tinny or false or vaguely suspect, a perception that builds and builds, and I soon find an irreparable flaw in the sentence. Either the language and/or the thought, the very premise of the story, and all of a sudden I think, What a stupid idea for a story that is! What the hell was I thinking? And soon enough the sentence, language, story, and premise, the whole damn thing bothers me, all of it, everything. Soon I can't stand the first sentence, and it suddenly appears the worst sentence I've ever read and/or the stupidest idea I've ever heard, and it might take a few minutes or a month, but inevitably I start over. The only variation on this theme is the half-finished story, which I usually forsake or abandon, until which time I can erase the entire file without giving it a second thought.

So instead of offering a complete work, because I don't see that happening anytime soon, I thought I might offer a working list of stories that I have recently or not so recently quit, abandoned, or forsaken, complete with short summaries of each failed effort, in order to give some idea of why they've been sent down. Besides, I like listing. It cheers me up. Listing gives me a sense of purpose and completion, you know. I don't have to feel alone: because I have a list! And I need never feel a sense of failure, checking off an item on any given list. Of course this particular list of failed stories will serve only as a sample of what I might've offered, had I finished any of these particular stories, and is no way intended to reflect the vast killing fields of my hard drive.

Most recently, as of this last month or two, I quit working on a story that's currently untitled. There are two reasons why this story doesn't have a working title; the first reason being that I rejected the first working title, "Animals Are Our Friends," and the second reason being that the second working title, though much improved, "The Second Coming of Ethel Merman," was likewise rejected. In any case, that story begins:

> *My daughter bats headless chickens out of the trees with an old broom.*

There's more to it than that sentence, like eight or nine pages more, but due to nagging syntactical doubts with the first sentence, I've put that story on the back burner for the time being. Long ago I bought into the idea that no one will read beyond a first sentence, so I put a lot of pressure on the perfect first sentence.

I used to finish more stories, or some at least, though not very good stories, and some were just lousy, and others were painfully bad, bad stories, really. But still, I finished them at least. Unfortunately, sometime shortly after I submitted my first story, I heard that you only get a paragraph. I heard that when you submit a story, any given reader at any given quarterly or little magazine or wherever will read the first paragraph of your story and then decide if it's worth continuing, or pitch the story in the reject pile then and there. Then, when the first story I submitted was rejected, rightly, I'm sure, I started thinking more about my first paragraphs. Then I heard somewhere that you don't get a paragraph, no, you only get a first sentence, and that's when I started fretting about my first sentences. Then, just to make matters worse, a friend told me not even, you don't even get an entire sentence, no: you only get five words. That's right: *five words.* My friend insisted the first five words were make-or-break. And I believed him. It seemed plausible, what with everything you read about our short attention spans these days.

So ever since then, for a good three, four years now, whenever I'm at a bookstore, I can't help but open book after book, and I read the first sentence, counting along, tapping the first five words on the fingers of my right hand. What's more, it's a hard habit to shake, and I don't get much reading done that way, and it's annoying, really. So I was talking to my friend recently, and he asked what I was reading, and I said not much, and I mentioned this behavior to him, and he apologized, because he had no recollection of saying that to me, what he said about the first five words. He gave it some thought, and he said he stands by what he said, somewhat, the first five words are important, yes, but he simply can't remember saying that to me. Well, anyway.

My daughter bats headless chickens out of the trees with an old broom—I can't say what, but something is just not right. Though I really don't know why I should start worrying about syntax now, I never have before, but still. And I wouldn't say I've abandoned this story just yet, I'd prefer to say its fate is undecided. Besides which, I'm extremely, extremely superstitious when it comes to my writing. I honestly believe that I'm really asking for trouble, talking about a story, even mentioning a story before it's finished, so as a rule, I never talk about my stories with anyone; and the closer the acquaintance, the more liable I am to failure. But anyone at all, really. Like when I meet people and they politely ask what I do, and I try to spit out something about writing, and if they should then ask about my writing, I just tell them, I'm sorry, I can't really talk about it, and we both seem relieved. Anyway, that's the second reason why I can't talk about this story or call it by a proper title, really, as I'm not ready to give up on it yet. Because every time I have ever discussed a story before it's finished, I've abandoned the story. Forget I mentioned it.

Coincidentally, the next story on my list also has a chicken theme, and it, too, falls into the category of unfinished-but-not-yet-completely-abandoned stories. It's a work in progress, a piece of nonfiction that I've simply called "Pinkie," for the lack of a proper title, and hoping to dodge the jinx, and so as not to confuse it with any other, for the past year or two. And, as of today, the story of Pinkie still begins:

Honestly, there was no Pinkie, and Pinkie was certainly not my grandfather, though there was a doll called "Pinky" and a man called "Winky." And the true story of Joe "Winky" Edmonds is this: As a child, no more than five or six, Joe Edmonds and his older brother were playing in the yard during the time of slaughter, when the boys noticed the ax left lodged in the tree stump. So the elder brother dared the younger brother to a game of chicken, to place his left hand on the butchering block, and the younger brother accepted the dare. Not to be bested by his younger brother, the elder dared the younger to spread his fingers wide apart, and the younger accepted the dare. All right, then, I'm going to give you to the count of three, and then I'm going to swing, the elder said, focusing his aim. He thought, of course, the younger would flinch as soon as he moved the ax, so the elder brother said, One . . . ? The younger didn't move his finger. Then he said, Two . . . ? But still the younger didn't move a muscle. Finally, the elder brother said, This is your last warning: Are you going to move your hand or not? And his little brother just looked him in the eye. All right, then, Three...? he called, before he swung the ax, severing his little brother's last digit to the palm. As for Winky, Joe got the nickname by winking his maimed hand hello and good-bye. No, though I once claimed Winky, or rather Pinky, to be my grandfather, he was not. Winky was my grandfather's lifelong best friend, and close to blood, but not really.

I haven't got a handle or even an angle, so the story trails off after this. What's more, what I've just shared happens to be the truth, so part of the problem is that there isn't exactly any fiction to the story, just yet. I have no idea where it might lead, once I begin to twist it into some form of fiction, but I think it's pretty flexible, and it could go in any direction.

A year or two ago, I told this very anecdote to a new acquaintance, who then, a few nights later—the very next night, in fact—accused me of threatening to castrate him. Before I could even tell him the truth, that Winky was not my grandfather, nor was Pinky. Pinky was a Madame Alexander doll I named in honor of Winky Edmonds, because she was suitably dressed in a pink chiffon gown with a pale pink bonnet and her precious little fingers were curled, such that the last fingers couldn't be seen...Well, before I could explain myself or the truth, my acquaintance accused me of threatening to castrate him. This gave me pause. I didn't know where to begin. I'm sorry, *when* did I threaten to castrate you? I asked, assuming he must be joking. The story of Pinky was obviously a threat to castrate me, he claimed, in utter seriousness, taking another bite of his cone.

Here's what I want to know: Why in the world would this man ask me out for a drink (and later ice cream) if he honestly—*honestly*—believed I was threatening to castrate him? Really, what would possess him? Something definitely doesn't sound right. And I'm not asking you to believe me, and I know I can be pretty roundabout, but still, if I were going to threaten to castrate a man, why wouldn't I just come out and say so? I tried to figure it out, I mean from his point of view—maybe he was thinking that I was insinuating that I was like the older brother and he was the younger brother? But even if that were the case, how did we get from his finger to his balls? I just don't see it. But still, part of the reason I backed off from writing about Pinky or Winky or trying to write anything related was the fear of how many male readers might also misunderstand and incorrectly assume I was threatening to castrate them as well. Still, I swear, if I were even going to try and fictionalize my threat, I'd just put my cards on the table:

> *Much to my surprise, John invited me out for a drink the day after I threatened to castrate him.*

For the record, John is not the man's real name. And of course I still deny threatening him, so. The only question that remains is, could there be a story in what I see to be the obvious answer to this guy's conclusion? I mean, that could be a pretty interesting story, some guy who invites a woman out for beer and Häagen-Dazs after she's threatened to castrate him. Don't you think? And I'd especially enjoy reading the story if someone else would write it for me. Really, comedy or horror, Southern Gothic, Western, or on the road, it could just be so fucked up and excellent, I think. I'm dying to know what's going on with him and his mother. What's that all about? Well, if someone wants to borrow the idea, by all means, be my guest. If you want, you can even borrow the first working title I rejected, which I was also considering rejecting as the first sentence of the story, before I abandoned the whole idea:

"Do you think it's because they don't get enough light over there, the English?"

But you know what, I'm not in favor of opening with dialogue. I don't know where this bias came from. Well, actually, I know perfectly well—no idea why I fibbed about that, either—it's no great secret that this dialogue bias came from some interview I read somewhere during an especially nonproductive period; an interview with some writer who said he hates stories that begin with dialogue. And I guess I thought, Oh god, I better not begin with dialogue, or there will be another person in the world who'll hate my story just as much as I do, from the very start. It was one of the Harrys who said that, either Harry Mathews or Harry Crews, and I used to confuse the two, but now I simply don't remember which. But to this day, I still don't open with dialogue, and I still get hung up on first sentences. Of course I realize I place far too much importance on writing a great first sentence, but since I write so many of them, the odds must be in my favor.

Well, as for the other nonfiction possibility, the tentatively working titled "The Red Hot Variations," which began, or rather, which would prove a painfully honest essay on the subject of cheerleading:

Of course there are some things that I choose to forget. In particular: cheerleading. Because I could never truly forget that I was once a cheerleader, I simply chose not to remember the fact. And in less than five years after the fact, I remembered having been a cheerleader so infrequently, it was as though I had completely forgotten; and less than ten years later, it was as though I'd forgotten cheerleading for so long that it had simply never happened to me. (In fact, I forgot so successfully that I only just remembered that I was not once a cheerleader, but twice actually: seventh and eighth grade; wrestling and basketball, respectively.) Regardless, for the past several years, I could hear or read mention of cheerleading, literally or figuratively, without any recollection, without any personal recollection of having once been a cheerleader myself. I could watch professional, collegiate, and high school cheerleaders, live or televised, with interest, curiosity, and bemusement.

For example, a few months ago (a year ago now), when an article in Women Outside *about the Collegiate Cheerleading Championship happened to catch my eye, I began to read the article, genuinely interested to know what compelled these young women to cheer. Coincidentally, my boyfriend D. was friends with the writer, and as he walked by, he noticed the article and remembered having heard mention of the assignment. How is it? he asked, glancing over my shoulder, seeming equally interested and enthusiastic.*

Well, I think Marshall's perfectly intelligent and, frankly, I expected more of him, I said, shrugging, then reading aloud:

Daytona Beach is a killing field—so smiles, people, smiles! Christie Neal, a University of Louisville co-captain, looks over at one of the hulking guys on her squad. She knows instinctively that he needs a word of support, for she has the experience. At twenty-two, she has been on two championship teams already, as many as any cheerleader ever. She is blond and ninety-six pounds. Her waist, from the looks of it, is seven epidermal layers thicker than a spinal column. She locks eyes with the boy, gauging the type of motivation he requires at this instant. A flurry of ideas and emotions races through her mind until a well-earned wisdom settles across her features. She leans forward; her shoulders recoil and the corners of her mouth begin to burst apart. "Get jiggy with it!" she shrieks instructively. *"Get jiiigggyyy with iiiiiittttt!"*

For she has the experience, I enunciated, nodding my head: A flurry of ideas and emotions races through her mind until a well-earned wisdom settles...Get jiggy with it. *Huh...Is—is that... sarcasm? I mocked, tapping my index finger against my lips, before losing all interest and tossing the publication across the table. You know, I don't think there's anything* wrong *with a little insight, once in a while, I concluded, sitting down beside D. on the couch, as he looked at me curiously for a moment, and then gave my shoulder a supportive squeeze. No further comment; the article was immediately forgotten. And to this day, my boyfriend still doesn't know the truth about my past. (Now he does, I had to tell him.) But now that I remember, and in all fairness to the writer, I should also admit that I've been asked, hypothetically, were I to have a daughter one day, what would be the most frightening, the most horrific idea of a daughter I could possibly imagine? To which I have answered, without hesitation: A cheerleader—that would be my worst nightmare, hands down.*

Part of the problem with writing this cheerleading thing was that I knew, as soon as I wrote even this much, I knew that it was really about cowboys; cheerleading was just the segue, because naturally I can't talk about one without discussing the other. Just forget that, too, the cowboy idea. See what I mean, though, I hexed myself with an actual title *and* discussion. Well, anyway, even though I didn't write enough to get to this part, the long and short of it is that last I heard, Ty Larsen, the one who used to hang his girlfriends from their Wrangler jeans pant loops from the top ledge of our school lockers, eight feet off the ground, he was still in prison for wife battery, out west, and that's why he was not able to attend the high school reunion.

I was talking to my friend B. one night. We went to high school together, and though B. was a year younger, I think he was the one who told me what had become of Ty Larsen. We had bought some beer and ordered a pizza and rented a video that night. While we were eating, I was telling B. that I had received an invitation to my ten-year reunion, and the invitation promised horseshoeing at the Saturday afternoon picnic or BBQ, and he must've told me then. I think B. had had several altercations with Ty, as well as just about every cowboy in school, really. B. was one of the four or five punk rockers our school had to offer, and of course the punks didn't get along with the cowboys. Usually, it was just your routine name calling and verbal harassment in the halls. Occasionally, B. or one of his friends would be slammed into a locker, while the halls were too busy for anyone to notice, but usually that was about it, as far as I knew.

As it turns out, I had no idea the extent of the harassment. Because B. then told me about the time that he was jumped one Friday night, sitting in Nelson's car. Nothing was going on that night, or maybe there was, and the two had just parked to drop some acid or something before the party. In any case, B. and Nelson were sitting, parked in Nelson's old silver Subaru wagon, across from Gopher Foods, not paying any attention, when a bunch of cowboys saw the two and parked their trucks in a circle around Nelson's car, closing them in. Apparently, someone had written "Ty is a fag" on one of the lockers at school, and the cowboys had all decided it must have been B. It's a long story, really, and Shane or Duane or one of those guys pulled a hunting knife on B., held the knife to B.'s throat, pinning him against the car seat, and insisting B. was the one who had written "fag." Even though B. swore he had written no such thing, and he hadn't, they insisted he had and accused him of lying, on top of it, and then said, Don't you lie to me, boy, or I'll kill you, so there was nothing B. could say.

And when he said nothing, in response, they insisted he admit what he had done. The cowboys were drunk and they just wanted an excuse to slit B.'s throat, and I think they actually nicked him, and it was then, at the moment that B.'s throat was nicked, that Nelson jumped out of the driver's side and charged the cowboys, the entire group. Ninety-pound Matt Nelson, the former child math prodigy who'd fried his brain on acid by the age of fourteen, he fought them off. Actually, Matt went ballistic and scared them off—he spooked them, basically, and in effect he saved B.'s life.

But, B. said, several years later, at a graduation party, Shane or Duane, whoever had pulled the knife, approached B. and apologized for almost slashing his throat. B. just wanted to enjoy the party, so he said it was all right, best let it go, let bygones be bygones, and Shane or Duane said no, he couldn't do that. He felt awful about it. Duane or Shane said he felt guilty about what had happened and he needed to know that B. truly forgave him and so he insisted that B. shake. B. didn't feel like shaking, I think he patted him on the shoulder and repeated that it was fine, it was a long time ago, and Duane or Shane said no. Duane or Shane said they had to shake on it, and B. said no, so Duane or Shane grabbed his hand and forced B. to shake. Even so, B. said, I had to admire him for apologizing to me, I know it wasn't easy for him.

Then B. went on to tell me how Stretch, Jim Lang, had died in Denver, a few years after graduation, in some bizarre drug deal; he'd been multiply stabbed to death. Or maybe B. told me about Stretch before he told me about getting jumped. In any case, B. said he'd always wanted to return to Denver to try to find out what happened. He knew Jim had been dealing crank for some time, and it haunted him.

Anyhow, I said I wasn't the least surprised to hear about Ty winding up in jail, and I started laughing, reminding him of that time Weaver tried to lasso B. in the school parking lot. It was one of my fondest memories of high school, and I had told the story repeatedly, whenever asked what it was really like to grow up in a small western town with real cowboys who were forced to remove their hats and spit out their chew before class began. God, I loved that story. I can see it, even now, and it was just so typical of our school. Huh, I don't remember that, B. said, laughing at my laughing. *What?* You don't remember the time Weaver tried to lasso you in the school parking lot on lunch hour? No. Tell me, he said.

It was probably Alex. He was always the instigator, either Alex or Tad. They were the ones who coined the term "cow love," drawling *love,* to describe the physical displays between the cowboys and their girlfriends in the halls. For instance, one of the cowboys might slap a girl's ass or grab her by her belt buckle and shake her, in greeting, and those two would simply shout, *Moooo!* So, one lunch hour, Ty rolled down his windows and blasted some C & W music out of his truck stereo, after shouting something like, This is *real* music!, in the direction of the punk pack. And I'm sure it must have been one of those two, either Alex or Tad, who shouted, *Yeeee-haaaa!* in response. Alex, I bet. Well, whoever, then, I distinctly remember this part, the two started clapping and stomping one foot, in a mock hoedown, chanting, in unison, *The devil went down to Georgia, he was looking for a soul to steal...* Well, Ty heard their taunting and he became furious, of course. So Ty turned over his ignition, Weaver jumped in the cab, and then the two started circling the parking lot. Naturally, Ty had several lengths of rope in the cab, and while he was circling, Weaver stood in the back and tied the rope, and as Ty picked up some speed, turning the corner, around the light post, then Weaver tried to lasso B., even though he had said nothing at all.

I believe Weaver had every intention of dragging B. behind the truck, if he managed to lasso him. But the thing was that Ty was so angry about the joke that he couldn't control his approach so that Weaver could get a good shot, and then Ty became that much angrier every time Weaver missed, because everyone was watching on the school lawn. And the whole time, B. simply stood his ground, watching them circle the parking lot, while everyone was cheering. Weaver had several rodeo trophies to his credit, so everyone else backed away, out of range, just watching the truck circle and circle, laughing, as Weaver kept missing B. This went on for a good ten minutes, and the entire time B. just stood there, watching them. He had such a calm expression on his face, that's what killed me. What happened then? B. asked. Oh, I think the lunch bell rang, and everyone just went back inside for sixth hour. You don't remember that? No, he said, returning to the fridge for another beer. I couldn't figure it out, how could he have forgotten that incident? I remembered it so vividly. Now I figure maybe he just chose not to remember.

I didn't attend my ten-year reunion, after all, but it was the reunion and that talk with B. that reminded me of cowboys and, thereby, cheerleading, and then, several months later, that article. But I just remembered her name, the name of the eighth-grade girl who Ty and several of his friends held down in the back of the bus and tore off her red cheerleading bloomers: her name was Andrea. I haven't remembered her in years. I remember telling my mother what happened to Andrea that night, when I got home. And was that ever a mistake. Well, there was more to it than Andrea being held down by several guys: afterward, the wrestling coach heard the boys joking about it as well, and the coach laughed along. My mother was outraged, of course, and she wanted to make a federal case out of it and told me she would call the principal on Andrea's behalf, if Andrea wanted some support.

My mother became so angry, I was afraid to tell her the whole story, which was that Andrea had first pulled down the sweatpants of one of the boys she liked. And then, in retaliation, several of the boys, four or five of them, held her down, each one taking an arm and a leg, and then they pulled off her bloomers. And so then, when the coach heard the story, having heard she started it, that's when he said, chuckling, *Mess with the bull, you get the horns...* The following Monday morning, when I told Andrea about my mother offering to call the principal on her behalf, Andrea started crying and begged me to call off my mother. She became hysterical at the very suggestion. Her parents were extremely religious, Baptists, I think, and she had had to plead with them to let her cheer, and they would have forced her to quit if they heard anything of the sort, or so she claimed.

Well, moving right along. Next on the list is "Naked." What's most unusual about this particular story is that I finished it—yes!—although, taking a second look, I simply didn't like it, and I soon grew to loathe the story, so I sent it down. It's pretty self-explanatory, but still, the story line is basically this: A woman answers her front door naked and the postman doesn't take any notice, and she feels such loss that she hits the streets. She walks straight out her front door. Now this story came out of a three-month dry spell; months passed without a single sentence on my computer screen. Friends tried to help, first by offering encouragement, then empathy, then sympathy, then condolences, seeing that I was inconsolable and I simply would not be convinced out of my thoroughly morbid funk. Finally, one night, talking on the phone, a friend suggested an exercise in spontaneity, to which I agreed. And I agreed only because I was so incredibly despondent and desperate, I would've agreed to anything, even that, even though it sounded hokey and kind of humiliating. That's how low I'd sunk.

In all fairness to my friend, let me digress for a moment and say that I've heard worse. Or, I would. About six months after this conversation with my friend, I hit another dry spell. At Thanksgiving I was invited to join my friend and her boyfriend and his family for a dinner at the house of an old family friend of my friend's boyfriend, if you follow. I agreed, giving it no further thought, and then, the week before Thanksgiving, my friend's boyfriend told me a little about this old friend of his family. He told me she was a guru, but she didn't like to be called a guru, but, nevertheless, that she was quite famous. He said I must have heard of her, and I had to admit that I'd never heard of her. Somehow, I'd missed the picture of the guru, photographed with Hillary Clinton, on the front page of the *Times*. I don't know how I missed it, guess I must've been out of the country or living in San Francisco at the time, I don't know. Anyhow, Thanksgiving with the guru.

My friend's boyfriend suggested I speak to the guru about my writing block, because she might have some ideas, and I became very excited by the possibility that someone might be able to help me. So dinner was a little wacky, and I didn't really have much to say, but then, finally, after dinner, I mustered the courage to speak to the guru about my problem. By that point, I was up for anything. I would've lit candles, welcomed magic spells, a sprinkling of fairy dust—anything. I was desperate. The guru was very kind and patient, listening as I detailed my block, and then she made a few suggestions, ranging from physical exhaustion to visualization techniques and hypnosis.

One last thought, she said. Yes? I asked, hoping this would be the one. Have you ever danced your story? she asked. I'm sorry? I asked. I didn't understand her question. She said, Instead of writing, have you ever danced your story? I said no, never. In all seriousness, in response to her question, I had visions of myself dancing my story, throwing my arms to one side, then the other, then stepping side to side, in a stiff box step, trying to get the rhythm, let it flow. Unfortunately, in my mind's eye, I looked more like a retiree stomping my feet in Jazzercise than a story dancer, and I thought, *Over my dead body*. No, I said, trying to sound open-minded. She said it was a good exercise, extremely effective, and I should try as soon as possible. I thanked her, dropping the subject, and then she gave me a tour of her house.

Returning home that night, I dismissed the idea as too absurd. Then, after another week or two passed without writing a single sentence, I was pulling my hair out. I was in such agony that I could barely hold a conversation. I couldn't stand to be around others, I couldn't stand to be alone: I had no choice, I had to take action. All right, all right, I thought, I give. So, home alone one night, I moved the living-room table and chairs, clearing an area on the floor, and I sat down to gather myself, removing my shoes and socks. Well, this is it, I thought, the moment of truth, and I asked myself: How badly do you want to be a writer?

Sighing, I looked at the open space in the middle of the room, and I gave the question serious thought. Then I stood, realizing I didn't want anything in this world that badly, and I immediately moved the furniture back. But, for the record, it worked wonders. The next week I wrote another story, from start to finish. I don't remember what, I probably killed it, too, but no matter. The point is that I honestly believe I managed to break through that spell out of sheer obstinacy. And to this day, the threat of dancing my story remains a surefire last resort. I recommend it to anyone in need.

Back to my friend. The idea was that he threw me a sentence, or even just an opening, or a few words, max, and I just had to respond; finish the sentence. He suggested, *A woman crossed the room...* What next? Your turn, he said. So, *A woman crossed the room* became *The woman crossed the room naked...* Good, he said. Well, actually, before that edit occurred, I asked him if he couldn't give me a better sentence, start things off on the right foot? He had to give me something better to work with, I said, and then I argued that I didn't like that sentence, and I wouldn't write that sentence to begin with; it didn't sound at all like the sort of thing I'd say. He managed to persist that time, even though I said *the* woman crossed sounded better than *a* woman crossed. And as to why the woman has to be crossing some nondescript room for no apparent reason, naked, write it off to yet another failure of my imagination. Nevertheless, against all odds, I finished that story.

I just looked a minute ago, but I can't seem to find that file or the printout. I must've thrown them both away. But I think it went something like this:

> *The woman crossed the room naked, but the postman took no notice, handing her a pink slip...*

Like I said, I sent this story down not only because I didn't like it, but also because it had no plot and not much action and nothing really happened. In short, it just didn't hold my attention from the very beginning. Before I rejected it, though, I submitted it to a reputable publication, and of course it was rejected, and then I simply agreed with that assessment. For a while after the rejection, I was thinking that maybe I'd rewrite the story; change the woman to a man, see what happened. But in truth, now I think that would interest me even less.

Maybe it was the naked story that led to "August" (absolutely no recollection why I titled it that, but I'm fairly predictable, so maybe I began the story in August?), which was loosely based on these upstairs neighbors I used to have. For almost a year, I lived beneath an NYU girl and her boyfriend, who were involved in the classic screaming sex/screaming argument cycle, waking me in the middle of the night, breaking windows, and leaving a trail of broken glass in my old courtyard. Cliché, I know, but, honestly, these two were so loud that I once heard their passion from the mail room—in another building. Three-hundred-square-foot studios separated by eight-foot ceilings, your neighbors are literally on top of you. And because I, for one, have never heard such a talker in my life—she really had a script, this one, you know: Oh god! Oh, there!

There, *there!* Do it to me! Stick your big hot cock...I always lost it with that "hot cock" bit, I couldn't help but laugh, so I'd cover my mouth, you know, and then I'd think, Why am *I* covering my mouth? Besides, how could they hear me if I couldn't even hear myself laughing over them?

The humor of the situation wore thin after a few weeks. I'd just be minding my own business, trying to drink my coffee, it just got to be too much...So the first time I heard them from the mail room, I thought it was a joke, you know, a bad porn imitation, with all the heat and the sticking, and never simply *pussy,* no. Always with the *my wet pussy*—it had to be a joke, I thought, but no. After a few months of that, those two were openly discussed among my other neighbors, returning from work, all of us checking our mail. Actually, it got to the point that I could call friends and hold out the phone, with my arm raised, the phone reached within a foot or two of their window, which was always open. If my friends were on another line at their respective jobs, I had ample time to call their personal answering machines. As for my neighbors, last I heard, they'd become engaged, apparently, because the girl wrote "The Future Mrs. So-and-So" across her name in the mail room. *Gag.*

Well, back to the August story. So far, it's proven to be a very short story, with the protagonist ending up on her fire escape, where a crowd's gathered to listen, and the crowd mistaking the protagonist for the source of the disturbance. I know that doesn't sound very interesting, and maybe I'm not describing it well, but at least there is an ending to speak of. I'm willing to give the ending the benefit of the doubt, because, having finished a complete draft, I showed this story to a friend and he said, "The ending's great, but the beginning's not strange enough." And I had to agree with him, there was a problem with the beginning, but then I couldn't think of anything particularly strange. Regardless, this story remains on my list, that is, accessible, in case a really strange introduction should ever occur. And as far as my questionable behavior, I do realize that I probably should've called the management company, but I didn't know how to state my complaint to Steve Gordon. Besides, he was kind of sleazy, anyway, one of those skinny guys who lives in New York and wears tight jeans with cowboy boots and plaid hunting jackets. He was nice enough but definitely on the sleazy side. The occupancy of our building was like 90 percent female, and I'd have to say, by and large, very attractive women.

The situation called for a level of maturity I lacked. So then I considered calling when Steve Gordon wasn't there, sometime after five, so I wouldn't have to feel awkward or embarrassed or like the sex police or something, which led me to thinking I should just leave him a message. Or, assuming he wouldn't be able to fully appreciate the severity of the situation, because it had to be heard to be believed, maybe I'd let him hear just how bad it really was, because those two kept all hours. I could call anytime, but then he wouldn't know who left the message, either, because I couldn't talk over them. Maybe that's where the story should begin, with Steve Gordon receiving an obscene voice mail at the office, but by now I'm at peace with its abandonment.

Next on the list, "Sleep." It's been awhile, and now that I look at it, I have no idea what this story is about. Sleep? Absolutely no idea what I was talking about. I don't know, maybe I wasn't even referring to a story idea. Oh—*right*! I remember. "Sleep"—of course, sleep-sleep, how could I forget the sleeping beauties story?

See, I once had an acquaintance who put herself through school stripping. I know it's pretty cliché, so far, but here's the catch: my acquaintance once told me that the worst thing that ever happened to her on the job was the day she fell asleep on the stage. Because she'd been out all night, and no one was there in the club when she got out on the stage around noon, so she lay down for a moment and then she dozed off…When she finally woke, there were a dozen men masturbating, simply watching her sleep, fully clothed in her Catholic school uniform or her cheerleading skirt or whatever she was wearing. For her, though, what an incredible violation of her privacy. But considering the way things ebb and flow, I've always been fascinated with the idea of a sleeping fad overtaking the strip-club scene. As if the industry were plagued with Ambien addictions, I don't know. Then again, I guess enough time has passed since she first told me that story, with so few details to work with and my own inability to translate her experience, or even my own experience of what she told me, that I'm no longer intrigued by the idea at all.

I'm currently at work on the last story on the list, and I'm playing with fire here, but I'll tell you a little about that story, anyway. Several years ago, I read this interview with a porn star who specialized in gang banging. The article included a photo of her at an event in which she had sex with about two hundred men at one time, or maybe more. I can't remember the exact number now, but it was a lot, two or three hundred men. And so there she was, photographed in the middle of the marathon, pictured on her back, smiling at the camera (a brunette, actually). I've never gotten that smile out of my head, it was so genuine; she wasn't porn pouting or anything and you could even see her gums. And sometimes, when I see something in the papers, like that former Wall Street investor who's being investigated for leaking information to a triple-X porn queen or whatever, I'll think of her smile. My only question—well, I have many, many questions, actually, but still—my first question is this: Where does one go from there? You know what I mean? So that's where I thought I'd begin. Right now, the unofficial working title is "The Former World Record Holder Settles Down." It's nothing fancy, but I have a first sentence as well:

I don't bowl for fun.

It's not going to win any awards, that sentence, but I think it's all right. Oh, and what's more, now that I look at it, that's five words exactly. So I have a good start on this story, and I'm hopeful. At least for the moment.

Sharks

She called me one Monday morning to tell me about her first weekend at the beach house, and to tell me about one of the shareholders in particular. He was a doctor, a neurosurgeon in fact, who, she said, had consumed copious amounts of marijuana, cocaine, and alcohol, then got up a few hours later and drove to work. That's where we started, anyway, but we moved on to how nice it would be to kick back on the beach all weekend. I hadn't been out of the city in a year.

You can come out during the week, sometime. It'll be fun, just the two of us, she said. I agreed, but then I thought about it for a minute, and I said that the thing was, I often lost patience with the beach. I'd get too hot, or I'd start to burn, or there'd be sand in my crotch or those awful gnats or biting flies, there was always something. I usually had a good five minutes at the beach, and then I was ready to go. Although I liked the idea of spending an afternoon at the beach, reading a book, listening to the waves, napping, it never worked out that way, really. And then there was the water, it was so cold until August, and I never really swam. Oh, I never swim, either, I barely go in, she said after I told her, but it's very peaceful just to get away, she said. Yes, I said.

I would like to swim, though. I haven't been swimming in ages, I said, and I used to be a swimmer. *I know,* she said, maybe we should go to a pool some night, wouldn't that be fun? We've never gone swimming before. I was already thinking maybe Chelsea Piers, even though it's pretty expensive, fifty bucks a pop. Kind of a rip-off, but it'd be fun. No, she said. You know how to swim, don't you? I asked. Yes, I can swim, she said. It's not that, it's that I'm afraid of sharks. Oh, I said, well, I'm afraid of sharks, too. Especially since the majority of shark attacks occur in shallow water, like no higher than your knee. I know, I know, she said, that's why I won't go in the water. I usually just stand as close to the edge of the waves, where I can't be knocked over or anything, and I lean over and splash myself, and then I get right back to my towel. I understand, I said, I only meant a swimming pool, here in the city. Maybe Chelsea Piers or down the street, I said, that would be fun. I'm fine with the Y, it's cheap, and we could go anytime. Then she said no again. Why not? Doesn't that sound fun? I asked.

I told you, she said. Sharks, she said. You misunderstand, I mean a swimming pool, I said. No, I didn't misunderstand, I know you meant a swimming pool, she said. Then I don't understand, I said. Haven't I ever told you about my fear of sharks? No, I said, I didn't know you were afraid of sharks, but that's okay. I am, too. That movie, I said, my uncle Paul took me when I was five, and after that, forget it, I said. I hear you, she said. Same here, never again. Oh, well, I can understand that much, I said. But I don't mean swimming in the ocean, I repeated. I know you didn't, she said, but I'm afraid of swimming, period. Even in swimming pools. Why? I don't understand, I said. I told you already, sharks, she said. In a swimming pool, I repeated, thinking I was still misunderstanding her somehow. Yes, she said. You're kidding, right? No, she said. This is amazing, I said, *I never knew this* about you. How long have I known you? I couldn't believe I never knew this about my best friend. Well, I'm sure I told you before, she said. No, you never told me. I wouldn't forget something like this, I said. I'm sure, she said. No, I'm telling you, you never told me about your fear of sharks in swimming pools, I wouldn't just forget that sort of thing. Well, anyway, she said, and then she returned to the subject of the other shareholders.

But wait, I said, interrupting her. About the sharks, I said… Yes? she asked, chewing on something that sounded crunchy. What are you eating? I asked. Dinner, she said. What did you make for dinner? I asked. Eggplant parmigiana. I made plenty. You want to come over? No, thanks, I said, I'm too lazy. Did you cook it through, though? I asked. It sounds a little underdone. *Yes,* she said, I cooked it through. I'm eating a carrot, she said. Oh, I said. So about the sharks, I said, you can't swim in a swimming pool for fear of shark attack? No, she said, that's right. I'm sure I told you this before, she said. *No,* I assured her. You never told me this before. Are you sure? Listen, I'm telling you, I said. I could swear, she said. No, I said. Well, anyway. Get down on it, she said, biting into another carrot. First impressions, and maybe that's unfair, but I don't think I'll be getting down on anything, she said. But wait, I said. What? she asked. Sharks...sharks can't live in fresh water, I said. I know, she said. Then we can go swimming at a pool, so let's go this weekend. No, she said, no swimming. It's not safe.

But you know sharks can't live in fresh water, or even pool water, right? They can't live in chlorine. They're saltwater dwellers, or whatever they're called, I said. Yes, she said, I know that rationally, but I have a fear of pools, just the same. You have a fear of sharks in city pools? I asked, clarifying. Yes, she said. But how in the world would a shark get in a pool, even if it could survive? At Chelsea Piers, it might be a little easier, being so close to the water. But it's not a simple thing, you know, it's not like, say, a rat getting into an outdoor pool, or something, I said. You know when I used to swim, I said. What? she said. It was an outdoor pool, right, and we had to swim at dawn, and half the time, when we'd show up, there'd be mice and rodents in the pool, little animals that slipped through the fence and drowned. They'd just be floating and our coach would have to fish them out before any of us would get in to start practice, I said. Gross, she said.

Yes, but, anyway, it's not like that, a shark isn't just going to slip into the pool at Chelsea Piers, it's glassed or something, there's a wall of some sort, I said. Are you sure I've never told you this before? she asked. I told you, I said, never. So how do sharks get into the swimming pool? I asked. It's complicated, she said. I'm sure. Go on, I said. Well, basically, scientists, she said. The answer is scientists. Sorry? I asked. Scientists release sharks into the pool, she said. And how do they do that, on the sly? No one notices them bringing the sharks in? I told you it was complicated, she said. Yes, I said, start from the beginning.

Okay. The scientists: there are these scientists experimenting on sharks, altering them or whatever. Wait, genetic engineering on *sharks*? I asked. Yes, she said, exactly. Don't act so surprised. They experiment on all other types of life-forms, why not sharks? Well, why would they? I asked. What I'm saying is that if they'll experiment on sheep, what's to keep them from experimenting on sharks? What's off-limits with these guys, you know? Far as I can tell, nothing. Nothing is off-limits, nothing is sacred, so sharks are not out of the question, she said. Okay, you got me there, I said. But why would these scientists want to release sharks into swimming pools? I asked. That's not their primary reason. It's during the experiment, see. It's an accident, really. They go at night, when no one is there, swimming, because there are only a few places in New York that are big enough, and even fewer that are deep enough. Anyhow, then the sharks get free, and the scientists can't figure how to get them out of the pool, she said. So are these scientists evil? Not necessarily, she said. I'm not saying their intent was evil, necessarily, they just wanted to know if it was possible, and that's why they started these experiments in the first place. So they didn't release the sharks on purpose?

No, no. They never meant to endanger any lives, really, but they just couldn't help themselves. They didn't think about what they were doing until it was too late, of course. Of course, I said. Yes, and so then the experiment just got away from them, she said. Happens all the time, you know. Yes, I know, I said. But what kind of sharks? I asked. Oh, all kinds of sharks, she said. Great whites, hammerheads, those little ones, you name it. Oh, I said. So why can't they just take them back out of the pool? I asked. *Because,* she said, they've become extra-deadly, these sharks. Extra-deadly? I asked. Yes, she said, lethal. Like biological warfare, that sort of thing. Once released, cannot be contained. You know how they have those top-secret labs with all kinds of diseases that could wipe out the entire population of the world? Yes, I said. But I still don't understand why these sharks can't be contained; they aren't airborne. They're right there, in the pool. So take them out, I said. No, she said, they can't do that. Because part of their experiment was perfecting their teeth, their jaws, augmentation or whatever. I don't know what they were thinking, really. But they do this on purpose, the teeth and everything? I asked. No, I don't think so, I think it happened unwittingly, as a side effect of whatever it was they meant to do. My guess is they told themselves they were doing a good thing, like they always do. In any case, whatever their reasons, these sharks have extra sets of teeth, entire sets, maybe a half-dozen or a dozen sets of teeth, and their teeth can chew through metal. And if they lose some teeth, no problem, they have plenty of extras. A human leg would be nothing, she said. Nothing.

Then how did they get them into the pool? I asked. In tanks, I suppose, she said. Oh, I said, right. But so why don't they take them out of the pool? I asked. Because the scientists didn't realize about the extra sets of teeth and strength of their jaws until they released the sharks into the pool. Right, I got that part, I said. Yes, and so then, once freed, of course the sharks didn't want to get back in their little glass tanks, when the scientists decided it was time to get them out, and then the sharks ate through every net. Now the scientists can't get any-where near these sharks without risking their own lives, and of course they aren't going to risk their lives or own up to their mistake, and inform the public and risk going to jail. No, of course not, I said. There you go, she said. What, so they just leave them there? *In the pool?* I asked. Yes, she said. That's right.

You honestly believe there are sharks at the Sol Goldman Y? I asked. It's not about believing; it's about my fear. This is my fear I'm talking about. I got that much, I said. Well, there you go, she said. You asked, I told you. No, you're right, okay. But tell me this, what happens if you get into a swimming pool? I asked. I don't unless I have to, she said. But if you went to a pool, wouldn't you be able to see the sharks, swimming around in the pool? I mean, wouldn't *somebody* notice that there was a shark in the pool? Or do they have a cloaking device, too? Very funny, she says, but the answer is no. No, you wouldn't neces-sarily see them. They just wait, she said. You mean the sharks wait somewhere in the pool? I asked, clarifying again. Yes, she said. Where? Where would they wait, the drain? I don't know where they might be waiting, see, *that's the thing.* They could be waiting anywhere. Of course, I said.

So when you have to get in a pool…, I said. I don't ever have to get in a pool, she said. But there must have been a few times when you had to get in a pool, or you wouldn't have learned how to swim, I said. Well, yes, I got in a few times, she said, but not often, certainly not anymore. So what happened those few times you got in? Did you look both ways, then jump in? I asked. Well, the few times I had to get in, I usually got in at the shallow end. I'd hold on to the side of the pool, facing the water, so I could see, and I'd hold on to the side of the pool and let myself down quickly, dunk under once, to prove I had gotten in all the way, then I'd turn around and jump out. I had to stay in the shallow end, so I could get out faster. And if I had to get in at the deep end, I held on to the ladder, sat on the steps, in case I needed to jump out at a moment's notice. In case you saw a shark, you mean? I asked. Yes, she said. But…, I said. Yes? But have you ever seen a shark in a swimming pool? I asked.

No, but I *felt* them. You felt a shark in the swimming pool? I asked. Yes, she said. And what did you do then, that time you felt it? I jumped out as fast as I could, of course. What do you think I did? So you were safe, I said, after you jumped out of the pool. Yes, she said, well, almost. There's more to it than that, she said. I'm sure, I said. Are you sure you don't want to come over for dinner? Thanks, but no, not tonight. Tell me what more, I said. It sounded like she was taking a pan out of the oven; I heard the oven door close. Well, it's not always enough just to get out of the pool, sometimes I have to run, she said. Sometimes? I asked. You run? Well, pretty much all the time, if I want to be certain, she said. Yes? I said. So, I have to run a certain distance away from the edge of the pool, out of their reach, because they can lunge, she said. Lunge? I asked. Yes, they might nip my ankle or my entire leg, and pull me back in, so I have to run to the wall before I'm safe. Wait, I said. First, how do you explain all those people who've survived, people who go swimming every day? Just lucky, she said. Luck, I said. Yes, she said, I don't know that I'll be so lucky.

I'm afraid I must have started laughing then, because she said, Oh, ha-ha-ha, I don't laugh and belittle your fears, you know, she said. I know, but I'm not belittling your fears, I'm just trying to understand. There must be something we can do to protect you from sharks, I said. Yes, I don't go swimming, that's what we can do, she said. No, I meant something so that you could go swimming, if you wanted to. But I don't want to, she said. But if you did, I said. Hypothetically, I'm saying. Like, I don't know, say, what if we wore those chain-metal suits that shark divers wear? No, she said, I've seen those shows on TV, and even regular sharks can bite through those suits, if they really want to. Not if we're in a cage, I said. It's not like we'll be holding out any raw meat, trying to attract their attention. We'll just wear the suits and get in a cage and splash around. Come on, it'll be fun! No, we can't do that, absolutely not, splashing draws attention, she said. Okay, fine. So we don't splash, we just relax in the cage, I said. And the cages, those only work with regular sharks, she said. I told you already, these sharks can bite through metal. If they want to, I said. Yes, she said. Well, what if we went to a different pool, I said, one far away from the ocean? Maybe we're just too close for comfort, I suggested. No, she said, no pool is safe.

I know, I said, what if we went home, could you swim in the pool downtown? We grew up in Colorado, in the mountains; there's no chance of sharks there. No, she said. I told you, no pool is safe. A thousand miles from the ocean, how's a shark going to get into the pool at home? *Land shark,* I said. What are you talking about? she said. You know, land shark, I said, the old *Saturday Night Live* skit, remember? No, I missed that. Probably a good thing, too. What are these land sharks? She sounded scared. You don't want to know, I said. Probably not, she said. So how do these sharks get from the Sol Goldman Y to Colorado, or vice versa? What, they walk? Were the transported by semi, and the truck crashed, and they were thrown over the cliff into a river, what? Could be, she said. It could happen in a number of ways. The scientists could make a mistake anywhere. So where are these scientists? I asked. That's the thing, she said, they could be anywhere. At any time. Oh, of course, I said. Are you mocking me? No, I'm not mocking you, I said. But what are they doing in Colorado? Breeding them to ski? Snow sharks? You said you weren't going to mock me, and that sounds like mocking to me, she said. I said I'm not mocking you, I said. Good, then don't, she said. Well, anyway, it's probably the safest place in the world for them to perform their experiments, no one would ever expect them in Colorado. No, I said, you're probably right. Yes, she said. That's brilliant, I thought. She's thought of every question, every possible angle. She's really got her bases covered here. I was impressed, really.

Besides, I wasn't safe there, either. In Colorado? I asked. Remember PE, when they used to make us go swimming? she asked. Of course I remembered having to go swimming in PE class; the final humiliation of the school year. Yes, I said. Well, that's why I almost failed PE, because I wouldn't go swimming. But you can swim, I said, you know how to swim, at least. Not very well, but yes, she said, I can swim. But I wouldn't stay in the pool as long as we were supposed to, and Coach Draker insisted we all swim two laps, and I couldn't do it. I would stand by the fence for an entire hour, with my fingers entwined in the fencing, holding on. He didn't fail you, did he? I asked. No, but almost, he threatened as much. So what did you do? I asked. I told him I had my period. For two weeks? I asked. Yes, I told him once, and then I'd just nod and hold my stomach, and he left it at that. I got off the hook. Coach Draker, even Coach Harris, they never contested menstrual cramps, they didn't want to risk some irate mother calling them and threatening to call the school board. I was just lucky it was him and not that woman, the other PE teacher, what was her name? she asked. I don't remember, I said. But swimming is supposed to be good for cramps, you know. Yes, I know, she said, good for cramps, but bad for sharks. I'd rather suffer than die. But you didn't really have your period, did you? No, she said, but if I had, there was really no way in hell I was getting in a pool then.

Didn't you ever want to get in the pool, seeing the other kids having a good time, splashing around? No, I never saw anyone have a good time, because I couldn't stand to watch, thinking that at any second, one of them might be pulled under, she said. Well, what if I go swimming, would you fear for my safety? I asked. No, she said. Oh, thanks a lot, I said. The thing is, sharks sense fear, she said. Blood and fear, so if you aren't afraid, which you aren't, then you aren't in as much danger as I am. You could come, see me having a good time, then maybe give it a shot, I said. No, then your life would be endangered, too. Simply by your being there, watching me? Yes, she said. Let me think, I said. Okay.

Let's go back to the part where you feel the shark, I said. Yes, she said. Where, and what do you feel? What's it feel like, the shark? It touches my ankle. Sometimes they graze my thigh, but it's usually my ankle. It stays close to the surface of the pool, and it's circling, or coming out of its hiding place, and I feel it on my ankle first. And what does a shark feel like? Pretty much like you'd imagine, slimy and fast—it's gone before I can see where it came from. You look? I ask. No, I don't have time to look, I have to move, get the hell out of the pool. So you actually feel it, and then you have to jump out and run to the wall for safety? Yes, she said. Look, all I can tell you is that I'm not safe until I'm out of the pool and back on the street. You mean you're not even really safe by the wall? No, not really, she said. What's it going to do, follow you into the shower? I just can't be sure how far he can reach, and I have to be sure, she said.

He? I ask. What do you mean? she said. You said he, I said. Yes, she said. So how do you know the shark is male? Oh, because they're all male, she said. They're bred to be male, engineered or whatever. Why do the scientists breed only males? So they'll be that much more aggressive, she said. Of course, I said. I don't think it's sharks we're talking about here. I don't know what you're talking about, but I'm definitely talking about sharks, she said. Well, what I was thinking was that it might be Freudian, somehow, but I didn't remember anything about sharks in Freud. Shark dreams, maybe. Did you ever dream you were attacked by sharks or have sharks ever appeared in your dreams? I asked, trying a different angle. Let me think, she said, hmmm...No, no. I can't remember ever dreaming about sharks. Are you sure? I asked. Positive, she said. Well, maybe you just don't remember the dream, or maybe you repressed the memory, because it scared you too much. Maybe, she said, but I'm sure I'd remember. Try to remember the last nightmare you had, I suggested. Okay...no, no, I remember the last nightmare I had, and there were no sharks. Are you certain? I asked. Yes, there was a shooting, a robbery or something, but it was on the street, there were no sharks involved. Mind if I eat while we're talking? Of course not, I said.

All right, fine, so we don't swim. We don't have to swim; we could just soak in a Jacuzzi or hot tub or something. No, she said. What, hot tubs aren't safe? I asked. No, she said. And they're dirty, too, she said, it's a well-known fact. I know, bacteria, who knows what, if you feel underneath the seat, there's the strange slimy feeling…Yes, but also they aren't safe from sharks, either. Oh? Any body of water is unsafe. I could sort of understand that, I used to be afraid of Jacuzzis, too. Hey, did you ever see that movie *Piranha*? I asked. No, what happens? she asked. I was surprised to hear she hadn't seen that movie. Really? I asked. Never saw it. Well, the details are a little blurry now that it's been awhile. But basically, the story is that piranha get into the water system of the city, L.A., or wherever. I don't remember how they get into the water system in the first place, but then, out of nowhere, they enter—well, I don't know if enter is the right word, but—all of a sudden, they swim into the swimming pool en masse. It's just this black cloud in the pool; seconds before, there's this frenetic image of the fish swimming into the camera in this pipe or whatever, and this awful buzzing sound, so you'd know they were on their way, and someone was doomed. Oh, that's awful, she said. Yeah, and then they'd cut from this person lounging in the pool, to the piranhas buzzing, making their way through the water pipes, as the piranhas were getting closer and closer…Then they'd enter the pool. In like a second, they'd enter and kill instantly, then they'd turn around and escape back out of the pool the same way they came. They'd head straight back into the water system and no one could figure it out.

A wife would be bringing a drink out for her husband, and he'd just be gone, and she'd call his name, say, Honey, where are you? Honey…? It was like people were just disappearing, because the piranha would eat everything—bones, hair, everything. Gone. You see what I mean, she said. Yes, but that was a movie, I said. But it scared you enough, didn't it? Yes, actually, for a few years after that, I'd have to check where the drain was in the pool all summer long. Then I'd swim on the opposite side so they'd kill someone else first, and I'd have a chance to escape. You see? You see what I mean? Yes, I said, and after that movie, I was even afraid of taking a bath, I wouldn't take a bath unless my mom would sit there with me. I figured at least she would know what happened to me if I died. I understand completely, she said. I was even afraid of the *toilet*. I'd have to check and make sure there weren't any piranhas in the bowl, and then I couldn't even sit down properly. I'd have to sit facing the tank. And then, a few weeks ago, a friend told me about this rat infestation he had in his apartment in Boston, and he had rats in his toilet. No! she said. Yes, I'm telling you. That's disgusting, she said. I know, so I've started checking again, just once in a while. Better safe than sorry, she agreed. Exactly, I said. Anyway, for a while there, as a kid, I'd have to watch the opening, for fear they might fly out at me or something. So you do understand, she said. Well, kind of, but I don't know what I thought, how they'd get me, exactly, but for a good year afterward, I was never comfortable peeing. So what happened? she asked.

Nothing. I forgot about it for a while, and then I heard about those prickly fish that can lodge in a man's penis, if he's peeing off the side of a boat. So, I didn't really think about the fact that I wasn't a man, and not in danger of peeing off a boat in Africa, I just focused on the fact that it happened to someone, somewhere, and so why not me? Aside from the fact that I wasn't a man peeing off the side of a boat on a river in Africa, why couldn't it happen to me, you know? Yes. So you understand, she said. Yes, but I was six or seven years old. I can swim now. Yes, but when you were a kid, did you ever jump out of the pool, fearing for your life? she asked. Well, yes. There you go, she said. It's not the same, though, I said. Yes, it is, she said, it's exactly the same. No, it's not, I said, I can swim now, and I pee comfortably. No, the fear is the same, your fear just isn't as developed as mine. I wouldn't put it that way, I said. You should be happy, she said. You can swim whenever you want to. But you could swim, too, if you wanted to. Yes, she said, but I don't want to. But if you got some help, I said. I don't need any help, she said. I think you do, I said, because if you got some help, you could swim without fear of sharks, and then you might want to, you might even enjoy swimming. No, she said, I don't think so. I've made it this far, just fine, without swimming, she said. I'm just trying to help, I said. I don't want help, she said. Fine, I said. Good, she said.

But just for the record, I said, experts say sharks are greatly misunderstood, there is a lot of misunderstanding about their behavior, you know. I know, she said. It's not like I want to hunt or kill sharks because of my fear — live and let live, that's all I'm saying. All right, well, maybe I'll think of something, I said. No, she said, you won't. I might, I said, give me a chance. I'm telling you, she said, you won't think of anything I haven't thought of before. I might, I said, don't be so sure. Well, I am, she said. I'm sure. Well, I might surprise you, I said. Well, good luck, then, she said. Same to you, I said. I have to go now, I need to clean up, my kitchen's a disaster, she said. Call you tomorrow. Okay, talk to you then. Okay, love you. Love you, too. Night. Good night. Bye. Bye.

It's been a good two years since we had that conversation, but it still bothers me. Nobody thinks of everything, nobody. I know that eventually, if I keep going over it and over it, I'll find something. Sooner or later, one day, I'll find her weakness, I will, and then I'll go for the kill.

Thieves

VISA Merchant Services
Claims Department
PO Box 15480
Wilmington, Delaware 19850

Re: #4118-4301-0007-XXXX

To Whom It May Concern,   July 26, 2000

I am writing in regards to your dispute of the four hundred dollars charged to one of your member's credit cards in June of 2000. I understand that you consider this matter a question of fraud, and that my employer has one month to prove the charges were not fraudulent. In the meantime, I would like to explain what happened that day, because I made that transaction and I am the responsible party.

It's a long story, but in short, I can tell you that a young woman had what I can only describe as a nervous breakdown in our store. In support, I can give plenty of details about this woman—I can even tell you exactly what time this woman entered the store, because I checked the clock on the computer screen. As soon as I saw her walk in front of the store, I thought to check, because the last time she came into the store, she stayed for well over an hour. On the day in question, she entered the store at 12:45, and my only hope was that she would leave by my lunch break, at 2:30.

So, as I said, this young woman had been in the store before. I knew her—I recognized her, at least. She'd been in twice before, and each time she'd spent a substantial amount of money, by our standard, approximately one hundred dollars each visit. She's a good customer, however trying, and, honestly, the store hasn't been doing well. I care about my boss, and I want to see his store succeed, and so when I saw her, I figured I'd put up with her and however long she took, if that meant a good day for the store.

There are several other reasons why I remembered this woman and, frankly, I remembered her because she was odd, to say the least. The last time she visited the store, her second visit, she brought her mother, and I will get to her mother, soon enough. First, let me describe this woman. She's blond, blue-eyed, twenty-six years old, five foot eight, and 150 pounds. I know this for a fact, because she told me her height and weight at some point in the afternoon. The reason she mentioned her size was because she'd gained thirty pounds in the past year, due to the medication she's been taking.

Well, from the moment she passed by, I knew it was a bad sign when it took her a good twenty minutes before she actually entered the store. Yes, for twenty minutes she sat outside, on the ledge in front of the store, smoking and checking her compact, applying lipstick; it was a bronze shade, and she was meticulous in her application. At first, watching her outside, I thought I might get off the hook, she just might leave, but no such luck. She finally entered the store, half an hour later, and I said hello.

She was excited, thrilled, really, about our new merchandise. It's an upscale stationery store, you see, and in all seriousness, this woman is obsessed with paper. This is not unusual; the store attracts a fair number of eccentrics. Paper fetishists, if you will. I've dealt with enough of these individuals that I can tell them a mile away, although I still make mistakes.

For example, once, last Christmas, a man walked into the store, and I was sure he was going to turn right around. He was tall, large, middle-aged, with dark slicked-back hair, a striped tracksuit, and gold chains. A guido, basically. So by all appearances, I thought the man would step one foot through the door and leave, but I was wrong. He entered, studied the store for a moment, turning in a circle, looking all around, and then he said, You have *very nice things* in your store. I thanked him and asked if he needed any help. He said, I need to buy some paper, I was robbed. I expressed sympathy, and then I asked him what had been stolen—I didn't quite understand what a robbery had to do with paper. They swiped his stationery, what? They must've really cleaned you out, I said. He said yes and no, all they took was his story: his story had been stolen, nothing else. So I asked him to explain.

He said that he was a writer and he had written a truly brilliant story and that someone had broken into his apartment and stolen it. As a matter of fact, he said, this happens to me all the time. And he was so matter-of-fact, I really didn't know what to say, so I asked him if he had a copy of this story, and he said no; he said they made sure to steal the original, the only copy. I suggested that maybe he could start a new story, in that case. He said, No, they would only steal that one, too. Then I asked him why he thought they stole his stories but nothing else, and he said because his stories were good enough to prompt theft. Those were the exact words of this man in the blue tracksuit, *prompt theft*. Brilliant, he said, shrugging and flipping one hand, as if to say, what can you do? So I asked him what these robbers did with his stories, and he said, They published my stories under their own names, of course! He said this in a tone as though I'd just asked a stupid question, like, *Duh*. As a matter of fact, he continued, I'd probably read one of his stories, except that they had changed the title and taken all the credit. I said, Those bastards. He said, My sentiments exactly.

By then, I was enjoying this exchange a great deal, as he went on to say that he really had to hand it to them, because they were smart, cunning. These vandals—yes, these *vandals* were so smart that they waited until he was working on *the last page. Capeesh?* Not quite, I said. Don't you see? They wait until I'm working on the last page, and then all they need to do is write the last sentence or two! *Anybody* can whip out a last sentence. I agreed that that was pretty smart and I wished I'd thought of it myself and I asked him where he lived, and he snapped, *That's none of your business.*

I was startled and asked if he'd contacted the police. He

sighed, and then he said that the police were of no use, because cops simply don't value literature. This is what he said, picking up different notebooks, studying the covers, feeling the different paper stocks. Maybe I had started to smile, I don't remember, but in any case, he looked at me and said, I'm not joking, and genius comes in many forms, so don't get smart with me, miss. I think I had to catch my jaw about then. Whatever my response, my coworker and boss, both working in the store that day, stopped what they were doing and stared at us. No, the man was not joking.

I apologized and then I asked if he'd like to see some of our stationery so that he could begin a new story, and he said no, because over the course of our conversation, he'd come to realize that it was no use. They knew where he lived, and even if he went to the police and they believed him, how could he ever prove the story was his? And if he started another story, they'd just steal that, too, because it'd happened so many times now, why bother? Every damn time, he said. Well, at least you're published, that's more than most people, right? I asked. That's one way of looking at it, certainly, but I don't think I can continue giving them my best work. You don't know what it does to me, he said. Then give them one of your throwaway stories, I suggested. No. No, he said, I can only give it my all—it's all or nothing with me, he said, pointing to himself, his chest, just above the light blue and orange velour stripes. That's just how I am, he said. He thought about it for another minute, nodded in agreement with himself, then he thanked me for my help, complimented the store once more, and he left.

My coworker Jonathan and my boss, James, stood staring at me, speechless, and I held up my hands. *Do you know that guy?*

Jonathan asked, dumbfounded, approaching the window, peeking to make sure the man had left. Never seen him in my life, I said, nodding. I thought it was a joke, that you knew each other and it was an old joke, he said. It might've been a joke, but I really don't know that man. *Creepy,* Jonathan said, returning to his work. Hey, what was up with the *tracksuit*? he asked, shivering. No idea, I said. To this day, Jon still talks about that man, the someone-keeps-stealing-my-great-stories man; it's a gauge for unusual behavior, and it's a joke as well, but only because it was so weird. You see, my point is that at first I, too, thought this man was joking, but by the end of the conversation, I knew I'd made a bad call. It happens, that's what I'm trying to say.

Anyhow, we change the store's stock four times a year, and the woman in question hadn't been by since we restocked the store in April. (I would guess her last visit was in early March— I remember that it was a mild day in March, because she wasn't wearing much clothing, certainly not a coat. I can even tell you why I remember this: because she wasn't wearing a bra. Apparently she never wears a bra, but I'll soon get to her breasts as well.) So the woman finally came in, exhaling and pitching her cigarette as she opened the door; I said hello, making it clear that I remembered her; and she said that she needed to treat herself to a new notebook. She groaned, repeating that she was in desperate need of something nice for herself; she deserved it. Then, without my expressing any curiosity as to why she needed to treat herself to a notebook, she proceeded to tell me that she hadn't slept all night, and that she hadn't slept in almost a week. She then told me that a man had been stalking her, and she was procrastinating returning home, because she didn't want to go to the police station to file a report, even though she knew she had no choice. She said that she had met this man at a club the previous weekend, and that she had spoken with him briefly, and then she'd left the club, and he must've followed her home.

I didn't ask what club, but in any case, she said that over the course of the following week, she had seen him several times, parked in his car, in front of her apartment building. She told me that she had problems sleeping, insomnia, and once, opening her window, she saw him standing in front of her apartment building at three in the morning. She called the cops, but they told her there was nothing they could do about a man parking his car in front of her apartment building. On a few other occasions, she called the police and the police sent a patrol car, but by the time the car arrived, the man had driven away.

Eventually, only a few days earlier, finding this man standing outside her front door, she had to call her boyfriend and tell him that some man she'd met at a club was stalking her, and she didn't know what to do. She said that she was in such a panic that she called her boyfriend in the middle of his radio show. I assumed that her boyfriend was a college disc jockey, at some college in New Jersey, maybe, but I didn't ask. She said her boyfriend was so concerned that he left in the middle of his radio show and drove to her apartment to pick her up, and they left together out the back entrance of the building.

Then she began to tell me about her boyfriend Josh. She said that Josh always tells people that he grew up poor in the Bronx, when, in fact, he was raised in London and on Riverside Drive, and that he's a rich kid. She said it's a total joke that Josh tries to behave as if he understands something of poverty and hardship, and he talks the talk, when, in fact, he doesn't have a fucking clue, she said. She sighed, and then she told me that their relationship would never work. She said that they had been under a great deal of stress lately, mostly because of her illness, and that it was only a matter of time before they broke up.

Well, it wasn't only because of her illness, she said it was Josh's family as well. I questioned whether or not they were serious, because she implied it was a religious issue, and so I asked if Josh's family was Orthodox or conservative, and if conversion was a possibility, and she said no. It's *Josh's family,* she repeated. I didn't understand her meaning, but I accepted their reservations, whatever their denomination.

She then told me that she met Josh shortly before she became ill. She'd been working in the film industry then, some position in the art department was my understanding, and that she'd been quite successful, her career was really on the rise until she became ill. She told me that she's made several short films, and there was a great deal of interest in her work. I congratulated her, but again, I didn't ask any further.

Another detail: her watch. She kept walking all around the store, playing with her watch. I remembered her watch, because it was very unusual, more like a large, thick silver bracelet than a watch. I had asked about her watch the last time she was in the store, with her mother standing by, and she told me that this guy had given it to her. He was just some rich guy, she said. They'd been friends once, she and this rich guy, but now they weren't. She didn't like this guy anymore, and she said she'd come to realize that he was just another asshole. She went on to call this rich asshole the Toad. And she said the Toad was so pathetic that when he heard that the designer John Galliano had commissioned a watch to be made for him to give to five hundred of his closest friends, her acquaintance did the same thing—on a smaller scale. He had fifty watches made. She said, *The Toad copied him*. Galliano. Can you even *believe* that? Isn't that about the lamest thing you've ever heard? I laughed, but I don't remember if I said yes or no, I think I simply smiled as if to express that I understood how unoriginal this man was to have dared copy a fashion designer's original watch idea.

Also, the first time I noticed her watch, when her mother was standing there listening, she continued to say that if I really liked the watch she was wearing that she would put me in touch with this rich man. I was simply admiring the watch, that's all, and I immediately said that wasn't necessary, shaking my head. She then told me not to worry, that I wouldn't have to have sex with him in order to get one of these watches, that he would just give it to me. In fact, she said, Don't worry, you won't have to fuck him or anything, he'll just give it to you, and I remember looking to her mother, who hadn't blinked, and I was at a loss. Actually, she was right, the thought had crossed my mind; she was perceptive, at least, or maybe I grimaced. He's really quite generous, in his own way, she said, but I didn't ask anything more about their relationship. I just thanked her again, and reiterated that it wasn't necessary. She then said that if she tired of the watch, she would give it to me, and I said that was very sweet. I wasn't interested in taking her watch, but there was something about her that made me think that she was actually the type of person who would randomly appear and give away a rare watch.

Which brings me to her mother. Well, what I found most striking was that her mother seemed so normal. Too normal, perhaps. Actually, a physical description would be difficult, she was so normal looking. She was average height, average build, and plainly dressed in jeans or beige pants and a plain blue felt coat. She had short graying brown hair, a nice-enough face, but nothing distinct, mid- to late forties, maybe fifty, at most. What was unusual about her, considering this watch exchange with her daughter, was how distant this woman seemed, especially considering her daughter's enthusiasms. Actually, her mother appeared bored, patient but bored, listening as her daughter spoke throughout their visit.

I remembered her mentioning film the last time she visited, the time she brought her mother. Because the entire time they were in the store, she kept searching for the perfect notebooks for a film project. She chose a red notebook for the obvious symbolic reasons: she was writing a script about a cutter. Cutters, self-mutilators, you understand. She bought another notebook or two as well, but I can't remember for certain, it was blue, I think. In any case, the blue notebook didn't matter as much; the red notebook was the crucial purchase. She began to explain to her mother why that particular shade of red was perfectly suited for the character and how the combination of lined and unlined pages would complement the story structure. Then she spoke further about the story line.

Which brings me to her mother, because her mother's reaction to the story line struck me as strange. I mean the fact that the woman appeared so indifferent while her daughter was going on, discussing her character being brutally raped, and the character, this cutter, then slashing her own forearms, immediately after the rape...Throughout, her mother just looked like she needed a nap. I'm serious: the woman was completely unimpressed with the graphic nature of her daughter's story. It wasn't that she seemed impatient, but rather that the woman simply accepted the fact that her daughter was her burden in this life, and she had no choice but to listen.

When they finally approached the register, the woman told me that our store was one of her favorites in the world, and that was why she'd brought her mother, and then she asked her mother for money. Her mother then removed her wallet and handed her daughter approximately one hundred dollars, in cash. As I said, it was a good sale, and I'm sure part of the reason why I remember was that it must've really added to the day's total. While I rang up her purchases, the daughter mentioned something of the money her mother still owed her, and that they could work it out later, after they had tea, and her mother agreed. After I handed the purchases to the daughter and thanked them, the daughter put her arm around her mother's shoulders and kissed her cheek. I seem to remember her mother smiling, as she received her kiss, but now I'm not certain about that.

Whether or not she smiled, I distinctly remember her daughter chirping, Thank you, Marilyn! because her tone was facetious. I must say that this woman has a very unusual voice, both wispy and husky, a slight drawl and somewhat slurred speech. Anyhow, the daughter continued talking the entire time, even walking down the street, past the store, I could still see her mouth moving, and her mother saying nothing, not one word. My impression at the time was simply what I have told you: an eccentric daughter and burdened mother.

So after all this talk about the stalker and Josh, she repeated that she needed a notebook, something so she could write down her thoughts, or she was going to lose her mind. Then she asked if she could use her mother's credit card number, charge her mother's credit card, without having the card in hand. I told her we couldn't do that, and she reminded me how much money she had spent last time and the time before, and what a good customer she was. She insisted that her mother always let her use her credit card, and that she had to sign all her Medicaid money over to her mother, and then she pulled out a small bundle of credit card receipts that she said were purchases she had made on her mother's card.

Before I could respond, she approached the register and showed me the details that had been written down on receipts from other stores: name, address, telephone, card number, expiration, and so on. She said that if I wouldn't let her make the purchase without a card in hand, she'd call and have her purchases sent mail order, so what was the difference? I knew better, but as I said, I agreed, and for the record, I am not on commission. She had been in several times, she loved the store, she had to rely on her mother for money, her mother had paid last time, and we'd never had any problems with her or anyone else ever before.

She said it would only be a hundred dollars, and I said, All right, this once, and then I asked this woman about her mother; I said I remembered her last visit with her mother. I even remembered her mother's name, Marilyn—probably because she had called her mother by her first name, not Mom or Mommy, except for that one kiss. In response to what I considered nothing more than a polite question, she told me that Marilyn was all right, other than the fact that Marilyn had left her and her father when she was eleven years old. Marilyn had run off with another man, the man to whom Marilyn is still married, and that Marilyn had left her eleven-year-old daughter with her father. The problem wasn't simply her abandonment, but that as a child, she resembled her mother. She said that her father had always had an ugly temper and a drinking problem, and he was hopelessly in love with Marilyn, and once Marilyn ran away, her father focused his anger on his daughter due to her striking resemblance to his wife.

She kept tugging at her tank top, and then I remembered how little clothing she had worn the last time she visited with her mother in March, which struck me as odd in itself. Again, as I said, the last time this woman visited, she wasn't wearing a jacket, and she wasn't wearing any bra. She wore a very tight knit halter top that tied behind her neck and pulled above her navel, and her breasts had a sort of pubescent triangularity to them, that doughiness that you see in girls who've started developing but have no definition. I remembered this because she wasn't the least self-conscious, and for whatever reason, it impressed me. I remember thinking, More power to her.

So she kept tugging at her top, and then she discussed her stepfather, saying that she doesn't get along with the man, but that he puts up with her because he loves Marilyn. She said Marilyn wants her to move back in with them, but she said she'd lose her mind if she moved back in with Marilyn, no fucking way, she said. Then another notebook caught her eye, and a few other customers entered, and the discussion was dropped, or so I thought.

After the other customers left, she told me more about her insomnia and this stalker, and I encouraged her to return home as soon as possible and head straight to the police department. I told her I knew it must be awful, but she had to file a report.

She had to have some record, for her own peace of mind. She agreed, saying, I know, I know, I know... Then she changed the subject, saying that her natural clock was off. She couldn't remember the word, and I didn't know what she was talking about, and then she piped, *Circadian!* I have no circadian rhythms anymore: it's the drugs. I lose all sense of time. I can't tell if two minutes or two hours have passed, she said, and that certainly seemed true.

Over the course of the next fifteen minutes, I learned that she'd been supporting herself since she was sixteen and that she now lives in a boarding house, an SRO in Montclair, New Jersey. Not the nice part of Montclair, she said, but not the worst part, either. It's what she can afford, and it was safe enough, except for this guy stalking her now, but otherwise, yeah. The real problem is that there are no locks on her bedroom windows, she said. So I suggested she have locks put on her bedroom windows, with or without a stalker, and she said that she doesn't have the money for a locksmith, and this is why she can't sleep. She thinks that this man might break into her apartment at night, and she's afraid to leave during the day, because he might be waiting outside for her. Then she began to tear, and I touched her arm.

By then, we were at the far end of the store; I was standing behind the register, and she smiled when I touched her arm, and she gathered herself. Then she leaned forward, over the cash wrap, and she mentioned the pain. I can't tell you how much pain I feel, every muscle in my body. She went to several doctors, doctor after doctor after doctor, who performed test after test, MRIs, CAT scans, trying to diagnose her condition, but her condition is extremely rare, she said. Finally, she found the world's leading specialist in this disease or disorder I've never heard of, but sounded too plausible for me to mention, because I would make it sound ridiculous, you see. (To be honest, I wanted to write down the name of her condition, even phonetically, because it sounded so plausible, and I'd never heard of it before. But of course I couldn't write down anything in front of her, and I told myself to quit being so perverse. Now I'm sorry I didn't.) Well, he wasn't the world's leading specialist, her doctor was the leading specialist's protégé, she said.

She then explained that her illness is similar to rheumatoid arthritis, but that her specialist believes the source is deep emotional trauma, inflicted during childhood. And as she began reading his research, she realized that she suffered every single complaint he listed on a very long list of complaints experienced by sufferers of this very rare condition. She said she loves her doctor, and that he is the only doctor who truly understands her suffering, and that he fucking rocks. But in order to get treatment, she needs ten thousand dollars, to fly to California, where the world's leading specialist, her doctor's mentor, lives and conducts his research.

She returned to the subject of her most excellent doctor and said that they have an unspoken agreement, because he charges three hundred dollars an hour, and she needs to see him several times a month, but she never receives any bills. Again, I didn't ask. She said that this world-famous California specialist's treatment has proven extremely effective, although it's uncertain how long lasting its effect. Typically, anywhere from three to six months and then patients need to return. She said if the treatment freed her from the pain for even a month, it would be worth every penny.

Then she remembered it was time to take her medication, and she said that she better take it while she remembered or she'd be in real trouble, and she removed several large plastic bottles from her purse. She asked the time, and I told her the time, and she gasped and said she would take her medication, pay for her purchases, and then she would have to leave. So I offered to get her a drink and quickly stepped into the office, to pour a glass of water.

She began piling a stack of notebooks on the counter, and then she mentioned the skirt she was wearing. At some point, I had complimented her skirt, I said I thought it was very pretty, and it was. It was a knee-length silk circle skirt, with a blue geometric print. She thanked me again for my compliment, and she said a friend of hers worked at a store on Madison Avenue and gave her the skirt. One hundred percent silk, she said. I said it was very flattering on her, and she said it was, wasn't it? Then she returned to the subject of her weight, the fact that if it weren't for people like her friend who worked at the store on Madison Avenue, she wouldn't have any clothes she fit into and thank god she still had a few true friends left.

She said that before she became ill, she was working all the time and that she was extremely thin. She looked down, frowning at her chest, and she said that she would have to buy a bra soon, if she continued gaining weight. She said that she'd never had to wear a bra in her life. Then, still looking at her chest, she frowned and said that she didn't understand them. Her breasts. She said she didn't understand her breasts, and I didn't know what to tell her. Well, she'd become a very big girl since her illness, she said, and I said I didn't consider her a very big girl. She said no, she wasn't *big*-big, but in comparison to her former self, yes, and then she referred to me as petite, fine-boned, grabbing my wrist in order to compare our sizes, and I didn't feel comfortable and I tried to change the subject again.

She said it didn't matter, about her gaining weight, at least not in terms of her boyfriend Josh. She said he was a really big guy, and sensitive about his weight, his fat gut, but that she liked big guys with fat guts and she patted her belly and pulled out the flesh and shook it to illustrate Josh's physical type. She was attracted to men who looked nothing like her Aryan all-American father, who stood six foot two and weighed 185 pounds, and I refrained from comment. I said her boyfriend sounded very sweet, to leave his radio show in the middle of the program and pick her up, and that maybe she should stay at his place for a few days, just to get some sleep? She said no, she couldn't stay with him, they weren't close enough anymore for her to stay with him and that she was worried that the stalker would resort to violence. She said she heard the man was violent, and she honestly believed Josh's life might be endangered if the stalker saw her with Josh. She didn't want to take any chances, and that's why she hadn't been returning Josh's phone calls.

She started detailing the differences between Josh and her father, piling more items on the cash wrap, and then she said her father sends her checks, guilt money, but it's not enough to pay her bills. She believed that he knew what he had done to her, beating her, and she really hated taking his money in exchange, but she had no choice. She said Medicaid covers some of her prescriptions, but not all. Then she said that her father had forced her to see a psychiatrist, and that by the time she turned thirteen, when she finally removed her shirt to show her psychiatrist the fist marks on her back, the psychiatrist called in her father. Without batting an eye, her father told the psychiatrist that those marks were self-inflicted. They were *fist marks,* she said, demonstrating with her own fists, so how did I beat my own back? she asked, and I said I didn't know and I was very sorry. Well, anyway, of course the psychiatrist believed her father. She said that she suspected the psychiatrist, who was female, had been attracted to her father, who looked like a model, just as every single woman over the age of thirty was attracted to her father.

She chose a few more items, carrying them around, and then she said her back was killing her, and she asked if I minded if she sat down on the floor for a minute, and I said no. Even if I felt no sympathy, which I did, what could I say? So she sat down, beside the cash wrap, leaned back on her arms, and spread her legs. Seated there, she sighed again and said that felt much better and then she told me that after her father claimed her bruises were self-inflicted, the shrink admitted her to a psychiatric ward for two weeks. She said she had to stay for two weeks until her mother was able to drive back to Wisconsin from the East Coast and have her discharged. Then she began to cry.

She said I couldn't imagine what it was to be accused of lying, of harming herself. She said that no one had believed her, they all thought she was insane, everyone took his side, and no one protected her, no one even examined her to see if he had sexually abused her. She said she knew her mother had tremendous guilt about leaving her with her father for those three years and the two weeks she spent in the psych ward, but that they were working on their issues, she said.

You want to hear something really sick? she asked, and before I could answer, she told me that Marilyn has propositioned

Josh, outright. She said Marilyn comes on to him all the time, and I wouldn't believe the things Josh has told her about Marilyn. And what's more, Marilyn has always been jealous of her boyfriends and any attention focused on her, really, and that Marilyn has never complimented her, never called her pretty or beautiful or even once said that she looked nice. She said that when Josh picked her up at Marilyn's house, a few months ago, she had dressed up for their date. When Josh commented on how pretty she looked, Marilyn said, You should have seen *me* when I was her age. I am still trying to imagine the silent plain-looking woman saying this to a tall, heavyset Jewish guy of about twenty-six years of age, and it's very difficult.

Then again, her mother was also a bit odd, and not the least maternal, that much seemed true. She never touched her daughter—she never even spoke to her daughter. Then again, there was something too sour about the woman for me to imagine her making a sexual advance on a guy half her age, or anyone, for that matter. Well, despite propositioning her boyfriend, she repeated that they're really working on their relationship, mother and daughter. They're trying, even though Marilyn doesn't believe that her daughter suffers any physical pain, and that Marilyn shows no interest in her illness. Marilyn simply tolerates her and takes her disability money, she said, but still.

Then she told me the name of her illness again, and she said how relieved she was that at least she wouldn't be disfigured for life. She hunched over, curling her fingers and wrists in order to illustrate how much worse her situation could be, and how grateful she was that that was not her fate. At that point she told me how fortunate she was, and that she knew her pain was nothing in comparison to what others suffered, and she had no right to complain about her lot in life. I told her there was no reason for her to compare her suffering to anyone else's, and she began to cry. Through sobs, she told me that she had never told anyone so much about herself before, she had never spoken of her father physically and sexually abusing her, and I believed her. Whether or not her story was true, she was obviously suffering a great deal, for whatever reason, and I simply couldn't refuse to listen or ask her to leave. I believed her, and I felt for her, and I thought the least I could do was let her talk. She struck me as someone in desperate need of a good cry—I thought it might make a difference.

God, I feel so much better, she said. I can't tell you how grateful I am. I said it was all right, and then I told her that she needed to talk to someone—someone she could trust. If what you're telling me about this illness, that it's caused by deep trauma, why don't you talk to someone about what happened to you and get off the morphine? I just don't want to go home, she said, and began crying again, raspy hoarse sobs. You have to go to the police station, file a report, give them some information, and then you can stay at your mother's and get some sleep. I think you need to find a therapist you can talk to, okay? I said. I'm sorry, I'm sorry for telling you, you were just trying to be nice, and no one has ever been so nice to me, and then she began to cry much harder than before. I knelt down, touching her arm, and I said, It's all right. There are plenty of people who can help you, if you give them a chance, but I'm not that person. She tried smiling; one of those disfigured, contorted smiles, and she nodded though her tears. Let's get you up, I said, and I helped her stand. She was obviously in pain and needed to grab on to both my shoulders in order to get her balance.

In fact, I noticed something odd about her body the first time I ever saw her. I mean, I could see the very thin woman inside her, just as she had said; and it was as though her body, every limb, muscle, and joint had been stretched beyond capacity. Like the arms of a cotton sweater that have lost their shape and dangle. Or like a small child wearing an adult's sweatshirt, hugging their arms inside the shirt, and swinging their prosthetic limbs about, pleased with the idea of having no arms. Really, she moved like a drugged rag doll. So I helped her stand and helped her lean over the counter, and she sifted through all the merchandise she had chosen. All right, if I let myself have these things, then I can do it, she said.

Her total didn't come to a hundred dollars, like she said, but she didn't bat an eye when I told her the total, and I didn't care anymore. I wanted her to pay and leave, but when I told her the total, I wasn't sure what to expect. In a perfectly calm voice, she said, Marilyn owes me, and I'll pay her back the rest. I'm receiving a check for a film treatment. The first check bounced, the guy is such a flake, but this one's sure to go through...Only now do I question the truth of this assertion, that she had written a film treatment that someone had actually optioned. But at the time, I didn't question the likelihood that she wrote a believable treatment on the subject of a self-mutilator who had been brutally raped, and that whoever had optioned her film had bounced a check, just as she said. It seemed perfectly natural. In fact, it seemed exactly the sort of story this woman would write, and write extremely well, and sell to some man in San Diego with financial problems of his own.

Well, I finally got her out of the store. I even carried her bags outside for her, and then she said she was just going to sit down and have a cigarette. I told her that I was going to have to close the store at 2:30 so that I would have time to make a bank deposit, which wasn't true, I never make the bank deposits, but I needed an excuse. She'd paid for her merchandise, so I didn't see any reason not to usher her out. I'd listened, I'd tried to be supportive, and I was faint with hunger. She asked if I'd be leaving soon, and I said I didn't know, because I was suspicious about her asking. She said if I was heading to the bank, she would join me, and I said she shouldn't wait, I'd have to do some work in the office before I could leave, and I wasn't certain how long that would take. She said, Oh, that's too bad, I'm so *sore,* and I'm not sure how I'm going to be able to hail a taxi, but never mind, she said, smiling. I'm sure it'll be no problem. I said, Are you sure? I could hail the taxi for you and carry your bags? She said no, she needed to rest and have a cigarette before she could muster the energy, so I said, Take care. She said, Hey, what's your name? I said, Courtney. She said, I'm Jen, and thank you so much, so, so, *so* much, you've been so good to me. No one's ever been so kind to me. From that point on, she started calling me numerous affections. Thank you, sweetheart; take care, honey; see you soon, darling. Anyhow.

I returned to the office and had a cigarette myself. My only hope was that she would be gone a half hour later, when I opened the doors again. But at 3:15, when I stepped out of the office, she was still sitting in front of the store. She'd put her hair in a ponytail on top of her head and she'd put on her sunglasses, and she looked prepared to leave, so I didn't return to the office. Her back was turned to me, and my motions didn't seem to rouse her any, not even when I unlocked the front door. She was still smoking, and then she started searching through her bag. It took a minute, riffling through the numerous items stuffed in her bag, none of which I could describe, because I was keeping my distance, but she finally found her lipstick, and she began applying lipstick again. I'd never seen anyone who took a half hour to apply lipstick, but she did. I know because I checked the clock again.

Finally, at 3:45, after she closed her compact, I stepped outside and I asked her if she wanted me to hail a cab. She said, You aren't going to the bank? I said, No, it's too late now. She said, *Oh...* Then she asked how much I thought it would cost to take a cab to Newark. She said she just couldn't bear taking the subway to the bus, and the bus to another bus. So she thought she might just take a cab to Newark, or maybe take the bus to Newark, then take a cab home. She said that she had been in this position once before, and a cab to Newark had only cost her thirty dollars. I told the man I had thirty bucks, and I figured I'd start the waterworks, if that didn't work. She said she'd do the same again, and not to worry about her, she'd be leaving in a minute. We said good-bye again, and she called me by an endearment again and told me that she'd have to bring a copy of one of her short films next time, one of her films that had been picked up by the Sundance Channel. I said I'd be very interested to see her work, and then I closed the door behind me.

For the next twenty minutes, I did my best to ignore her. Other customers came in, I helped them, and then, while I was ringing up another transaction, Jen returned inside. I hadn't been paying attention, and she hobbled toward the register, explaining that her heel was bleeding. The other customers left, and then Jen said that she had blisters from her cheap shoes and asked if she could use the bathroom to rinse off the blood, and I agreed. She was bleeding and she needed to use the bathroom, I couldn't refuse. But needless to say, it took her awhile. With the door cracked, she stayed in the bathroom for a good fifteen minutes, and then she reappeared and sat back down on the floor. Before I could speak, she said she needed to clean off her feet, then she'd be on her way.

Riffling through the pills in her bag, she proceeded to remove a Wet Ones, a very large Wet Ones, or whatever it was. I remember because I'd never seen a Handi Wipe that big. I wondered where she got them; they looked surgical, or at least I'd never seen them in the podiatry section of my neighborhood Love's. She then removed the sterile wipe from its seal, tearing it open with her teeth and spitting the torn corner on the floor, and she proceeded to clean her feet.

Then she started complaining about her shoes. She told me she'd bought them at Nine West and showed me where the shoes had cut her ankle, and then she began complaining about the low quality of Nine West shoes. She asked me if I had ever bought Nine West shoes, and I said no, and she warned me against them. Then she began scrubbing her feet, right on our floor, scrubbing the black dye off her sole. Her feet were black from a cheap dye job, it was true, and the wipe began pilling, little black dirty-foot pills, all over our wooden floor, and I was hoping she would think to clean them up so I wouldn't have to. Really, I am not a squeamish person, but it kind of grossed me out, to be honest, even though I was trying not to worry about it, and the entire situation was so bizarre, I didn't have a chance to worry.

Finally, Jen finished cleaning her right foot, and I thought, *Thank god,* she's going to leave now. I'll help her stand, and then she'll leave. I'll walk her out the door again, and it'll be done...No. Just as I was about to offer her a hand, pull her up by her arm if need be, she removed another Wet Ones from her purse, tore it open, spitting again, and then began cleaning her shoe. Her shoe. First, the sole of her shoe, then the ankle strap, the heel, around the sole, the sole, again, scrubbing the shoe and inspecting her work.

I checked to see if there was any traffic on the street, if anyone might be able to see her sitting with her skirt jacked to her waist and her legs spread, but there wasn't much happening on the street, and, thankfully, no one else was in the store. I don't know if she noticed my gaze, but at some point she realized that she was exposing herself, and she said, I should probably pull my skirt down, huh? I don't think I said yes, but I gave the impression it might be a good idea. Her underwear was blue, midnight blue satin bikini underwear, and she felt no self-consciousness about this, either. Honestly, I probably sound uptight, but I'm not squeamish, and I'm not prudish, really. I was just leaning over the counter, propping my chin with one hand, watching her on the ground. I wasn't uptight—it was just a little disconcerting.

Still working on her ankle strap, she asked if I'd ever been sick, really, really sick, sick for days on end, and if I could remember that feeling, forgetting what it was to be healthy, and I said yes. She said that's how it was with her pain, that she could no longer remember what it felt to live without pain or who she had been before she became ill. She talked some more about her morphine intake, and how ineffective the drug had become, that she'd developed such a high tolerance that they couldn't give her enough without the risk of her overdosing, and that was why they had put her on all this other medication. Combinations of medications that caused all these side effects, that made her gain weight, and caused her to lose her bladder control, and constipated her, and left her unable to sleep for weeks on end, even when she wasn't being stalked.

She asked if I'd ever read any Buddhist tracts, her exact word, and I said I'd read some, and she said Buddhism had saved her life. She had suffered such intense pain that there was a time when she wasn't sure she wanted to go on living that way, but then she remembered something she had once read about not attaching to pain, not attaching to negative thoughts and emotions, and it had freed her. Really, she said. That's how I'm able to stand and smile and act normal, even when I feel as awful as I do, every single day of my life. And that's why people don't believe me. I just wish they really knew, I wish someone knew… As she said this, she stood and asked for the trash to throw away her Wet Ones, and she cleaned up the pills of dirty wet paper that had accumulated on the floor. Then she asked if she could wash her hands, and before I had a chance to answer, she had already opened the door and stepped into the office, heading straight into the bathroom.

Once she closed the bathroom door, I called my boss, but he wasn't in the studio. I left a message at the studio, and then I tried him on his cell phone, but he didn't answer, and I had to leave a second message, explaining that he needed to call me as soon as possible. Then, after another twenty minutes of Jen in the bathroom, I began to worry. I could hear her moving, the water running, but at thirty minutes, I began to panic.

You have to understand, I live in the East Village, and when someone stays in the bathroom for a long period of time, I think overdose. I hadn't given any thought to Jen being a junkie, because of her weight, and because she didn't have junkie skin, that plasticity you sometimes see in the skin of a waiter or waitress. Anyhow, I hadn't given it any thought, but then I began to worry. I didn't know what else to think but OD. I thought she must be shooting up, and that she might overdose in our bathroom, and that I'd have to call an ambulance. I tried to stay calm, figuring that if she had already passed out, St. Vincent's was just down the street. So all I had to do was break down the door, slap her, throw water on her, and if that didn't work, if necessary, I would drag her outside by her ankles and hail a cab. If I could just get her to St. Vincent's, they'd take her, they had to, or I was going to throw the most ungodly fit they'd ever seen. I certainly felt capable, and it was reassuring, so I figured, Save it: I'll get her to St. Vincent's, if I can just get the door open. Just deal with the door...

Well, in the meantime, I thought to keep her talking, because as long as she was talking, I wouldn't need to break down the door. I could still get myself out of this mess, and suddenly the door swung open, Jen reappeared, and then she said good-bye and she left the store. Just like that. I couldn't believe it— I'd been saved. More customers entered, I became distracted, and less than two minutes later, Jen entered the store for the third time that day. I have to use your bathroom, she said, squeezing her thighs together, and she went right in. I was speaking to a customer, and there was nothing else I could do but leave the door to the office open.

Ten minutes later, still no Jen, and so I started knocking

every few minutes, and she would answer and she'd say, I'm just washing my hands, or, I'll be right out, or, Almost done, and I figured that as long as she was speaking coherently, everything would be all right. I kept the door open and after the store emptied again, I started talking. I didn't like the idea of talking to her while she was doing her business, if that's what she was doing, but talking was far less disturbing than the idea of calling an ambulance. Five or ten minutes later, I finally asked her to open the door. I called her by an endearment this time, speaking in the sweetest possible voice. I said, Jen, honey, will you open the door so I can be sure you're all right? Then the door swung open, and there she was, with her silk skirt pulled and tucked into a ball in the crotch of her underwear, propping her foot in the bathroom sink, inspecting her toenails. Be right out, she said. I was stunned. Okay, I said.

When she finally stepped out of the bathroom, forty minutes later, almost six hours after she first passed the store, she slumped over the register, putting on one shoe, and warning me again to never buy Nine West shoes. Because even though they looked all right, they were cheap pieces of shit, and then she got the shoe on her foot, much to my relief, and she said the medication they put her on caused her to lose bladder and bowel control whenever she wasn't constipated. She told me it was her first bowel movement in a week, and I tried not to think about it, honestly. I think I said I was sorry to hear that. Then she left. She went outside and sat on the stoop again, but at least I was alone for a minute, so I locked the office door, just in case.

What should I have done? Throughout her visits to the bathroom, people kept coming into the store, and with Jen in the bathroom, I was trapped. The most I could do was leave the office door open, so I could hear her and stay at the register, in case anyone had a purchase. I couldn't call my boss, as I had wanted to do since I first tried him around 3:45. I wasn't able to try him again until close to 6:00, when I finally got Jen back outside for the last time. But even then, she was still sitting right outside, and once I did have a chance to call my boss again, he still wasn't at the studio, and his cell phone wasn't turned on, either, but I left more messages, repeating that he needed to call me right away. When he finally called me back, Jen was still outside, but there were more people in the store, and I couldn't speak. I had told him it was urgent he return my call as soon as possible, and then I had to tell him that I'd call him right back, and he sounded confused, but he agreed. So by the time I was finally able to call him back and say that I couldn't talk, but he needed to come right away, he said he'd be there in less than ten minutes.

At first, I was afraid that James wouldn't arrive in time, and that he'd think I had made the whole thing up. I was also afraid that he would send her away, and she would know that I had told on her, and that she couldn't trust me, and she might not trust anyone else again. Somehow, I wanted her to trust me, but I also wanted to be freed of her. I just wanted her to go away. And by the time he arrived, less than ten minutes later, Jen wasn't sitting in front of the store anymore. Before I could speak, he asked if she was wearing a blue skirt with a pattern, and I almost shouted, Yes! That's her! She's down the street, sitting on the steps of the Y, he said.

He asked me what happened, and I told him about her breakdown and her needing to use the bathroom and lying about a deposit just so I could get her out of the store, then escorting her out of the store, offering to call a cab, and then her returning, again and again...I was very upset. My boss said that I shouldn't have allowed her to use our bathroom. I said I knew better, but she'd been in the store before, and she'd just spent four hundred dollars, and that she said she might lose bladder control in our store if I didn't. I said I didn't have any choice, and he said, All right, but never again. He said it was a security issue. Did she threaten you? he asked, and I said no.

Then he stepped outside and walked down the block to check on her. When he returned, he informed me that she'd moved inside, and she was just sitting in a chair, alone in a room. She had all her shopping bags with her—that's how he identified her. I was just relieved that he'd seen her. Then I asked permission to leave. It'd been over six hours since she first appeared, and I couldn't stay there any longer, and he said of course. I didn't tell him about agreeing to ring up her purchases without a credit card in hand, because I still believed her. I didn't even think about it, to tell you the truth. I felt too exhausted. Stepping out the door, I checked to make sure she wasn't in sight, and then I left, walking in the opposite direction as fast as I could.

I returned home and thought the matter was forgotten. James sent me an e-mail, a few days later, apologizing for not being more supportive, and I thanked him. But then, this last Sunday, I arrived at the store to find a note my coworker Jonathan left for me. He wrote to say he'd call me later in the day, because the saga of the poor little rich girl continued, and I thought it could be a number of different customers. So when he didn't call, I didn't think much of it. I called him the next day, Monday, at noon, and Jon told me that your company was disputing the four-hundred-dollar charge that this woman had made. I can't tell you how sick I felt. He said, Don't worry, don't worry about it, you haven't done anything wrong.

I hung up with Jon, and I immediately called my boss, James, and I told him that I rang up that charge as an EDC sale. EDC, as you know, is the term for a charge made without a card in hand. I punched Marilyn's card number, the expiration date, and that was all it took. It was a mistake, I know, but I never thought that it would come to this. At most, I figured it was something that Jen would work out with her mother, whatever their financial arrangement. James thanked me for my honesty, sighed, and said he would call me later. I hung up, sat for a moment, stood, and then I threw up. I became so upset that I threw up and had to lie down for several hours, with what remained of my day off.

A few days ago, after I heard that James would have to make a case in his own defense, I asked him if it wasn't possible to call one of your representatives, explain that a woman who had been to our store several times had told me that she had permission to use her mother's card. I hoped he could explain that the fault was mine, not his. Well, James said he didn't feel that was possible; he would simply have to gather what proof he had and proceed. In the meantime, he was going to look for the receipt and see if he could decipher the name signed on the receipt. His hope is that Jen signed Marilyn's full name, and he might be able to find Marilyn and explain what happened and see if any of the merchandise can be returned. My feeling is that even if he can track her down, Marilyn will not help us, she will say that the fault is mine and that I shouldn't have allowed her daughter to use the card. Fine.

Honestly, I don't care anymore. By now, I don't care if I was conned, I don't care if Jen was lying, and I'm not sure I care if she was telling the truth. Let Jen keep the notebooks, credit Marilyn's account, and my boss can drop his claim. I don't have four hundred dollars. I don't have twenty, for that matter. But I will figure a way to repay the store, and I will never perform another transaction without a credit card in hand, all right? There's nothing more to be said or done. Please, can we just forget about it now? Thank you for your consideration.

Sincerely,
Courtney Eldridge

Summer
of Mopeds

S ay there's this woman whose accountant makes her cry. Say there's this woman who wakes, showers, goes to her accountant's office, and he says, What's that look on your face? And then the woman starts to cry, or she leaves his office and then she cries. Or, say the woman wakes, showers, gets dressed, goes to therapy, and then goes to her accountant's office. Then her accountant says, What's that look on your face? And the woman says, What is what look on my face...? Then they fight and the woman leaves her accountant's office, shaking with anger, and she almost starts to cry, waiting for the elevator.

Or, say she wakes, showers, gets dressed, goes to therapy, and then walks to the subway. She catches the subway, walks to her accountant's office, and then passes his building. The woman walks right past her accountant's office, distracted, and then realizes that she's missed her accountant's building. She turns around, walks back, and grimaces, entering her accountant's building. Then she gets in the elevator and pushes the wrong button, but doesn't realize her mistake until she steps out into the penthouse suite, looks up, and thinks, *Where am I...? Whoops—wrong floor.*

She turns around and gets back in the elevator and pushes the right button, waits for the doors to close, then pushes the DOOR CLOSE button, waits, and then pushes DOOR CLOSE again, sighs, and says to herself, What the fuck? She pushes the button a few times in rapid succession, as if to teach the button a lesson, and the doors close. Then the elevator stops at her floor and she swears, getting off the elevator, and walks down the hall.

She enters her accountant's office and sits down in the chair in front of his desk, then he says, What's that look on your face? She takes offense and says, What is *what* look on my face...? They fight about Social Security, and then she leaves, shaking with anger, and she almost starts crying but doesn't, because she doesn't want to give her accountant the satisfaction and because there are too many people on the elevator for her to cry freely.

She thinks of possible insults to keep from crying, as if she could do it all over again and insult him first, but can't in either case, then returns home and calls her friend who recommended this accountant. He is *such a character,* her friend had said. And then her friend said that this accountant was cheap and charming *and* he had a voice like Barry White. What's his name? she asked, and her friend said, Klaus. Klaus Winchester. And she said, A CPA named Klaus who's cheap and sounds like Barry White? And her friend said, You'll love him. So she calls this friend and tells her friend that, Barry White or not, if the man ever speaks to her like that again, she'll go *off*.

Or, say she wakes, showers, drinks a cup of coffee, and checks her date book. Then she dreads her appointments, thinks of canceling, thinks her new accountant is mean and he scares her, thinks, *Yes, he does, but not as much as the IRS,* then she nods, grabs her keys, and goes to therapy. At therapy, then, she talks about a suit; she thinks to mention a red-and-white horizontal-striped one-piece bathing suit she wore as a girl. She says, I loved that suit. Then she talks some more about swimming and high school girls she knew and kids she looked down on, growing up, then feels badly, and then she cries, dries her eyes, thanks her therapist for her time, leaves, and walks to the subway.

At the subway, then, she waits and steps forward and looks for rats, then down the tunnel, sees nothing but a single blue track light, and then quickly steps back. She puts the image of herself being shoved in front of an oncoming train out of her mind, crossing her arms and leaning against a metal beam, and listens to other commuters complain. *Fuckin' A,* says one guy, and she rolls her eyes, wishing the other commuters would just shut up.

She clenches her jaw, hearing the announcement that the R train is having electrical difficulties and passengers should... etc., etc., and thinks, *Thanks for fucking telling me, like you couldn't,* etc., etc. Then she leaves in a huff and runs down the stairs to catch another subway and almost trips, headfirst. She catches her breath and steps on the subway, sits, and smiles, feeling pleased. Then she realizes she's headed in the wrong direction and gets off and catches the subway headed in the right direction.

She gets off the subway and walks up the stairs to Canal Street, then smells something rank and covers her nose. She crosses the street and walks in the right direction, and then walks past her accountant's office, wondering what ever happened to that suit...? She looks up, notices the numbers on a building, and turns around, swearing at herself again, etc., and walks two blocks back to her accountant's building. She grimaces, entering the front door, gets on the elevator and pushes the wrong button, and ends up at the penthouse, with fresh calla lilies and a receptionist wearing an ivory silk blouse, and she thinks, *Where am I...?* Etc.

She gets back on the elevator, sighs, checks her watch, pushes DOOR CLOSE, etc., then waits as more people get on the elevator. The elevator stops several more times and several more people get on the elevator and someone steps on her and she shouts, Watch it! Then she gets pushed by more people getting into the elevator and keeps her mouth shut this time, and then grimaces again, recalling the thousands of fingerprints she saw on the glass doors when she entered the building. And again she's disgusted by the idea of thousands of dirty hands touching the glass in the middle of flu season and couldn't they pay someone to clean the front doors once in a while...? She steps aside once more as the doors open and she waits as more people try to get on the elevator and she wants to tell them it's too full! *No more fucking people, all right?*

She takes a deep breath and scolds herself for having thought, while being pushed and stepped on, that because every other person on the elevator is Chinese, they don't mind being sardined together. Then she feels ashamed of herself for having such thoughts and tells herself to calm down, considering she wouldn't be here if she'd pushed the right button in the first place. Push the right floor next time and this won't happen, will it? No, she tells herself, and then tells herself, Okay, then.

And then she says, Excuse me, excuse me, please, *Jesus,* etc., gets off the elevator, and rings the buzzer outside her accountant's office. She enters his office, sits, waits in the waiting room, and then walks into her accountant's office. She sits down and then her accountant says, What's that look on your face? And she says, What is *what* look...? Etc. They disagree about Social Security and then they fight, and she leaves shaking, and almost cries but doesn't, because, etc., etc., and then she tries to think of an insult that would reduce the man to tears, but can't. She returns home and calls her friend and says, Who the hell does he think he is? And then she becomes angry with her friend as well.

Or, she wakes and rolls over, closes her eyes, and dreads the day ahead. She gets up, showers, dresses, pours a cup of coffee, then looks at her date book and thinks about her accountant, etc., etc., then nods, grabs her keys, walks to therapy, and waits in the waiting room. She leafs through *Newsweek* and *Food & Wine* and thinks, *God, I want to go home. I just want to go home and go back to bed and I want this all to be over...* Her therapist walks into the waiting room and smiles at her and she smiles back at her therapist and returns the magazines to the coffee

table. She follows her therapist down the hall, into her therapist's office, and then she sits in her favorite chair, the one far-
thest from the window.

Her therapist sits and smiles and says, How are you? How
was your week? And she says, Fine, fine, and then she smiles,
and her therapist says, Good, good, and nods and waits. She
looks at her hands, thinks, ignores the thought, and then
she mentions a swimsuit she wore as a girl; a red-and-white
horizontal-striped one-piece bathing suit. I loved that suit, she
says. I loved that suit so much I slept in it all summer long, she
says. Then she talks some more about the striped suit and
swimming and high school girls and her brothers shouting,
Two for flinching! Two for flinching! Then her therapist nods
and asks a question, and then she nods and tries to answer her
question without crying but only cries harder. Then she stops
crying, dries her eyes and blows her nose, thanks her therapist,
and closes her therapist's office door behind her. She checks
the mirror in her therapist's bathroom, wipes the mascara off
her cheeks, and leaves.

She walks to the subway and waits and frowns, watching a
guy check out some teenage girl, standing nearby, wearing
stretch jeans and white patent platform boots, as the guy's
friend hawks and spits onto the tracks, then she steps forward
and checks the tunnel again. She listens to other commuters
complain, *Fuckin' A,* and, What the hell is taking so long? I
haven't got all damn day, and then she hears the announcement
that the R train is etc., etc. In a huff then, she walks back upstairs, then downstairs, then she almost trips, grabs the rail and
gasps, and steadies herself, etc. She catches the subway in the
nick of time and sits down, only to realize she's heading in

the wrong direction, and thinks, *Oh, goddamnit*... etc., then smacks her forehead with the palm of her hand.

She gets off the subway headed in the wrong direction, then she gets on the subway headed in the right direction, and then she gets off again and walks up the stairs to Canal. She smells something and checks the street signs, etc., and walks in the right direction, etc. Then she walks right past her accountant's office, distracted by thoughts of that bathing suit and whether or not her mother threw it away after she got her brother in trouble or if she threw it away or...? She stops, notices the numbers on the building in front of her, swears at herself again, and then turns around and walks to her accountant's building and grimaces, etc.

She gets on the elevator and pushes the wrong button and ends up in the peach penthouse with the beautiful Asian receptionist, who reminds her of an ex-boyfriend. Then she gets back on the elevator and gets pushed and shoved and checks the elevator's weight capacity and thinks racist thoughts about Asians as more people cram onto the elevator, etc. Then she yells, Watch it! at an old lady and scolds herself for yelling and for getting shoved in the first place. Then she excuses herself, snaps, Jesus, gets off, and makes it to her accountant's office, only five minutes late.

She enters and waits in Klaus's waiting room, overhearing him talk to another client, as the two men enter the waiting room from his office. Then she tries not to stare at the man with whom her accountant is surprisingly cheerful, not at all like he is with her. Then, watching the two men on the sly, she wonders why her accountant doesn't seem to like her when he likes her friend and even her friend's two coworkers, neither of whom she particularly likes. Then she tries not to take it personally and decides that it doesn't matter because she disliked her accountant first, anyway.

Then the black man—or rather, the very handsome black man—the very handsome black man wearing a tailored pinstriped suit and purple dress shirt and a dark gray silk tie with a handkerchief, says good-bye to her, and she realizes she's been staring at him the whole time. She says, Good-bye, after he's already turned and opened the door, and then she worries that the delay in her response has made her seem unfriendly and she frowns again. Then her accountant invites her into his office and tells her to sit, and she does, not caring for his tone.

Then he says, What's that look on your face? and she says, What is *what* look on my face…? Etc. Then she removes a letter from her purse and asks her accountant to take a look at the letter and he does and then they fight about Social Security. Then she leaves, shaking, etc., and almost starts to cry but doesn't, because or because etc., etc. She returns home, thinking of something mean she could say about his face or his person or his ugly tie, as if she could, but can't, and can't think of anything particularly mean, either, etc.

Angry again, she calls her friend and says, I don't give a fuck who he sounds like. Barry White or not, I think he's a total fucking asshole. And if he ever, *ever* speaks to me like that again, I'll go *off.* Her friend starts to speak, and she interrupts and says, I should call *him* boy, see how he likes that. Hey, *boy,* finish my taxes yet…? Then her friend says, You just have to get his sense of humor, and then she becomes that much angrier with her accountant and her friend and she hangs up the phone.

———

Or, she wakes, rolls over and wants to hide, knowing that it's going to be a long day, sighs, and finally gets up. She showers, dresses, pours a cup of coffee, dreads her appointments, and wonders why in the world she scheduled these two appointments on the same day. Crazy.

Then she remembers that her accountant gave her no choice and left her a nasty message on her answering machine. And she remembers how she had tried to break the ice with her accountant the first and only time they met, by confessing her fear of being audited, and instead of showing any compassion, he treated her like an idiot. And then she remembers that afterward, when she mentioned her fear of this new accountant to the friend who recommended him, her friend said, Oh, you just have to get his sense of humor, that's all, and she really didn't care for the insinuation that she didn't get the man's sense of humor, either. She assures herself she has a very good sense of humor, nods, grabs her keys, and heads out the door.

She walks to therapy, buzzes, waits, dreads, and thinks, *I just want to go home and go back to bed,* etc. Her therapist walks into the waiting room and she smiles at her therapist and follows her down the hall and sits in her favorite chair and then scans the room, checking the time and the Kleenex box and the candy basket and whether or not there are flowers on the metal stand in the corner, near the window? But no, no flowers today... Then her therapist sits in the chair across from her, etc., smiles and wipes her nose with a pink Kleenex, and says, How are you? Then she says, Fine, fine, and her therapist says, Good, good, etc., and waits. Then she looks at her hands and says, Well, to tell you the truth, I was dreading coming here today, and her therapist nods again and asks why.

She thinks for a moment, ignores the thought, and then she mentions a swimsuit she wore as a girl, a red-and-white horizontal-striped one-piece bathing suit. A Speedo—it was a Speedo, she says. I loved to swim so much that I slept in my bathing suit all summer long. Then she smiles and says, So I was riding my bike home from the pool this one day. I was walking my bike up the hill, and this friend of my dad's drove by and he stopped and offered me a ride home.

Then she talks some more about the man and the summer of mopeds and her brothers and how her brothers teased her, making her stand by the television for hours sometimes, during severe thunderstorms when television stations used to broadcast the emergency message, PLEASE STAND BY, because if she didn't stand by the TV, the storm would never end and it would be all her fault for being so damn lazy, so get your butt over there, they said. And then if she refused, they'd tackle her and play typewriter or, simply, tappers, as they called it, and her therapist leans her head to the side, curious, and asks, Tappers? And she says, One of my brothers, whoever got me first, would pin me down on my back by straddling my chest and digging his kneecaps into my shoulders and then tapping my chest as hard as he could with his fingertips until I screamed, and then *bang*! He'd slap me upside the head like he was returning on a manual typewriter…Then she starts to laugh, then she starts to cry, etc., blows her nose and dries her eyes and leaves, etc.

She walks to the subway, waits, sighs, steps forward, looks, loses patience, etc. She rolls her eyes as a guy wearing a navy cotton sun visor turned upside down and backward on his forehead says, *Fuckin' A,* while his friend checks out some hottie with a spit curl on her forehead and red lips lined in a black liner. Then she hears the announcement that passengers should etc., etc., and she walks back upstairs and catches a subway headed in the wrong direction, etc. She gets off and on and off the subway, then walks to the street and smells something rank, etc. Then she walks past her accountant's building, distracted, thinking of her brother calling her a lying bitch and how they never really got along after that and feels bad and wishes she could talk to him, really talk, but still, the suit. No idea what happened to that suit…She looks up, frowns, turns around, and walks back to her accountant's building, swearing at herself, etc. She gets on the elevator, pushes the wrong button, and ends up at the penthouse, with the beautiful Asian secretary looking at her as if she's obviously in the wrong place, and she nods in agreement.

She gets back on the elevator and smiles at the receptionist and then steps away from the open doors, worrying that her face is still puffy from crying, then pushes the right button and waits and gets shoved and stepped on and yells at an old woman and snaps, Jesus, etc. She gets off the elevator and walks into her accountant's office and sees her accountant talking to a very handsome man whose shirt is more like lavender, and she whistles to herself. Her accountant laughs at something the man has said and says to her, Be with you in a moment, and she smiles and says, Fine, no rush, then she wonders why her accountant isn't as nice to her as he is to this man or her friend or etc., etc., and the handsome man says good-bye to her and she etc., etc. Then she follows her accountant into his office, and he says, Sit, in a brusque tone, and she tries to smile.

Yes, she smiles, although she's very nervous about what her accountant has to say about how much money she owes the government. And she wants to protest, simply because her accountant told her last time that she probably owes several thousand dollars this year. If you're lucky, he said. If I'm *lucky*? she asked. Then he sent her away late on a Friday afternoon, he waved her off, after telling her that she'd find a way to pay. Then she asked how she was going to pay her taxes if she had no money? And then he shrugged and threw her file on top of a pile of manila files, waist-high and haphazardly stacked in a corner of the room, behind his cluttered desk.

Just to top it off, her accountant turned around, looked at her, frowned, and then told her she should be grateful and to get out and have a nice weekend. There are more important things in life, he said. And she wanted to say something barbed in response, but she felt too sick to her stomach. Though she did manage to protest, asking him if he was certain she was going to owe this year? Then he said, We'll see what we see; and she asked him what he meant by *we'll see what we see*? Then he said, Just go. Go on, git. And she thought he might smile, speaking to her in that tone of voice, but he didn't, and she couldn't respond except to do as she was told.

Then she smiles, anyway, sitting down, still scolding herself for not having said good-bye to the very handsome man in time, because she wants Klaus to like her even if she didn't like him first. Then he says, What's that look on your face? And he says this not in a good-humored way but rather insultingly, she thinks, like there's an ugly expression on her face, and she says, What is *what* look on my face? And who are *you* to talk about looks, anyway...?

She begins to shake, realizing what she has just said, feels the blood rise to her face, then her accountant stares at her for a moment, considering her comment, and then she looks down and removes a letter from her purse. He says, What's that? Then she shows him the letter and then they disagree about whether or not she should call the Social Security Administration. Then they fight about his payment and she leaves his office, shaking and thinking of saying something insulting about his freckled mulatto face or his ugly tie or his filthy windowless office and its fake wood paneling and piles of shit everywhere, that little shithole in the middle of fucking Chinatown...etc., etc. She can't think of anything, becomes angry again, and returns home.

She then calls her friend and tells her friend what Klaus said to her and she says, Who the hell does he think he is? And she interrupts her friend and says, Well, you know what? I don't care. I don't care who he thinks he is. And then her friend suggests he was just trying to be funny. You just have to get his sense of humor, her friend says, and then she becomes that much angrier with her accountant and her friend and she says, Yeah, well, you know what? I *don't,* okay? I don't get his sense of humor. Guess that means I just don't have a sense of humor. Then she gets in a fight with her friend and hangs up the phone and thinks, *Some friend.*

Or, she wakes, rolls over, dreads the day ahead, gets up, showers, and drinks her coffee while looking at her date book. She bites her nails and stares off, wondering why her accountant sends her friend her friend's tax forms and her friend's coworkers their tax forms, but her accountant won't send her tax forms. Why? Not even after she called and left a message sweetly requesting he send them to her, because that day was really not going to be a good day for her to make the trip to his office right after therapy. Her accountant simply ignored her request. Or rather, Klaus called back and left a message telling her to stop by and pick up her tax forms, no matter how inconvenient the trip might be. He said that her busy schedule *really wasn't* his concern; he was her accountant, not her secretary. Then, chewing the skin of her ring finger, she worries if her request made him feel subservient for any reason. She was just asking if he could mail her forms to her, that was all, but no time to fret about that now, seeing as it's April 14. She'll just have to go, like it or not.

Well, then, no, she doesn't like it, and she thinks he's mean and etc., etc., nods and leaves, etc. She walks to therapy, buzzes her therapist's office, enters and waits, etc., and then her therapist enters and smiles and she follows her therapist to her office. She sits and scans the room and her therapist sits and smiles and throws her pink Kleenex in the wastebasket beside her chair and says, How are you? Etc. And she says, Fine, fine, etc., and her therapist says, Good, good, etc. Then she looks at her hands and says, Well, to tell you the truth, I was dreading coming here today, and her therapist nods and asks why. She looks away and shrugs and mentions a red-and-white striped suit. It was a Speedo, she says, a racing suit. But my dad said it made me look like a tan candy cane, she says, and smiles.

Then she says, The best part was when we used to get out of the pool during Adult Swim and lay down on the hot cement for five minutes. And by the end of the summer, the front of my suit was shredded from snagging on the cement. It was a rag, but I was so proud, I still wouldn't take it off…So I was riding my bike home from the pool, and there was this hill. I was pushing my bike up the hill, and this friend of my dad's drove by and stopped to offer me a ride. Well, he wasn't a friend, really, he was just someone who worked with my dad. Then she talks some more about the man and her brothers and her family and about being the only girl and the youngest, etc. Then her therapist asks a question, and then she tries to answer the question, but she can't, and then she tries not to cry but only cries harder. She dries her eyes and blows her nose, fishes two individually wrapped green Life Savers from the candy basket and leaves, etc.

She walks to the subway and waits, etc., etc., and gets annoyed with the fat guy with the baggy jeans to his knees checking out the hottie's ass, and she thinks, *Oh, as if,* and then his friend, the guy with the upside-down and backward Nike sun visor steps forward and snorts and hawks and cocks his chin and spits on the tracks. Disgusting. She winces, rolls her eyes, checks the track again, then hears the announcement and thinks, *Thanks for fucking telling me,* etc. She runs upstairs, then downstairs, then almost trips and breaks her neck and jumps on the wrong train just in the nick of time, etc. She realizes her mistake, swears at herself, gets off the wrong subway, etc., etc., and walks up the stairs to the street, etc. Then she walks right past her accountant's office building, distracted, just can't remember what she did with that suit. She remembers her brother saying, Hey, Ugly, where you been? And she remembers telling him to fuck off, and his tackling her, and her crying because it hurt so badly, and she started crying, telling him to get off, he was hurting her, and he said, Oh, you gonna cry, baby? Let's see you cry, then, cry! And then she started screaming at him to get off and her mother ran in and yelled at her brother, telling him to get off, but then...? She stops, turns around, walks back, and enters her accountant's building, grimacing, etc.

She gets on the elevator and pushes the wrong button and ends up at the penthouse with the crystal vases on the reception desk and the beautiful secretary with the high-collared silk blouse and her hair pulled in a bun, looking like some tourist ad, she looks so perfect, sitting there, she thinks, and steps away, etc., etc.

The elevator stops again and again and more and more people get on, and then someone steps on her foot, someone very heavy, and before she has a chance to look, she yells, Ouch! Watch it! Would you watch where you're stepping next time! Then she looks down to find a very old lady with a little boy who looks like he must be the woman's grandson. Then the little boy hides from her gaze, as if she's a mean woman for yelling at his grandmother, and she wants to convince him that she's really a very nice woman, but he won't look at her, so she looks away, too. Then she feels guilty, because it is her fault, really, that she got stepped on in the first place, etc., as more people get on the elevator and etc., etc.

She excuses herself, snaps, Jesus, and gets off the elevator and buzzes her accountant's office, enters, and waits while her accountant talks to a very handsome man, and she notices he's so well dressed she can't imagine what he's doing here. Then she thinks that she would have sex with this man. And then she wonders why Klaus is so nice to this man and her friend, etc., and then chooses not to think about why her accountant doesn't like her. And, instead, she wonders if this man would have sex with her, too, and feels much better. Then the handsome man says good-bye and then she says good-bye as he closes the door, then frowns, having missed the opportunity to make eye contact before he closed the door and swears at herself again, etc.

She enters her accountant's office and he says, Sit, and repeats himself. Sit...Sit...Then she thinks that apparently Klaus is big on the sit and git, and she almost smiles and then remembers her last visit and his response when she said she was afraid she might be audited. I'm a little nervous, she said the first time she sat in his office. And since he didn't ask, she added, I'm afraid I'm going to be audited. Really, he asked or said, furrowing his brow, looking over the receipts she had Scotch-taped to blank sheets of Xerox paper, causing her to worry that she hadn't taped them correctly or maybe he thought it was a bogus expenditure or something, what?

She peered to see what receipt he was frowning at and she said, Yes. I just have this feeling. Then she sat back and said, I guess everyone probably worries about being audited, right? He stopped, looked up her, and said, No, not really. Then, still looking at her, he took off his wire-rimmed glasses and put them on his desk and said, Don't flatter yourself. And she said, I didn't mean to flatter myself—, and he said, Don't interrupt me, please, and she said, I'm sorry, I—, and he interrupted her and said, Listen. You don't make enough money to be worth their time, and she said, I know, but a friend of mine— And then he waved his hand and said, I'm not here to discuss your friends. Save it for your shrink, and she balked, and then he told her to have a nice weekend, now git.

I said sit, he repeats, and then she sits and keeps smiling, remembering the shrink comment and the message he left on her machine last week, the secretary comment he made, as well as his having told her to get out and enjoy her weekend the first time they met, after he basically dropped a bomb on her personal finances and then he behaved as if she were overreacting, etc., etc. Then she hears her accountant say, What's that look on your face? And she answers, What is *what* look, and who are *you* . . . ? Etc., etc. She gets in a fight with her accountant over Social Security, and she tells him that she's going to call, and he calls her a fool and tells her to do as she pleases, then, and she says yes, that's exactly what she plans on doing, thank you. She signs her returns and then she leaves, shaking and thinking of something scathing she could say to make him want to cry, too, as if she could do it all over again, but can't, etc., etc.

Then she calls and tells her friend what her accountant said and she threatens to call him boy, see how he likes that, and again her friend says, You just have to get his sense of humor. Then she says, That's fine, but, you see, I don't, okay? I *don't* get his sense of humor. I think he's a fucking asshole. And if he ever, *ever* speaks to me like that again, I'll go *off*. Her friend insists that the man was just trying to be funny, and then she becomes that much angrier with her accountant and her friend, and she asks her friend why she's defending him, and her friend says she's not defending him, she just thinks he was teasing her, and she says, How would you know? You weren't there, were you? Then she fights with her friend, hangs up, and tells herself never to listen to that friend again. The woman obviously doesn't know what the hell she's talking about.

———

Or, she wakes, rolls over and sighs, gets up, showers, drinks a cup of coffee, dreads her appointments, thinks, then thinks, etc., etc., then grabs her keys and heads out the door. She walks, buzzes her therapist's office, waits, etc., etc., smiles and follows her therapist to her office, down the hall. She sits in her favorite high-back chair, locates her therapist's Starbucks grande latte cup, etc., and her therapist smiles and says, How are you? and she says, Fine, fine, and her therapist says, Good, good, and nods, etc.

Then she looks at her hands and says, Well, to tell you the truth, I was dreading coming here today, and her therapist nods again and asks why. And she thinks, *Because I've talked about this before and it doesn't change anything, not a damn thing, so this is basically an incredible waste of time, that's why. I think my being here is a waste of time and your being here is a waste of time and I don't really believe talking changes anything. I think people are the same, and it's the same fucked-up world and nothing's improving, anyway, and it's just so self-obsessed. Person after person after person who thinks they're the center of the fucking world? The whole cliché: I talk and you listen and the whole, oh, poor me, poor me, blah blah blah, it makes me sick, it really does. Turns my stomach...* Then she sighs and looks away and shrugs and thinks to mention a striped Speedo racing suit that her dad said made her look like a tan candy cane.

She says, When I was a kid, I went to the pool every day. Every single day of the summer. I loved to swim so much I even slept in my bathing suit. I showered and took baths in my bathing suit. I wouldn't take my suit off. I couldn't be talked out of my swimsuit...

I was always the last out at night, and so I was riding my bike home from the pool, wearing nothing but my swimsuit, with my towel wrapped around my neck. She says, And there was this hill. It was great going down, on your way to the pool, but on the way home, back up the hill, it was a bitch. So I got off, and I was walking my bike up the hill, and this friend of my dad's drove by. He wasn't really a friend, he was this guy who worked on one of my dad's crews and came over sometimes, with some of the other guys. But, anyway, he stopped and offered me a ride.

Then she crosses her legs and says, I didn't really like him, but it was getting late, so I said all right. And her therapist says, Why didn't you like him? And she says, Because…Because he always complimented me. He used to compliment me, she shrugs. And her therapist says, You didn't like him because he complimented you? And she says, No, I didn't like him because he complimented me and I liked being complimented so much. Nobody ever said stuff like that in my family. That's not the way we talk in my family, don't you look pretty or whatever. I mean, just the opposite. You mean one thing, you say another. If you want to say, You look pretty in that dress, then you say, Hey, fat ass…And my brothers—, she nods. We'd be in the car and a sign would say CATTLE CROSSING, and my brothers would make me get out and walk back and forth in front of the car, and then she laughs and looks at her hands.

So I said yes and he got out and put my bike in the back, and I climbed in the front seat. He asked if I wanted to go for a drive and I said, No, I should probably get home. Then he said, Well, that's too bad, because he was thinking maybe I'd want to drive his truck and he asked if I'd ever driven before, and I said no. He said, Well, I was going to let you try, but if you don't want to…and I was like, shit, I want to drive, so I said,

Oh, okay. He smiled and said we'd have to find a back road so no one would see me driving, and I started to get really excited. He stopped the truck and he said I'd have to sit on his lap and steer, and he'd do the gas. And he said, What's wrong? And I just shrugged...

Then she says, There was this one time, sometime the year before, and I was sitting on the kitchen counter at home. We weren't supposed to sit on the counter, but I was. I was sitting on the counter, and then I jumped off—I kicked out my legs and pushed off the counter, but I didn't look below. I didn't see the cupboard door was open beneath me, and I landed with my legs spread on the cupboard door. Right on my crotch. I thought that was the worst pain I'd ever felt. I couldn't even scream, it hurt so bad.

Then her therapist talks and asks her a question, then she tries to answer, but she can't form the words, she's trying so hard not to cry that she can't speak, and then she starts to cry. She sobs, answers the question, blows her nose, and dries her eyes. She stands and thanks her therapist for her time because she doesn't know what else to say for herself, closes the door behind her, heads to the bathroom, etc., and leaves.

She walks to the subway and waits, etc. She catches the wrong subway and gets off, etc. She walks up the stairs to Canal Street and walks right past her accountant's office, etc. Then she grimaces, entering his building, and pushes the wrong button on the elevator and ends up at the penthouse, etc. And then she steps out, looks up, sees the gorgeous woman sitting behind the lilies, and wonders how much the woman gets paid to sit there and look beautiful or do whatever it is she does and what the nature of this company is, anyway, and thinks about an ex-boyfriend who had an Asian fetish, which is probably why it didn't work between them—well, that and several other reasons—and wonders what her ex-boyfriend is up to. Then the receptionist catches her looking at her and she smiles and looks away and pushes the DOOR CLOSE button again, then more and more people get on the elevator, then she snaps and pushes her way out of the elevator.

She walks down the hall and enters her accountant's office, sees her accountant and another man talking, thinks the man very handsome, wonders why her accountant doesn't like her, etc., and then thinks about having sex with the man and then feels much better. Then the handsome man catches her eye and she stares at her feet and wonders why she's never had sex or been in a relationship with a black man before and answers her own question, Well, probably because you're a racist. She frowns, stares at her feet again, feels her toe throb, and wishes the old woman would have been more careful where she was stepping.

Then the very handsome man says good-bye, but she hears the man too late to realize he was paying her any attention, and she says good-bye to the man a few seconds too late and she looks very rude, she knows, thinking, *Oh, swell, racist and rude to boot.* But why can't you at least smile when a handsome man smiles at you? What's the matter with you, are you *retarded*? Then her accountant asks her into his office and tells her to sit, he says, Sit, which reminds her of her last visit, when he told her to git, which reminds her of his response to her fear of being audited and the secretary comment after that, etc., etc. Then her accountant asks about the look on her face, and she says,

What is *what* look and who are *you* to talk...? Etc. They fight and she leaves, shaking with anger, etc., etc.

She calls her friend and tells her friend what her accountant said and swears, If he ever, *ever* speaks to me like that again, I'll go *off.* Then her friend starts to speak, and she interrupts and says, I should call him *boy,* see how he likes that. Hey, *boy*... Finished my taxes yet, boy? Her friend laughs and says, You just have to get his sense of humor, and then she becomes that much angrier with her accountant and her friend. Well, that's fine, but I don't. I *don't* get his sense of humor. Besides which, I'm paying him to do my taxes, not some fucking stand-up routine, all right? Her friend laughs as if she's making a big deal out of nothing and she says, Look. You know what's funny? What's funny is that I don't remember seeing you in the room. And then her friend starts to say something and she interrupts her friend and says, You weren't there, were you? No, she answers her own question. No, you weren't there, so how do you know? She hangs up the phone and thinks, *Some friend.* She doesn't like her accountant, and she doesn't like her friend, and she wonders why people can't just leave her alone. Then her phone rings and she thinks, *Whoever you are, go away.* Please. *Just go* away.

Or, she wakes, dreads, etc., showers and dreads, etc., pours coffee and thinks, etc., grabs her keys and walks to therapy and waits and smiles and follows her therapist down the hall, etc., etc. Her therapist sits and smiles and says, How are you? Etc. Then she looks at her hands and says, Well, to tell you the truth, I was dreading coming here today, and her therapist nods and asks why, and she sighs. She looks away and shrugs and then she mentions a red-and-white horizontal-striped Speedo racing suit and her dad saying it made her look like a tan candy cane. And then she smiles, thinking of her dad and any number of things he'd say over and over, never tiring of his own jokes. And how he used to say, You look like a giant candy cane in that suit, or, Christmas in July, huh...? Etc., etc., and she nods, rolling her eyes.

Then she says, I loved to swim. My parents would get us all season passes when we were kids. So instead of getting your hand stamped for the day, you just walked through the front doors and yelled, Season! And I thought I was so cool, you know. I thought I was so much better than the country kids who came in once or twice a year, swimming in cut-off jeans and doggy-paddling in the shallow end. Afraid to get their faces in the water because they didn't know how to swim. I really looked down on them, plugging their noses with their fingers if they wanted to dunk their head beneath the water...That wasn't very nice. It was just the one time of year that I got to feel rich, you know?

She stops and looks at her hands and says, So my suit. One summer, when I was about eleven, I had this bathing suit— I loved to swim so much I slept in my bathing suit. She smiles and nods and says, Yes. Just so I wouldn't waste time, I even show-ered and took baths in my bathing suit. My mom used to beg me to take it off, but I wouldn't take my suit off. I couldn't be talked out of my swimsuit...Anyhow. So I was riding my bike home from the pool, wearing just my swimsuit. I had my towel wrapped around my neck, whatever. And there was this hill. It was great going down, on your way to the pool, but on the way home, back up the hill, it was a bitch. All the kids had to get off and walk their bikes up the hill…So I was walking my bike up the hill, and this friend of my dad's drove by. Then he stopped and offered me a ride home. Well, he wasn't a friend, really. He was this guy who worked on one of my dad's crews, and he'd come around with the others, whenever we had parties…

It was really hot that day, the end of August, and I didn't really like him, but I said all right. And her therapist says, Why didn't you like him? And she says, Because he always complimented me, that's why. He used to compliment me and I loved it. Part of me, at least. He'd say, You have such pretty hair. I always remembered that, too, and I'd show off my hair. This one time, he was over for a barbecue or something, and he said, Your hair always looks so pretty, the way it blows in the wind… It sounds so corny, I know, but nobody ever said stuff like that in my family. My brothers — my brothers teased me mercilessly, that was affection in our family. We'd be in the car, and a sign would say CATTLE CROSSING or DIP IN THE ROAD, and they'd make me lie down in the road, and she starts to laugh but begins to sob. I liked him saying how pretty I was and it confused me. So then I'd ignore him or I'd be openly snotty, just because I knew I could, and she shrugs.

So it was getting late and he said, Come on, I'll put your bike in the back. I didn't say yes right away, I had to think about it. The hill or the guy? And finally, I said all right, and then he got out and put my bike in the back, and I climbed in the front seat. Then he did something. I remember thinking it was weird, but I didn't ask when he U-turned. It was no big deal, but I didn't know where he was going. So I said, Where are we going? And he said, I thought we'd take a drive, and I said, I don't want to take a drive. And he said, Oh, well. I was going to let you drive, but if you don't want to…I didn't know what to do, because I wanted to drive the car, so I said, Oh, all right. Like I was huffy, you know.

He started making small talk, asking about the pool and my friends and was I ready to go back to school. And we had just gotten out of town when he said, You never take that suit off, do you? And I said no, and he said, Then you must be really dirty underneath, and I said no. I soaped up in my suit, I was clean. And then I told him how, by the end of the summer, when I took the suit off, you could see stripes, from where the fabric had worn and the sun would shine through the white stripes, and he said, Really? You mean your skin is striped? And I said yes.

She tucks one foot beneath her legs and clears her throat and says, He smiled and then he said we'd have to find a back road so no one would see us driving, and I started to get really excited. I saw myself cruising down the dirt road…He drove over to the fairgrounds and took this turn, then he stopped the truck and he said I'd have to sit on his lap and steer, and he'd do the gas. I said I wanted to do it alone, but he said my legs would never reach, so I agreed. He turned off the engine, and I moved over and sat on his lap, and then he asked if he could see the stripes. He said he wanted to see this striped skin of mine. I said no, I showed him my tan lines at my shoulders, but I told him I couldn't show him the stripes without pulling down my suit. And he said, It's just me. No one was going to see. And then I didn't want to drive anymore. I got off his lap and I just wanted to go home at that point, and I told him. And he said, What's wrong? And I just shrugged.

I said, Nothing. I want to go home now. And he said, Why are you being such a crybaby all of a sudden? I give you a lift, I offer to teach you to drive, and you act like a spoiled brat. There was nothing more shameful in our family than being called a spoiled brat, so I didn't know what to say. I felt really ashamed, and I must've looked pouty, because he said, Stick that lip out any farther and a little birdie's going to come along and shit on it, or whatever that saying is. I hate that saying. Then I felt angry, you know, and he poked me in the ribs, and I said, Don't. Then he poked me again, and he started laughing, and I said, *Don't do that,* and I told him to leave me alone. He poked me in the ribs again and then he squeezed my knees, and I slapped his hand away. I told him to stop it and he did it again, and I started to hit him and he caught my hand and clenched it in his palm.

He moved the seat back and pulled me back over on his lap, and I could feel his erection beneath my butt, my thigh, right here, but I honestly didn't know what it was. I kept moving around thinking there was something in his pocket...

My brothers, the oldest two, Tim and Jaime, they once tried to get me out of my suit by pinning me down and then my dad walked in and he pulled them off so fast. Oh, the veins in my dad's neck were bulging—it was scary. Then he told them if they ever did that again, he'd beat their asses so hard... Jaime almost started crying and he said, We were just teasing, Dad... And they really were teasing, they'd never have taken my suit off. They just wanted to hear me scream. So I thought—I kept thinking he was teasing or he just wanted a reaction, too. At worst, I kept thinking he'd get tired of my screaming, like my brothers always did, or he'd stop when he saw my stripes. But he didn't.

Then she says, There was this time, sometime the year before that. During the school year, I guess. I was sitting on the kitchen counter at home. She smiles and her therapist smiles and her therapist nods and she nods and she says, But I was sitting there, on the counter, and then I jumped off—I kicked out my legs and pushed off the counter, but I didn't look. I didn't look below. I didn't see the cupboard door was open beneath me, and I landed with my legs spread on the cupboard door. Right on my crotch. I thought that was the worst pain I'd ever felt, landing on the cupboard door, but it hurt worse than that... She says, Have you... Says, Have you ever taken a cotton sheet in both hands and torn it...? Her therapist stares, says nothing. It was like that sound, but inside, she says.

Then her therapist says, When did you know? And she says, When did I know what? And her therapist says, What was happening? And she says, The whole time, in a way. I felt it in my stomach from the time he pulled me on his lap, this sort of queasy churning. But I don't— Because even when he pinned me down on the seat and he was pulling off my bathing suit, I kept thinking, Please don't rip my bathing suit. Please don't rip my suit... I didn't—I, no. I'm sure I knew what he was doing, I knew what it was called, but I don't remember it being discussed, or, you know—no. No, she says, and nods her head. She says, He had Wet Ones in the glove compartment. I remember he had all these fast-food ketchup packets, and those little salts and peppers, too. The ones they throw in your bag at fast-food places. And napkins, he had a ton of napkins in the glove compartment. And so then he cleaned me up... I remember getting out, or him opening my door after he took my bike out of the back, but I don't remember driving home. And then her therapist says, Did you tell anyone? No, she says, and her therapist asks why not. And she says, Because I decided there was nothing *to* tell.

She shifts in the chair, tucks both feet beneath her butt, and she says, I locked myself in the upstairs bathroom. The window was open and I heard some girls drive by on mopeds. It was the summer of mopeds; everyone had them, all the cool girls. She smiles, remembering. Then she says, I heard a couple girls drive by outside, I heard their voices for a moment, yelling at each other, and then I remembered something I'd heard one of the girls say on the bus. One of the coolest high school girls. Missy Thorstad. We took the same bus together, and one time, in the back of the bus, she said it smells like fish when you have sex. We didn't have much fish, Mrs. Paul's or an outing to Red Lobster once a year, that was about it, so I didn't really understand. But then, lying on the bathroom floor, I realized I didn't smell any fish, and I thought, thank god. I got all excited, and I sat up and got off the floor, and I started smelling my arms, just to be sure. I smelled the top of my arms, then underneath, my shoulders, and then my hands. She says, All my fingers, my knuckles...I kept sniffing and sniffing, making sure there was no fishy smell anywhere, and then I leaned over—to smell between my legs, my crotch, and I almost puked. He'd missed some blood.

She says, I keep trying to figure out what it was, what he enjoyed. What did he enjoy? She says, Was it my size? Because I was so small or was it my...She says. She says. She says— When...? What moment did he get hard? Or was it...She can't say the word. She stops, thinks, *Say the word. Say it. Terror. Say terror. Say, Because I was terrified? Can't*— She says, Was it...

Again. Says, Was it...Starts to cry. Can see the word, but can't say it. She can't say the fucking word. Again. Says, Was it because I was so terrified? Is that what I did wrong? She starts to sob. I just want to know, she says. Was that what he enjoyed? What got him off? And which moment was it, then? she says. When he pulled at my swimsuit straps? Or was it when I slapped his hand? What if I hadn't slapped his hand then, or the next moment? Or what if I'd laughed when he kissed me instead of shoving him away? What if I'd kissed him back, would he have left me alone? Because there has to be a moment, there's always one moment when you can turn back, but I missed it. I can't figure out when it was.

She takes a breath, uncrosses her legs, frowns. Says, If I could figure out what it was and which moment, I think I would be all right. Was it any one thing I did or was it all of it? Says, If I hadn't screamed, you think? Says, What should I have done? Says, I know there's something. There must be something. Maybe if I'd kept swimming. Or if I'd left earlier with my friends. Or if I'd said no. If I wasn't so lazy. Or if I'd kept riding straight instead of turning left at the hill. And her therapist says, You think that would have changed anything? She says, Yes. Yes, I do. If I hadn't been there when he drove by, it never would have happened. And my entire life would've...Would have what? Would have been completely different, she says. Everything would have been so different. So you think it's your fault, then? She starts to answer then begins to cry again and says nothing or says yes or—

She cries, dries her eyes, blows her nose, thanks her therapist, and shuts the door behind her. She wipes the mascara off her cheeks, leaves, and walks to the subway. She waits on the platform, etc., etc., then gets on the wrong subway, etc., etc., then she turns around and gets on the right subway, and gets off again, etc., etc. She walks to the streets, sighs, etc., etc., checks the street sign, etc., etc. She walks to her accountant's office, then walks right past her accountant's building, etc., etc., etc., distracted, etc., etc., and afterward, after she took a bath and put on a pair of sweatpants and made her way to the TV room and her eldest brother, Timothy, said, Hey, Ugly. Where you been? And she said, Fuck off. Her brothers stopped and stared at her before Tim tackled her, and later she told her mother Tim tore her suit and she cried and cried and her mother told her to calm down, calm down. No use crying over spilled milk, and then Tim got in trouble and wouldn't speak to her for weeks and called her a lying little bitch. But after that, what became of the suit…? Then she stops and frowns, turns around and walks in and pushes the wrong button, etc., etc., etc.

She enters her accountant's office and sits down, etc., and he says, What is that look on your face? And she says, What is *what* look on my face, and who are *you* to talk about looks, anyway? And she feels the blood rush to her cheeks as he stares at her.

Then she removes a letter that Social Security has sent her and asks him what he thinks of the paperwork. He says he thinks she should ignore it and forget about Social Security, even though it says she must call their offices immediately be-cause there is a problem with her Social Security number that could complicate her return, etc., etc., etc. Ignore it, he says, handing the letter back. She protests and says it might be im-portant and he says, All right, all right. Let me see that again, and she hands the letter to him, and he looks at the paperwork and then he says, No. Don't call them. Waste of time, and she says, I just want to know what the problem is. Why would they—, and he says, Doesn't matter. It's a waste of time, throw it away, and she says, I'll call them, just in case. And he says, No. What did I just say? She says, I heard you, but I want to make sure they have my correct Social Security number on file. And he says, You're acting like a fool. He says, Don't be an idiot, all right? And she says, I'm not. That's why I'm going to call. Then he says, If you aren't going to listen to me, what are you paying me for? And she says, My taxes, I think. Are they done? And he shakes his head, in disgust. Then her accountant hands her two stuffed envelopes from a stack of forms on his cluttered desk, removes her tax forms from their envelopes, and tells her where to sign, handing her a Bic pen. Here and here, he says, and then he removes his glasses and rubs his eyes and with his eyes closed, still rubbing.

She looks at the forms and then he opens his eyes and says, Are you done signing? And she says, No, I was just looking them over. I'll sign later, when I get home. And he says, No. Sign them now, and she says, I said I'll sign them when I get home, and he says, No, there's no use not signing them now, and she says, No, I'll sign them—, then she feels the blood rising to her cheeks again and her hands shaking, so she signs her tax forms. There, she says. Then she hands him back his pen and he gathers her forms and puts them back in their respective envelopes, and then he says, Why am *I* doing this? They aren't my taxes. You can do this! And she says, I didn't ask you to, and he says, You didn't ask me to? She says nothing, stares at her hands, and then he says, And here's your bill, and he jots down a number on a piece of paper and hands the paper to her, and she says, Oh. And he says, Oh, what? What oh?

And then she says, Oh, nothing. Nothing, and she searches for her wallet in her purse, then finds her checkbook first, and he says, Didn't you bring cash? And she says, No, why? And he says, The rule is pay when you pick up, and she says, I will pay—I have my checkbook and plastic. And he says, I don't take plastic and I don't take checks from first-time clients. Can you bill me, then? she asks. And he says, Didn't you hear me? The rule is, pay when you pick up, he repeats. And she says, Yes, but when did that rule begin? Her friend Kate assured her that he need not be paid right away, in fact, her friend said she still owes him for last year's tax return and he'll understand, and he says, That's always been the rule here. And she says, Maybe, but not with my friend, you—, and he says, Nonsense, and she says, I couldn't agree more. I apologize. It's just a little unusual to have to pay cash, but if that's your rule, then we wouldn't want you to break your rule, would we? And he stares at her, sitting back in his chair, holding a pencil above his chest.

She stands, fumbling with her purse, and says, I'll run to the cash machine in the lobby, if you need cash now, and he says, Don't bother. She says, If that's your rule, just let me run out—, and he interrupts her and says, I said don't bother. I said no need, didn't I? I seem to remember saying— Then she interrupts him and says, First, you say it's the rule, when it's not, or at least it's not the rule for everyone, and then when I offer—, and her accountant stares at her and says, Get that look off your face, and she says, *What look* would that be, Klaus? Then he says, Don't give me that lip, and she says, You don't want the lip, you don't want the look, what *do* you want, Klaus? Please, tell me now so we can get it out of the way.

He says, Quit fussing yourself, girl. And she balks and says, Don't ever call me girl. Don't *ever*…Don't, she says, shaking her head. And he stares at her and then she says, Why don't you let me do as you ask, and we can be done with this now? The only reason I didn't bring cash was because I didn't know you needed to be paid in cash. I don't know many people who insist upon cash in these situations, besides which, my friend said you could take a check. But now you say no check, no credit cards, so why don't you let me —, and he says, Take it and go. Just take it and get out of my face. Git.

She sits and stares, and he says, I said git, go. Then she says, Fine, and she stands and takes her two envelopes and her bag of receipts, and leaves without saying good-bye, or maybe she says good-bye, she doesn't remember anything but slamming the door behind her. She presses the elevator and she waits in the hall, shaking, trying not to cry, thinks of secretary and git and that look on your face, etc., etc., gets in the elevator, the elevator stops, more people, more people, gets off, leaves the building, what look? Returns home, calls friend. Then her friend says, He was just trying to be funny. And she says, No, he wasn't trying to be funny. He was trying to be an asshole, etc. They talk some more, she hangs up, thinks, *Some friend,* etc.

Her phone rings and she thinks about letting the machine pick up, she's too exhausted to talk. Then she decides to answer, because it might be her assistant, and there might be a problem at work, so she answers the phone and hears Klaus's voice and wonders, *What the hell do you want, you sick fuck?* And she says, What can I do for you, Klaus? Then he asks how she knew it was him and she thinks of telling him what her friend originally told her about his Barry White voice, and she says, I'm very good with voices. Now what can I do for you?

Then he says that he's surprised she knows his voice that well, since he's only spoken to her twice in person and once on the phone, and she thinks, *Plus the obnoxious secretary message.* She says nothing in reply and thinks, *Fuck you, Klaus. Fuck you,* and then he says, I'm calling to apologize for earlier today. And then she says, What about it? And he says, For how I spoke to you in my office. I feel bad. I'm under a great deal of pressure right now. I haven't slept in days. It's a terrible week for me, and I'm sorry about what happened earlier. And she thinks, *You have no idea.* And he says, I wanted to apologize, and— Then she interrupts him and says, Don't worry about it, and he interrupts her and says, No, really, I—, and she thinks, *Stop. Just leave it alone,* and he keeps talking, and she thinks, and she thinks. She wants him to stop talking, she wants him to leave her alone, she wants him to shut up, and she thinks, *Yes, say it. Say it now, tell him, give it to him,* and then she says, Thanks for calling, I appreciate it, and she hangs up the phone. Etc.

Becky

Oh, hi, Rachel, this is Becky. Um, I'm the girl in the wheelchair. Um, you know, the lunch seems a little bit too much for me. A little bit. Maybe because I went to lie down, kind of—I'm *tired,* you know. And I have a hiatal hernia—I don't know if you know what that is—and I'm only supposed to eat small bits of food at a time. And I'm lying here in bed and I don't *feel* so good and I really have to sit up. But I'm a little concerned because the dinners are so big. You know, sometimes that's too much for my stomach at one time. I don't know, I have a doctor, I'll talk to him about it, see what he wants me to do. But other than that, I'm with the food plan, you know. I'm not eating so much, you know, dairy every time I'm turning around and a million other things for breakfast. And although I've loved it, I don't think I've lost a pound on this program. And when I was at FAA, you know, well, maybe because I'm so sedentary. I've been going on the Exercycle… Anyway, my number is 212-477-1232. I'm glad to see you, you know, in this program and, you know, you're so beautiful and it was so nice to see you. It's nice just to look at you. And, uh, I just thought you'd be home. It's about 3:41 or a little earlier. 3:41, I think. Okay. Bye-bye."

"Hello, Rachel, this is Becky. How are you? I thought, uh, since it says I could call anytime that perhaps I could reach you around this time. Um, I'm doing well in my program. I hope you are, too, and, um, I'm making just a program call and good to hear your voice. Your voice is pretty, too. My name is Becky, or Becky Sue. I'm at 212-477-1232. And I tend to be home, you know, rather late. You know, it could be nine or ten. It could be seven, eight, nine, or ten. It could be six—six is good, too, but I'm usually eating then, but six is fine, if you need six. And it could be like anything, you know. I don't know if I'm—sometimes I go to other programs at the Realization Center. Um... you know, they have ACOA, and they have CODA—CODA's only on Wednesday night, at, um...I think it's seven forty-five, but tomorrow, at six, they got ACOA, but, um, I mean today or tomorrow. Tomorrow I go to the doctor, you know. My internist is tomorrow at 11:00 A.M., so I've got that first thing tomorrow morning. So just not tomorrow morning at eleven, but any other time, if it's not too late. It could be anytime but tomorrow morning, because I won't be here then. Or I could call you back. That reminds me. Okay. Take care. Be well. Bye-bye."

"Hi, Rachel, this is Becky Goldberg, at 477-1232, 2-1-2-4-7-7-1-2-3-2. I'm doing a lot of *crying,* I'm *upset,* I don't know what to *do.* Um, yes, I'm holding my food and I guess my body just needs to adjust to this plan, all these salads and vegetables. It's a shock to my system, you know. Uh, I don't know what to do about going to Jeremy Robinson and this doctor, Dr. Weinstein. They're both food-addiction people, you know, and the people I have now, I'm very comfortable with, but they're not food-addiction people. But I don't know if I should leave what I have. I have a good psychiatrist, I don't want to leave him, and I have a good internist, I don't want to leave him. But this Dr. Weinstein is, um, some sort of medical doctor. As a Jewish man, he seems very nice. He's up by Bloomingdale's. I'm sure you know where that is, Bloomingdale's. I don't have the address right here, but I'm sure you know where it is. I thought I might see you at Bloomingdale's, but I didn't see you there today. I just popped in after my appointment, but I didn't see you at cosmetics or perfume, so I turned back around. I think you'd know me if you saw me, if you saw me there. I'm Becky Sue, I'm the one in the wheelchair, you know. But, um, Jeremy Robinson, he, uh, he — I get the feeling he's very *hard.* I don't know, he upset me, he said he didn't think I was very serious. I'm as serious as death. Just that if it gets too hard for me, I lose interest. Okay then, that, too. Okay. Bye-bye."

"Hello, Rachel, this is Becky Sue. I'm at 477-1232, that's 212-477-1232. I'm just calling to say hello, how are you? I just want to know if you have trouble with all these vegetables. And the beans, Jesus Christ, they put me over the top, you know. So my stomach's been a little bit upset, too, you know. Um, I tried to get on the Exercycle but then I felt too *gassy,* like I was about to explode. My doctor said not to push it, just a little every day. Um, I think it's the vegetables. It's the healthy things that give you the worst gas, in my experience. So I might try later today, we'll see how I feel a little later. It's just this awful pain in my abdomen. And I was talking to my doctor, that one I told you, Dr. Weinstein, I was talking to him about you today. I happened to notice that he has no ring on his finger and I told him I know a very beautiful woman he might like to meet. I don't know if you're Jewish or not, but you're so beautiful I said you were. He's a little bit older, maybe forty, or mid-forties, but I'm sure he's very stable and he would take very good care of you. Because he has very clean hands. And good teeth, although I noticed some fillings, so he might eat too much sugar himself but, um. I told him you seem like a very clean girl, too, I don't see any piercings or tattoos to worry about. Your earrings are very pretty, too. I think earrings are fine. I like earrings myself, now and again, just nothing cheap, you know. It can't be anything but twenty-four-carat gold or my ears get all infected and *pussy*. Ugh, what a mess. What can you do, though, you know? So as I was saying, then I looked at the phone list, after my appointment with Dr. Weinstein today and, um, your last name's not exactly Jewish, but maybe on your mother's side? Rachel's a Jewish name, so I'm sure. And you said you have a cat, a little cat. Wasn't that you, with the cat? I like cats all right. I would get myself a cat, but I have these allergies. Like pollen, and I'm also allergic to furs. Um, not like coats, like cat fur. And dog fur, you know. I just get all swollen and puffy and sneezy, like I'm retaining water or something. But I think it would be nice to have something to pet and hold, like a little something that didn't want to have sex with you whenever you pet it. But I

have Arthur, my helper. He's almost as good. Um, as I was saying, I told my doctor you were so beautiful, he should really
think about it, because he must be into his forties or mid-
forties now, and he's not pick of the litter anymore himself. I'm
not saying he's too old for you, just yet. Soon, maybe, but. I
don't think it would be right, like ethical, you know, for me to
get sexually involved with my own doctor. Because then I'd
have to look for another and I don't have the time for that, it's
just too draining, what with where I am right now. And, uh,
well, he's not going to get the chance to meet too many beautiful women like you anymore. I told him there comes a time
when you have to take a leap of faith. Women might like that
hard-to-get business, but there comes a time when a man is
nothing she's going to want to tell her friends about if he's fifty,
for chrissakes. He's got a good two, three years left in him, max,
and then it's going to be a cold, cruel world, he's going to get
something of a wake-up call himself, and I told him so. Women
know, they can sense it. That old man smell, you know? I think
it would be good for his practice, too, if he had a pretty picture
or two of a beautiful woman like you in his office and he could
tell his patients when they asked, he could say, That's my *wife,*
you know. I think patients would trust him more, to know he
was stable and loving. You know, when you go to the doctor,
you aren't supposed to be worrying about whatever the hell
their problem is, and I have to wonder about that when I don't
see any pretty pictures, you know. He's there to help me, you
know, and I should feel reassured about him being loving and
stable, so something needs to be done about that. I don't know
what he is, because he doesn't wear a ring. He might just be di-

vorced. But I'm sure he likes women, I think. Maybe he likes them too much, but like I said, you gotta have faith. I'll find out for you, okay. That's good. Well, now I best go birth this gas baby, so…Well, yeah, okay, then. Bye-bye."

"Hello, Rachel. This is Becky. Yes, I forgot to talk to him about a discount, though. Well, my insurance covers most of it, or a lot of it, but I still have a hard time with all these bills he keeps sending me, every other time I turn around. They upset my stomach, you know, worse than the dairy. It's really hard to stick with the food plan when he keeps sending me all these bills, every time I open my box. And he's a food-addiction person himself, so he should know how these things upset me. What sorts of things happen if I get too upset, you know. I was thinking maybe if he couldn't give me a little discount, or he might take me to temple and you could come with. He would probably have enough room in his car, if he has a trunk for my wheelchair. He should probably have a car if he's a doctor, you know. You would think, huh? Because I wouldn't want to taxi, though, if he doesn't have a car, that gets too expensive unless he offers to pay. You'd think his mother taught him manners, he'd know how to treat a lady, for god sake. Well, if not, he could drop me off first, then pick you up, and you could have some time to get to know each other. Um, that's another thing, sometimes when we talk about God or our higher power, I see how you get all those little wrinkles in your forehead and you stare at your hands or you pass. You're still very, very beautiful, though, even with those little wrinkles, and I'm always happy to see you. Stick to the big book, and just keep coming back, keep coming to the rooms, you know. It works. Okay, bye-bye."

"Hi, Rachel, this is Becky or you might know me as Becky Sue, I go by both, whichever you prefer...Uh, I don't know, it could just be indigestion. My stomach feels *bloated* and I feel *sick* and I ate a *chicken wing* today. I don't know if that was such a good thing, um, eating the barbecued chicken wing. My stomach's *hurting* and I just took a lie-down, but nothing's helping. My psychiatrist hasn't called me back yet, and I just paged my other doctor, but I've got these horrible pains, you know. I don't know if it's my hiatal hernia or if I'm having a gallbladder attack. Those things come on fast with rich foods. I've got to watch myself with the sauces, barbecue and hollandaise. Ugh, I love the hollandaise, like eggs Benedict, *to die*. But, uh, I'm thinking maybe that's what's caused this, maybe the chicken wing was too rich? Or maybe the meat was bad? Because I don't usually eat chicken for my protein. I don't know if I'll be able to keep my metabolic down at four o'clock, if I have to go to the hospital. I should probably talk to my sponsor about all this milk and chicken. I like my sponsor all right, but she's very, very strict with me, like if I call five minutes late to hand over my food, she gets on my case, and I think there are times when we have to bend the rules a little if it's not working. Because she needs to remember, I'm in a wheelchair, you know, it's not the same. And if I feel this bad, that can't be right. And I don't like most fish, and, you know, but Mrs. Paul's I like, and McDonald's Filet-O-Fish, but that's the thing, because fish leads to french fries. Turkey, maybe. Or I could try a little sliced turkey breast. Or maybe some honey-roasted ham. Not now, you know, but maybe next time. Okay, I just thought you might be home, but I guess not. Bye-bye."

"Hello, Rachel, this is Becky. I did a little time on the Exercycle and now I'm going to try to eat my lunch. But nothing's wrong, I'm just calling to ask if you were at Bloomingdale's today? I thought I saw you, and I tried to follow, but I couldn't keep up. And you shouldn't walk so fast like that, because it's always so busy there, and I'm in the wheelchair, you know. Um, it gives me a *cramp,* it, um, it hurts my *wrists,* and with my arthritis, if I have to try to keep up with you and you're walking so fast. It's hard for me to keep up with people who walk like that unless it's on a quiet street. And I have to be very, very careful with my arthritis, not overdoing it. So I paged Dr. Weinstein about it, but he didn't call me back in time. If he had been there with me at Bloomingdale's, I would've made him run ahead so he could introduce himself to you. I'm still waiting for him to call me, but you can call me back, anyway. I'm at 477-1232, that's the 212, 2-1-2, area code, maybe in an hour or so. You don't have to worry, I have call-waiting, in case my doctor calls while you call, so it shouldn't be a problem. Um, so I'm going to try to eat my lunch now. I think I'm ready. Bye-bye."

"Hello, Rachel, this is Becky Sue, at 212-477-1232. I just ate a green salad at dinner tonight. Fresh lettuce, I tried to eat those sprouts, like people are talking about, but it tasted like *dirt* and

I had to rinse my mouth out, I thought I was going to gag. I went out to dinner just the other night, like last night, and I made doubly sure they put the dressing on the side, but sometimes, I don't know. I tried to ask, but the waitress wasn't very nice when I asked her to help me with my scale because my wrists were hurting me. She upset me, you know. I think it's the cold, too. I thought maybe you could recommend some restaurants to me where people are friendlier and more understanding. I know you must go out to dinner all the time. But I don't want anything too fancy, you know. Nice, but not *too* fancy. Uh, and I was wondering if you wanted to meet for lunch at Bloomingdale's. I can meet you there on Thursday afternoon. My doctor's office is right up near there, and maybe you could just pick me up at his office? Maybe this Thursday, about one or one thirty. Sometimes he runs late, but I'd wait for you. Last week he kept me waiting an hour. Or if you eat your lunch earlier than that, I could change my appointment to midmorning. But I think if he just sees you, he'll know what I said was true. Or maybe we three could go out to lunch at a nice place you know. He seems very nice. I'm sure he's smart, too, to be a doctor like that. So, let's see, it's 7:38, or there about. I'll be up late, nine or ten or so, you can call me then. Okay, bye-bye."

"Oh, hi, Rachel, this is Becky, at 212-477-1232. I'm sorry I missed your call. I was out. Uh, I'm very sorry you won't be able to meet at Bloomingdale's this week, but maybe next week? We can go any week you like. Um, next week or the week after next week or anytime we could work it out. My hiatal hernia seems a little better, you know, you don't need to worry about that. One day at a time. Maybe a little better, I can't tell what it is, between this new food plan and my new doctor and all the changes. It's hard on a system, all this shock. Because I need a regular program, or things happen like this. It's hard for me to tell what's upsetting me the most. Yesterday I was crying and crying. I couldn't get out of bed. I didn't know what was wrong, just everything seemed *wrong*. Uh, I think it's because I don't have two metabolics anymore. If there's no ten o'clock metabolic, I get anxious. I start worrying at dinner. I don't know if that's going to work for me. I want to stick to this food plan, but I need more metabolics or my blood sugar goes haywire, and then I think I'm gonna lose my mind. And with my diabetes, you know. I have to go now. Be well. Bye-bye."

"Hi, Rachel, this is Becky. And you walked out while I was saying that my mother was very *critical,* you know. Um, she was pick, pick, pick, pick, pick. Always picking on me. She was a very critical woman, my mother. I never really felt like a part of my own family, even though it was only the three of us, you know. I think my father wanted a boy, I don't know. They had me much later in life, and I talk to my psychiatrist about this. How they probably got used to the idea of not having a baby, and then I came along. I try to understand, you know, like if I found out I was pregnant today, that would be the death of me, so I imagine that's how she must've felt, my mother. I think forgiveness is very important, and I'm trying to forgive her, but it's hard when she's no longer alive, and I can't tell her how angry I am. Um, and she made me eat food I didn't *want* to eat. Prune juice every breakfast. Every goddamn morning. That's why I have a hard time giving it up to a higher power. Because I don't want to *eat* things I don't want to eat. I still don't like breakfast even though this food plan doesn't make me drink juices. I think someone's going to criticize me when that happens, though. When I think about breakfast, I start to think about prune juice, and I don't feel so good, you know. I'm feeling okay now, I got through breakfast all right. I'll be up late again, so you can call me at nine, as late as ten or so. Ten is fine, too. Um, I haven't been sleeping very well. I can't tell if it's my stomach or my heart. The pain starts at my heart and goes all the way down to my stomach, I don't know. It could just be indigestion, but it feels like my heart, like a big knot, not like heartburn, but I don't know what. I paged my internist, and he should be calling me back soon. Okay. I hope you're doing well. Bye-bye."

"Hi, Rachel, you're a very, very attractive woman, and I'm sure you go out on a lot of dates. My name is Becky, I'm at 212-477-1232, 212-4-7-7-1-2-3-2. How do you handle it when someone asks you out on a date and takes you to a fancy restaurant, and you gotta eat exactly what's on the food plan, and maybe they have something gourmet that you'd like to taste? I mean, I may not—y-y-you and I may be very different, maybe you don't mind if you don't get noshes every—or you don't get bagels and lox. Or you don't get um, *breast of chicken with mushrooms,* or you know, or—or you don't get an apple *fritter* at Theresa's Restaurant. Maybe you don't care about it. I don't know, like to me, I'm missing *the whole world*—if I can't have a particular item of food when I'm on a date, I—I go crazy. I go out of my mind. And then when I want to binge, the bingeing seems like the most important thing in my life that I want to do. And if I'm on Atkins, I can eat and eat and eat and eat, which, I don't know, Rachel, I need to talk to you—but I don't want you to tell me what to do, okay. I want you to share what *you* feel, and what *you* go through, and how you are able to stay in these programs. I'd like to know how you do it. Is it like the love in the program that keeps you there? That makes it not necessary to get the love of the food? I would like to understand it. Oh, by the way, I started doing my writing again. See, it was at CEA-HOW, I had Andrea as my sponsor, she's not my sponsor anymore—I-I don't know if I can do these programs. My doctor wants me to go on the Atkins, which I lost 112 pounds on. One hundred and twelve pounds! And I did the Atkins, it was a miracle. I don't know why I did it. I don't know what made me stay on that, and I stayed on it, Rachel. But like with the CEAHOW, I started gagging on all the vegetables, you know, and three days, you got fifteen cups of frickin' vegetables, you know, whereas on Atkins, you're not counting your meat, and you do the best you can, and you get a lot of bacon and eggs. When I first went on CEAHOW, I-I-I cheated right away, I had six pieces of bacon with my two eggs. I felt—you know, now I—I'm with the CEAHOW and I'm—you know, I'm still doing the CEAHOW on my own now, and I'm making the calls in the program, and maybe I'll come back to the meetings—I don't know, I can't go to the meetings when there's steps—you know that, right? Maybe I would get out of the wheelchair if I stick to something, you know? But—I—uh, I'm angry at CEAHOW. I like Atkins better, but I eventually got angry at Atkins. But what I really want is my freedom, and I want to be able to choose what I want to do when I want to do it, and that's—that's the major problem. And last night I had like a spiritual awakening, and I understood if I'm in the group, I'm supposed to do what the group is doing. And that's where my strength is supposed to come from. But my feeling is, do I *want* to be in the group? You know, I was extremely rebellious my whole life and I'm not saying it did me bad, it did me a lot of bad, at times there were terrible things that happened, and in other ways, I-I became a very open-minded person who learned a lot about the world that the—90 percent of the people don't live the way I do, and then I feel it's because I'm an artist, and that's part of it. I think artists are very open and they don't put themselves into so much, uh, structure, but my lack, the lack of structure has hurt me, too. The lack of structure actually hurts. But I-I-I-I can't stay on any structure too long. I—I go *berserk*. Anyway, I wanted to talk to you about it, I wanted to hear what *you* have to say. If you can identify with anything I'm saying, and what *you* feel, but I don't want you to preach at me, all right, Rachel? Well, I also had lack of structure, but now I'm in CEAHOW, and I'm so great! *Great!* Well, great, *great, GREAT*! Last night I didn't binge, I wanted to binge. I had brussels sprouts and—and a fish, and I didn't binge! But I wanted honey, and put that butter on there, and then I was thinking about ordering some stuff from Passover, and I wanted that egg nosh? You know, I could go *wild* with jelly on the egg nosh, so you know, I have it all planned already, terrible, *terrible*…And, anyway, take care, sweetheart, bye-bye and— well, please don't be afraid to call me back, oh—there's the—"

"Hello, Rachel, this is Becky. Some people call me Becky Sue. I'm the one who just called a minute ago, and your machine cut me off. It's fine, though, don't worry about it. I spoke to Dr. Weinstein about my discount, and he said he'd think about it. Well, I'm thinking about it, too, and I'm thinking maybe 20 or 25 percent off would be enough. I don't know. I told him that or temple, and he said he'd get back to me on that, too. He seems like a smart man, so I know he'll do the right thing. He's a food-addiction person, and he's also some sort of medical doctor, you know, and he says he sees no problem with the *chicken wing,* but if it's upsetting to my stomach, I probably shouldn't eat the chicken wings then. And he says it's probably the milk that's causing all these mucous problems. Maybe I'm allergic to dairy. I talked to my sponsor, but she said if I want to go off dairy, then I have to get a doctor's note, but I forgot to talk to my doctor about the doctor's note. I think if I ask him for the note, then he'll probably want to take a lot of tests, and that'll be expensive, and I'll get more bills from him, and that'll upset my stomach more than the milk, so, um...I don't know. I lie down, but I can't fall asleep if my stomach's upset like it is. And I feel so *phlegmy,* you know. It's my chest and my sinuses, all the phlegm, then with my bowels, I can't take it. I try to spit it up but it doesn't help and it hurts my stomach more. Okay, well, bye-bye."

"And all of my life, as far back as I can remember, all I ever wanted was to be as beautiful as you are, Rachel. Just to know for one day what that felt like, to look like you do. To wake up and look in the mirror...You know, for people to like, say, just to *look* at me, and see me as *beautiful* and want to be next to me, and touch me, and to want to have sex with me when they look at me, and for me to be able to look back at them, at all the people looking at me and wanting me, I mean. Or just to be as beautiful as you are and then to be able to look back at me and think nothing of it, just continue about my business. I'm telling you, Rachel, I would've *died* or given up my right arm, my left arm, both these legs, my soul or whatever, you know, whatever, just for one goddamn day. So...that's why I'm calling, really. I just want to know, honestly, what's it like? I want to know. I'm telling you, I'm serious, I want you to tell me how it feels to be you, to get to take it all for granted. Because there are some days that I wish you could know what it was to be me, too. I really do. So you would know. Because sometimes, the way you look at me when you catch me looking at you in a meeting, and all I'm thinking is that I want to be as pretty as you are. Because I can tell you don't know what I'm thinking. Or, I don't know, you know, maybe you do know what I must be thinking. Maybe that's the only time you're grateful and you don't take it for granted, all you have. When you're looking at me, you know? Because it's like, I'm a *Cosmo* girl and all. I read what those cover models have to say about their awful childhoods, how no one paid attention to them, or called them names, and all the teasing they took...*Puh-lease,* like I don't have enough troubles, I have to hear them yammering on, I mean, look at them, or look at you, and look at me...Because, you know, I don't think I've told you this before, but when I was a little girl, I wanted to learn how to fly. I was never very healthy, you know, and all I wanted to do was fly. So I used to go down to the basement in our house, and I'd try to learn to fly down there, jumping off the fourth or fifth step, flapping my arms. And every time I'd fall on the ground, my mother would shout down, What was that? Becky Sue, what are you doing down there?! Come up here now, so I can see what you're up to. And sometimes I think those falls might've contributed to my health problems now. It probably would've been better to learn to fly in the front yard, but we didn't have a front yard or grass or anything. I mean, you'd think, where was I going to fly in the basement? Oh, I don't know…Maybe every kid thinks they can fly, but it was like the most important thing in the world to me. I thought I'd show them, my parents, and then they wouldn't be sorry anymore. I'd be the girl who could fly and my mother could tell all her friends and everyone could watch me. Well, anyway, that's all I wanted to ask. I just want to know how it feels to be as beautiful as you are, if you ever think about it, or what? You can be honest with me, too. I'll understand. Okay, that's all. Hope you're well, honey. Bye-bye."

"Hi, Rachel, this is Becky Sue. I'm at 212-477-1232. And my helper, Arthur, he's like my personal assistant, I brought him to the meeting last week. Um, you might have seen him sitting by me in the back? He helped me, and I took him to meet Dr. Weinstein, and, uh, Arthur thought he seemed like a good match for you. I pointed you out at the meeting, so he knows who you are. Arthur, he said, what with your looks and the father's brains. And, um, you wouldn't have to get a *tutor,* if your kids had questions about math or science. I needed a tutor, but my parents couldn't afford to get me one, so I had a hard time. That leaves scars, you know. You'll be spared that. Or you could always ask Arthur for help; he does all my taxes, every year. Taxes are a bit complicated with my disability, you know.

Arthur's not really a food-addiction person, but he comes to meetings as part of my network. If you're too shy, we could all go out together. Dinner, maybe, the four of us. Or lunch or dinner. Or breakfast or lunch or dinner. I just can't wait until brunch, you know. That's too much, too late, but they'd understand. You might not want to get involved until you have one year under your belt, but if Dr. Weinstein could only *see* you, I'm sure he would wait. Um, he's waited this long, what's another year? All right, then, be well. Bye-bye."

"Hello, Rachel, this is Becky Sue. And Dr. Weinstein said maybe he could arrange a ride for me next week, so maybe you should just come meet him this one time, tomorrow, pop your head in and say hello, then he'll decide to drive me himself. I think you two would have a lot to talk about, with him being a food-addiction person and you being a food addict. I didn't tell him that about you, don't worry. You can tell him yourself, and maybe if you have any questions about your meal plan, he could give you his advice. I don't think he'd charge you if you were dating, or you could charge him back for looking at you, you're so pretty and all. I keep telling him that, but he doesn't seem to believe me. *Uh,* I have to go have my lie-down now, or I can't get myself to my meetings, you know. I want to make it to CODA, but I just feel so *tired* on this meal plan and sometimes I just want to cry and cry and I can barely get out of bed, you know. I'm not feeling too good today. And I have some information on a singles group that I thought you might enjoy because I can't use it, you know. I could probably go with you, though, just to have a look. We'll see. Well, I hope you're well. Bye-bye."

"Hi, Rachel, this is Becky. I got your message. I'm at 212-477-1232, and I got your message. I just got home from the doctor and I'm home now if you want to call me back. But I, uh, I didn't really understand what you were saying, what, with the thing about your not being Jewish? Are you saying you won't go out on a date with my doctor, Dr. Weinstein? I don't understand what you're saying. Are you saying you're anti-Semitic? I don't think you have any business pointing fingers. If that's what you're saying, I think you should take a long, hard look in the mirror. And you're very, very pretty, it's true, but still. Don't think that's all right with me. I'm just asking for a little help. I know I need help and at least I can admit it and ask for it, but you—I'm just asking you to keep an open mind, that's all. Because if you can't do that, then what's the point of your being in the program? The rooms don't need you with that uppity attitude or yours, with your skinny ass and your nose up in the frickin' air like that. I know you'll at least meet him, that's all I'm asking, because you can help a friend. It's not ideal, but you could always convert, so don't worry. Just keep an open mind. Don't be afraid to ask for help. Okay, I hope you're well. Bye-bye."

"Hi, Rachel, this is Becky, or Becky Sue. I'm just wondering what you know about this Oprah Diet. Oprah Winfrey, you know her? I don't know if you've been on this one, it's the one where you have two set meals per day. And they're very, very set meals, you know, really strict, but then you get one hour of the day when you get to eat anything you want, you know? Like one hour, you have to time it. When you hear the bell, then you have to stop eating, though. That's the rule. So I'm working this one now, you know. Arthur sets the timer for me, and I spend most of my day planning my free hour. I had a row of mushroom knishes lined up, they were so good, and I had a strawberry upside-down cake, and I had a bag of salty pecans, and then I ate as much Jiffy Nut as I could stand. Sweet, then salty, you know. And ten links of spicy sausage, too. I love the spicy sausage. I don't know how you feel about it, but my life just isn't the same if I'm not allowed sausage. Arthur fried it up for me, while I was working on my Ho Hos. And I swear to god, it was the best sausage I ever ate! Um, and my friend Jean, she says it really works, this plan, she's already lost twelve pounds, if you can believe it. Swear to god, she did, but Jean, she's not a food-addiction person, she's just fat, so I don't know. I know she's a spiritual person, and I think she's making some real headway in that direction, along her path, but I'm not sure if Oprah knows what sort of effect this plan can have on a food-addiction person, as I am, because I can't think of anything but my free hour, and what I'm going to eat, and getting everything prepared for my hour. I like to save my free hour for later in the day, like five or six, so I have something to look forward to, to keep me going. But still, you know, even if I haven't lost any weight yet, I get the structure and I get the freedom, so it seems a good balance for me. Structure and freedom. I don't know how to reach her to ask, though, I don't know how, but maybe I'll write her a letter or call the number they give on the show. I think they have a 1-800 number, I think. *The Oprah Winfrey Show,* if you watch that ever? Ugh, that was my stomach. You heard for yourself, didn't you? I'm hungry and I'm just waiting for my free hour, you know. Watching the clock, every second I'm a little closer. But I was outside today, and I passed a newsstand, and I saw a recent picture of Oprah, and she's not looking so thin herself, so I don't know, am I supposed to believe it works if she's on the heavy side? Looks like she packed away her thin jeans for the winter. I don't know what's going on with her program, if she's sticking to it, but if she's taking two hours, only giving us one, I don't think that's fair. Well, I hope you're doing good on whatever program you're doing, sweetheart. Oh, another thing, Arthur took a picture of Dr. Weinstein for you, so you can see what he looks like. Arthur caught him pushing me, as we were coming out of the exam room, and Dr. Weinstein looks a little surprised in the picture, and the flash made his eyes red, but you'll see. His first name is Irving, so you know. Irving Weinstein, MD. Okay. Bye-bye."

"Hello, Rachel, this is Becky. My number is 212-477-1232, and I'm trying not to get discouraged about not losing a pound. I'm rotating between the Oprah Plan and CEAHOW, but I'm not feeling very good today. I'm overjoyed to be back in meetings, but I'm feeling very *upset,* you know. The structure is such a shock, and I have to hand over my food, and I don't know if that's what I really need. But I really appreciated what you had to say about the milk today, but what was it you said about soy milk? I couldn't hear very well because I have to sit at the back of the room, you know, because of my being in a wheelchair, and there wasn't any room on your side. I thought I might give that soy milk a try, because, uh, what the dairy does to me. But I heard somewhere that too much soy isn't good. That the body can develop an allergy to it. So I'll need to be careful, keep an eye out. Um, but I just wanted to know what brand you buy of soy milk, what kind did you say it was? Is it low-fat? Because I can't take all the fat, you know, especially when I'm not feeling so good. Okay. I'm Becky, you know. I was wondering why you sat in the back and then you got up and walked out before the meeting was over. I don't know what your problems are, but I don't think you should be isolating. It's not good to isolate when you're not doing well with your program. We all have pain, trust me, I know all about that. I have pain you can't imagine, it's so bad. My pain is so bad no one can begin to imagine what I experience in a day. I wouldn't wish that on anybody. I don't even know why you're in this program, you're so beautiful and all. Uh, I'm a little tired, so you probably shouldn't call too late, like after nine or so, but I'll be okay. I just need a little rest. Talk soon. Bye-bye."

"Hi, Rachel, this is Becky. I'm Becky Sue, at 212-477-1232. I'm serious about this program, but if I don't have *support,* I see people not calling me back, not doing anything, and I don't know why, you know, what's wrong, you know. I'm trying to help you, but you won't help *me*? That's hateful. I, I-I-I'll tell you this, I have more days of abstinence than you do, so who the hell are you to look down on me? Where do you get off, missy? Jesus fuckin' Christ, because I-I called *you,* I called Carol, I called—well, I did—Mary wants to speak to me, and Robert and Vicky have both spoken to me. But I don't know what you all want me to say that you don't call me back. You know, what, I'm not *perfect* enough for you? I'm sorry. I'm really, really sorry that I can't be more perfect than I am. I'm a very, very sick girl—you shouldn't have what I have. I have a right, because whatever is wrong with me, I don't know what it is with you, if it's bingeing or purging, whatever you do—that's somewhat controllable, but my hip is not controllable. I have no control over my arthritis and artificial limbs and pain. I don't have control over that, you understand? *I don't have control over that!* You have no idea what it's like. Just thank your lucky stars you don't know my pain. You hear me, Rachel? I have to wait for a ride in the pouring *rain,* stuck in this motherfucking wheelchair, getting soaked to the goddamn bone just so I can get to all these goddamn *doctors,* who never even pick up the goddamn *phone* when all their hands seem to work just fine to me. They go to school to become doctors for all those years, but they don't understand what pain means, they have no idea, those fuckers. Treating me like I'm an animal, like I'm a piece of meat, I-I-I'm *nothing*? Nothing, nothing, *NOTHING*? For starters, how am I supposed to trust all these people when they don't even call me *back*…? So there's that, too. Um, all right, anyway. Let me go now. Thanks for calling. Bye-bye."

Unkempt

Poor Michael. I must've hung up on him…three, four
times, maybe? But you have to understand. I was just
watching TV in bed one night—it wasn't that late, but I
was having the worst week at my job. Anyway, the phone rang,
so I answered, and this man says, Hello, Mrs. Pollard? That was
the first time I hung up.

Then the phone rang again, a few seconds later, and this
time he says—same guy—and he says, Hello. I just called a
few seconds ago, and I think I got disconnected. I'm trying to
reach Peg Pollard? So I said, Excuse me, it's Connor. It's Peg
Connor, I said. Who is this, please? And he said, I'm sorry. My
name's Michael. Michael something, and I said, All right. What
can I do for you, Michael? And he said, Well. Actually, I'm
Jenna's boyfriend— *Whoosh,* that really knocked the wind out
of me. Very funny, I said, and I hung up on him a second time.

Then he called back again, and by that point I'd had it. I
didn't even say hello; I said, Listen. I don't know what you

want, but joke's over, okay? I was about to hang up, when he said, Please, Ms. Connor—if you'd just give me two minutes, I can explain; and he sounded so sincere that I agreed. All right, I said, you've got two minutes.

So then he goes on to tell me—well, first he says, obviously some things have changed in the past few years, or there've been some changes in Jenna's life, however he put it. But he said Jenna would probably want to discuss all that with me, herself, and I'm thinking, Probably not. Anyway, he said he was throwing Jenna a surprise party because she's getting her doctorate—she's going to be a doctor. PhD, not MD, but still. Then he said, I'm so proud of her, and that was rough. The whole thing was strange, but hearing that, I don't know. Jealousy, I suppose.

Anyway, I wanted to tell him to back up, start from the beginning, because all I could think was how many times Jenna'd told me, over and over again: Mom, this is not a phase. I'm not experimenting here, and this isn't some phase that I'm going to grow out of, okay? That's what she'd always told me, so what was I to think? I mean, I believed him, I really did. Then again, you don't just stop being a lesbian, do you? Well, I don't know. Maybe lesbians have boyfriends these days. I've been wrong before, so. He says he's her boyfriend, okay. Fine by me.

But then, when he said he knew Jenna'd want me there, at her party, it was too much. No, really, that was just too much. So I said, Michael, I think there's been some mistake, and he said no. He said, Ms. Connor—, and I said, Peg. Please, everyone calls me Peg. He said, All right, Peg. Thank you. He had very good manners, but anyway. He said, Peg, I know it's been a long time—no, no, he said, *some time,* that's right. He was very tactful about the whole thing. He said, Peg, I know it's been some time since you've spoken to Jenna, but I can't tell you how much it would mean to her if you could make it.

So I told him I'd think about it. I said that that was the best I could do, and he said, I'm glad. I'm glad you're at least willing to consider it. And he sounded genuinely pleased, he really did. So then we chatted awhile, and I told him about my move and my new job and about my little house...We had a very nice conversation. And before hanging up, Michael gave me all the information, their address and the name of a hotel he said was affordable, not far from where they live in Oakland. So I wrote it all down, and I told him I'd get back to him.

Then, as soon as we hung up, I got up and I called and made hotel and plane reservations. I was thinking I'd go for a long weekend, fly out early Friday and return early Monday. But once that was done, and I had a minute...I panicked. All I could think was, are you *crazy*? My stomach started churning, my bowels—terrible. And this whole huge...I don't know what. This, this—fantasy I'd had talking on the phone with Michael, this idea of the two of us being reunited, starting over. Well, that went right up in smoke. Because as soon as I had a moment, I thought, Oh my god, he doesn't know. No, Michael must not know. Because how could he invite me if he knew?

This is Jenna's college graduation I'm talking about, not high school—her high school graduation was fine. No, this was college. First of all, I had to fly into Chicago, change planes, then fly into Boston, and *then* take the train from there, but anyway. The whole flight out, I couldn't stop worrying. I mean, Jenna went to school with a bunch of rich kids. She even showed me pictures of kids from her school in fashion magazines at the checkout—right before she'd groan, but still. I couldn't stop worrying about my hair, my clothes, everything. I was afraid she'd be embarrassed of me, basically. So I'd barely stepped foot off the train, and the first thing Jenna says to me is, *So*. She has that forced smile on and she says, So. Still perming your hair, huh? Well. What more did she need to say?

Then, the next day, at her graduation—well, first of all, it was so hot that day, just unbelievable. And the humidity was worse than the Midwest. I'm serious. So once Jen got her diploma and we got through the pictures, first thing I did was sneak off to find a ladies' room so that I could peel out of those damn hose. I hate panty hose, I really do. The only reason I wore them was because I hadn't seen my ex-husband Ron since Jen's high school graduation and I wanted to look as thin as possible. So after I ditched the hose, I decided I'd wear my *summer undies,* as my grandmother used to say. I figured I'd just go without. Of course I checked to make sure you couldn't see through my dress and you couldn't, so.

But it wouldn't have mattered what I wore. I just didn't belong there. It's true. I mean, I'd been dreading this thing for months, and the time had finally come, and there was nothing I could do but buck up. So I kept telling myself, You just have to get through this. You just gotta soldier through... And we were doing our best, Jen and I. We both knew what was up: she had to invite me; and I had to be there. That's just how it was.

So once we got back to the Rainbow House—I don't know if that's what it was really called or not, but that's what I called it because they had this huge rainbow flag hanging from the balcony of the second floor. I mean, it was just enormous, this flag. Anyway, they had a big backyard, and they'd set up a sound system and they had all this food and a full bar—they did a great job. And there must have been at least two hundred people there, but I kept to myself pretty much. I just didn't have anything to say to anybody, really.

Then, maybe an hour after we got there, this man came over and he introduced himself. At first, I thought he was gay, but anyway. He seemed nice, so we got to talking. We were just chitchatting, you know, the usual; he told me about his son, I talked about Jenna. Then he offered to get us some champagne. But I'd promised myself. I swore I wasn't going to drink, so I said no thank you. Then he said, Come on, Peggy, it's a celebration. Have a little champagne with me, come on…Loosen up! That's what he said to me. Loosen up. Then again, he was the only person who'd tried talking to me besides Jenna's friends, so I said okay. All right, I said, one glass.

Well, we probably had a couple glasses, and then at some point, he brought me a drink instead. I said, What's this? He said, Scotch, and I was about to pass, when he leans over and says, You look like you can handle it. And it's true; I was pretty loose by then, so I downed it. So we had a couple drinks, and I felt fine. Really, Jenna even came over to check on me and she gave me a little hug. No, I was fine, right up until Bill or whatever his name was, he says, Hey, Peggy— He kept calling me Peggy, too—and I am definitely not a Peggy. My full name's Marguerite, but anyway. Bill said, Let's dance! Then he grabbed my hand and pulled me into the middle of the yard.

Lots of people were dancing by then; we weren't the only ones. God, no. But the man—no, first, first, let me tell you about the pants. They were plaid. Pastel plaid. Like I said, at first I thought he was the gay one, but then he kept trying to do the bump with me, and I finally realized that he was hitting on me. I wasn't exactly flattered, but I have to admit it made me feel better. I thought, What was all the worrying for? I have as much business being here as anybody else does. I was actually starting to have a good time.

Then Bill swung me around a couple times and we were doing fine, right up until he tried dipping me—without giving me any warning. So when he dipped me, I automatically arched my back and lifted one leg up in the air…and then I don't know what happened. No, I honestly don't know if I tripped or he dropped me, but whatever it was, I fell. I did, I fell flat on my ass.

It was a few moments before I realized I'd caught my dress under me and you could see everything. I mean, everything— my crotch—awful. It was just awful. When I looked up, Bill's eyes were the size of two saucers; then I looked down and saw that I'd popped a couple buttons off the front of my dress, so I tried looking for them, patting the grass, but there were too many people standing around…

Next thing I remember was waking up in my hotel room with this throbbing headache and a swollen ankle. Something was flashing, I think that's what woke me. So once I sat up and figured out where I was, I turned on the light on the bedside table and saw that the phone was flashing. Ron'd left me a message saying that Jen didn't want to speak to me, and she'd asked I leave her alone for the time being. He said I could call him, but after everything that'd happened, I could at least have the decency to do as Jenna asked.

It was after two, but I called Ron at his hotel anyway. I had to—I couldn't stand it, just lying there, trying to imagine what he meant by *after everything that'd happened.* No, I had to. I didn't even know how I got back to my room. I'd obviously woken him up, so I said, I'm sorry to call so late— Are you alone? he said. Yes. Of course, I said. Ron paused, and then he said, Anyhow. It's late, and I don't want to talk about this now, Peg. Please, let's not get into this now, he said, and I said okay. Call me in the morning, he said, and I said, I will. Good night, I said, but he'd already hung up.

I sat there, on the edge of the bed, trying to remember what had happened, but I couldn't remember anything. So I checked the bathroom trash, the toilet, and I didn't see any signs of Bill—or anyone else, for that matter. All I knew was that I had that white terry cloth hotel robe on and that I'd woken up on top of the bed, on one of those slick floral bedspreads that disguise everything. So there was just no telling.

So there I was, sitting on the edge of the motel bed, fingering myself, sniffing my middle fingers, just to make sure I hadn't had sex with some strange man I'd only just met at my daughter's graduation party. I mean, he was nice, but the whole thing made me sick. The thought of Bill made me sick—the thought of sex, period, made me sick. I thought I was going to retch, but I couldn't even do that properly.

No, I kept picking up the phone and dialing my friend Joanna, because I knew she'd talk me down; she'd say something like, Oh, big deal, Peg. So you tripped and flashed a bunch of gay guys, you think they care? I knew what Joanna would say, but then I kept dialing and hanging up, until I realized I didn't really *want* anyone to tell me it was all right. Because it wasn't all right, it was obscene. So if I felt like shit, well, I made my own bed. That's what you get.

Honestly, there are nights I wake up, and maybe it starts with stress at work or some problem with my house, but I always end up there. Eight years later, and still—it *still* turns my stomach, just thinking about that day. But there was no way I could face anyone after that, no way. So first thing next morning—I barely slept, but first thing, I called Ron. Sonya answered, wasn't that a treat, but anyway.

Sonya said Ron had taken the kids—I assumed she meant their kids—out for breakfast; and that it'd probably be best if I called back and she didn't answer, so I could leave Ron a message. Rather than her relaying the message, right. She just didn't want to speak to me a second longer than she absolutely had to. And for a moment there, I thought about asking Sonya to tell me what happened after I fell, because it was the most humiliating thing I could imagine, but I didn't. Sometimes I still wish I had, but anyway. I called back and left Ron a message, asking him to tell Jen how sorry I was and to tell her that she could call me anytime, day or night, collect of course... Then I flew home that afternoon. I wasn't even there forty-eight hours.

So after I got back home, I thought I should wait for Jen to call me, leave the ball in her court, but she didn't call. A couple weeks went by, then a month. Fourth of July, Labor Day... By September, I knew she'd moved to California, and I was sure she'd call once she got settled, but still no call. I was really beginning to think she was never going to speak to me again, and I didn't know what to do. I thought of writing her, and I tried, but whenever I sat down, I couldn't figure out what to say. I'd sit there for hours, staring at the page, a complete blank.

Then, in November, finally, she called. Well, the end of October or the beginning of November, I can't remember.

Anyway, Jenna called one night, and the strangest part was that she acted like nothing had ever happened. She said, *Hey!* It's me. How are you, Mom? She sounded really good, too. I said, Fine, Jen. Fine. It's so good to hear from you! She said, You, too. How's things? I said, Same ole, same ole. But tell me about California! Then she said sure, but she wanted to talk about Christmas first, because she needed to book something. And I thought, You're actually coming home for Christmas? I said, Of course. What's the plan?

Then she asked if I'd mind her bringing her girlfriend home with her. That's what she said. She said, Mom, would it be okay if I brought my girlfriend home for Christmas? So I thought she meant she wanted to bring her girlfriend home to *meet me,* you know. I was so excited to hear from her, and then, on top of that, she was finally bringing someone home. I mean, she'd never brought anyone home, so I said yes. Of course I said yes; I couldn't wait.

I said, So what's her name? And Jenna said, Frankie. And I said, Frankie? Her name's *Frankie?* Jenna said, *Mom.* I knew that Mom, too: she'd fired her warning shot. So I said, I'm sorry, sweetheart, I wasn't sure I heard you correctly. She sighed and then she said, It's Francesca, but she prefers Frankie. Well, I can understand that, I said. Well, there you go, she said, and I could tell she was starting to get annoyed with me, so I said, Whatever her name is, Francesca, Frannie, Fran…Jenna said, Her mother's name is Fran—please don't call her Fran, okay? I said, Okay. I just meant she's welcome to join us. Really, we'd love to have her, I said. I don't know why I said *we,* but anyway.

Then she said, Thanks, Mom. This means a lot to me; and I said, Of course! What are you talking about? She said, I was worried you might say no, and I said, Why would I say no? She said, I don't know, I just...Her voice softened, and I thought she was going to talk about how long it'd been since we spoke and tell me what she thought of the whole situation. But then I had to go and open my big mouth. I said, Jenna, you could bring a dog home far as I'm concerned—so long as the dog doesn't mind.

I was only trying to lighten things up. What I meant was... well, I don't know what I meant, exactly, but I certainly wasn't comparing her girlfriend to a dog or calling her a bitch. Never. But sure enough, Jenna got her nose bent out of shape. There was that awful moment of silence, and I knew it was going to be bad. Then she goes, Excuse me. Are you equating homosexuality with bestiality? Exactly. Are you e-*quating*...? I said no. No, that's not what I meant at all— She wouldn't hear a word. But honestly, I've never equated anything in my life. All I meant was that so far as I was concerned, as long as it was consensual, she could do whatever...Never mind.

I finally got her to calm down, but if it hadn't been for her Christmas plans, I doubt she would have listened. So after that narrow escape, we never talked about graduation. I mean, I sure as hell wasn't going to bring it up, at least not then. And I wasn't trying to avoid anything; I just didn't want to make waves before we'd had a chance to see each other again. That's all.

I'll never forget the first time I saw Frankie. Actually, I heard her before I saw her, because Frankie was wearing all those chains on her leather jacket. I mean, I was waiting there, at the end of the terminal, and then, along the top of the heads, I see this mohawk. Although, I have to say, Frankie's hair didn't stick up like a mohawk, it was flatter, more like a pelt. And I don't mean that in a bad way, but anyway. I'd assumed it was some weirdo, just some guy, you know, then I saw that it was a girl, and then I saw her talking to Jenna…My chin practically broke a toe in the fall.

Frankie had this thick leather wallet in her back pocket, attached to this heavy chain, swinging from her belt loop, and those lace-up boots, with her jeans rolled up to the knee. And, man, was she solid. I think that was the first time I understood what they mean by butch. I mean Karen—my cousin Karen—she plays softball and has a couple dogs and a pickup, the whole thing. But Frankie was *really butch*. Is that an awful thing to say?

Well, it took me a minute to take it all in, that there was my daughter with her punk-dyke girlfriend or whatever she was, and here we were, all together. I stood and smiled, trying to get their attention, and Jen pretended she hadn't seen me, even though I knew she had. But I could tell that Frankie had been looking for me in the crowd. And when she saw me, I mean she had the biggest smile you've ever seen. Like this little explosion, the way she lit up—amazing. She completely won me over, then and there.

You must be Peg! she said, and I said, How did you guess? Frankie said, I can see the resemblance, and I said, Really? No one ever said that about us, so I looked at Jenna, to see what she thought, but she was looking away, making that sour face of hers. I'm Frankie, she said, and held out her hand, and I said, Nice to meet you, Frankie, I'm so glad you could come. Then Frankie leaned forward and kissed me on the cheek, and that was a little awkward. I know women kiss in the East, but we don't, really. So I was just a little surprised, that's all.

Then, when I leaned over to give Jen a hug and kiss—and I was about to tell her that her hair looked nice, because she'd dyed it again. She'd gone platinum blond, and it looked great. Then, when I leaned over, Jenna went stiff on me: *Would you please quit gawking?* She practically hissed in my ear, before pulling away. Maybe I was gawking, but still. I said, Why don't I go get the car? Good idea, Jenna said, looking away again.

You should've seen them on the way home, though. I mean, we made small talk most of the way, because every time I tried to have a real conversation with Frankie, Jen'd change the subject. Anyway, we were entering town limits, when Frankie slaps the window: *Oh my god!* I thought you were kidding! she said, pointing. So then Jenna sat up and looked out the window and said, You see! You see! What did I tell you? I'd never seen two people get so worked up over a billboard before. I mean, I know it's corny, WELCOME TO SIGOURNEY, IOWA...JUST NATURALLY FRIENDLY! But, really, I didn't think it was worth mentioning to anybody.

Anyway, the way they grabbed hands and started bouncing over the billboard, squealing like that, you'd have thought they were thirteen years old. No, they sounded just like a couple of teenage girls playing chic or freak? Whatever that game was. And it wasn't until that moment that I realized I'd been waiting twenty-three years to hear that sound coming from the backseat.

So many things started racing through my head that I wanted to say. I wanted to tell Frankie about the year Jenna tried detasseling or how much she used to love to walk down to the middle school to watch the old-timers square-dancing on Thursday nights…But then I thought, No, leave it alone, so I did. I just tried to enjoy the moment, take it in.

Well, Jenna worshipped Frankie. She absolutely worshipped her. I'd never seen anything like it. Honestly, I'd never seen my daughter laugh and smile, joking around like that. Giggling even. And the way she doted on Frankie's every word. Jen had this funny thing she did, where she ended all her sentences on a high note. Kind of chirpy, like, Don't you *think*? Wouldn't you *say*? Everything sounded like a question, like she had to ask for Frankie's permission or something. But it was very sweet, it was. I thought, Wow, Jen's really crazy about this girl.

And of course I wanted to be accepting. I wanted them to know I was perfectly A-OK with their relationship. So once we got home and carried their bags inside, I said, I've got an idea. Why don't you two take my bed, and I can sleep in your bed, Jen. How's that? Well, no…No, that's not exactly true. God, this is so painful. What I said was, If you two lovebirds want to take my room, I'll just sleep in Jen's room, how's that?

I mean, if you'd seen them together, the way they held each other's hands—they were practically cooing…but no. There's no excuse. I knew I'd really screwed up soon as the words came out of my mouth. Frankie stared at her hands and Jenna was staring a hole in the carpet. Then, in a perfectly calm voice, Jen said, Frankie, would you excuse us for a minute? Frankie nodded, got up, and went to Jenna's room. The whole time I was waiting for Frankie to close the door, I wanted to say, *Please don't go, Frankie!* Because I knew what was coming.

How could you do this to me, in front of my best friend? How. Could you. Do this to me…? she said. And I told her, I said, I was just saying— What? You were just saying what, Mom? You were saying you've got an idea? No—, I said. Well, you're right, she said, you have *no idea*. I said, Jenna, I was just saying that it was fine if you wanted to— If we wanted to what? she said. What, Peg…?

She has this temper. And once Jenna gets started, there's no turning back. I don't think she could stop even if she wanted to. At least that's one thing we have in common, but anyway. I could see it happening, and I started getting that dizzy feeling I get when I know her words are picking up speed, and any second, I won't understand what she's saying. Because I'm just the opposite: I don't know what to say when I get upset. And then that infuriates her all the more, see. No, there's nothing I can do.

What do you *think,* she said, that every woman I'm close to I fuck? Is that what you're trying to say? I said, No, it's not. I'm sorry. I just didn't understand the situation, I said, and then she goes, Because there is no situation, okay? There. Is. No. Situation. Do-*you*-under-*stand*-what-I'm-*say*-ing? she said, mouthing her words like she was speaking to a retard or something. Then she answered her own question: Well, probably not, because you never understood. So what are you telling me? What, Mom? But I just stood there. Speak! Fuck sake, Mom, *speak*! Then she stopped.

It was the strangest thing: Jenna nodded her head and then she walked away. I'd never known her to walk away before. I was even more shocked when she calmly turned and went to her room. No parting shots, no last words—she just closed the door, like it was nothing. I have to say, standing there alone was worse than her shouting. I couldn't take it.

So I decided I'd leave for a while, clear my head and give them some space. I left them some pizza money with a note saying I'd be back late, but to leave me a slice. I got back, I don't know, sometime after two, maybe, and when I got home, the money was still there. Frankie had left me a note saying they'd gone shopping, and she'd made some dinner, and there was a plate for me in the refrigerator. Lasagna, my favorite. Frankie even signed her note, No worries, Peg. XO, Frankie. I was so touched by that, I really was.

She was right, though, Jenna. Of course she was right about my being out of line with that comment. God, it was just so stupid, *stupid.* Was I trying to be cute or...? I don't know. But she was also right in saying that there was never any understanding to begin with. It's true. We never understood each other; we never saw eye to eye on just about anything—you name it. Jenna was just like my little sister, Maureen. They always talked about books, those sorts of things. Not to say we didn't get along, Maureen and I. No, we got along fine. We were just very different: Maureen liked to read, and I liked to have a good time, that's all.

One night that Christmas Frankie was visiting, I stayed out late, and when I got home, I found Frankie, sitting at the kitchen table, leafing through a magazine. It was the first time we'd been alone together—I think Jen was afraid I'd lure Frankie with my evil ways, but anyway. I said, Are you all right? Frankie said she was fine; she just suffered from insomnia. So I asked her if she wanted some tea or maybe some hot milk—I didn't know if we had any milk, but anyway—Frankie said, No thanks. I said, Then how about a nightcap? She had to think about it, so I knew Mother Jen must have said something. That's what I used to call her, Mother Jen—as in Mother Hen, right.

I'd been calling her that since she started talking. Because she was always on my case about something, always, as far back as I can remember. What, either she didn't like the way I talked, or...Oh, perfect example. A few days after Christmas, I was going to cook a real meal for a change. So I was putting away the groceries, and I started telling the girls about running into one of Jen's old classmates at the grocery store. Then, right in the middle of the story, Jenna says, *Mom,* and I thought, Christ. What did I do now? I held up my hands and I said, What? She looked at me, and then she turns to Frankie and says, Want to know why everyone looks so old in the Midwest?

I could tell they'd talked about this before. Next thing, she'd be saying, *D'ja git enough t'eat?* That's what she always told people, like it was some great hardship that where she came from, we don't say, How was your food, sir? No, here we say, Did'ya get enough to eat? Don't—don't get me started. Anyway. Want to know why everyone looks so old here? she said, and I said, Jen—, and she said, This is why. Because it takes them a year to spit anything out. I'm telling you, there are dog years and there are *Iowa years*— What is *wrong* with you? I said. Nothing, Jen said. I just wish you could get from point A to point B without stopping to ask someone their life story or offering your own. Is that too much to ask? she said. I didn't answer; no use.

One night, I was late for work and I couldn't find one of my shoes. So I hobbled into the living room and I said to Jen, I said, Honey, have you seen where my shoe's at? Then she got on my case about that, too. She started in again on the black student. You know, the one about the new freshman, the black kid who stops the stuffy old professor and says, Excuse me, sir, can you tell me where the library's at? And the professor gets his feathers ruffled, and he says, *Young man,* here at Princeton, we don't end our sentences with prepositional phrases or whatever, however he puts it. So the black kid says, Oh, okay. Excuse me, can you tell me where the library's at, asshole?

Jen's telling me this for about the hundredth time, right. I said, Jen, what do you want me to say? Excuse me, have you seen where my shoe's at, asshole? I'm serious, if Francesca hadn't been there, I would've said, Excuse me, but I really don't need a lecture from my snot-nosed daughter who thinks she's so much better than the rest of us, my god. I mean, really. Well, then Frankie started laughing, and the look—oh, the look on Jenna's face…to die. I mean, I knew thirteen was going to be rough, but I didn't know it was going to go on for ten years.

I'm sorry, but it's true. I was vulgar, I had the mouth of a sailor, I didn't enunciate or I talked too slow or I watched too much TV and I never used my brain, on and on. She was constantly nagging me about something. So at nineteen, I basically went from having an older mother to a younger one—and I told her that, too. I did. I said, Listen, I really don't need another mother, okay? One was plenty, trust me.

Anyway, I could tell Mother Jen must've said something about my drinking, and that Frankie was about to say no, but then she changed her mind. So we had a drink, and then Frankie started telling me how hard it was at Christmas. She told me about her parents kicking her out after she came out to them, and how they'd kicked her out at sixteen, at *sixteen*. And despite everything, Frankie said she still wondered if she should have kept her mouth shut just so she could see her family once or twice a year. Even if it meant lying, she said, who cares? I didn't know what to say. But she was so matter-of-fact, so open that I could see why Jen admired her so much. I would've had a crush on her, too.

So I told Frankie how Jenna'd written a letter her sophomore year—that's how I found out she was gay. But what really amazed me was that Jen wrote the whole letter by hand. I mean, I was so impressed she could do that, sit down and just write like that, without any screwups and nothing scribbled out. Nine pages and nothing was crossed out, there were no arrows pointing to what she meant to say or circling a few words she wanted to add somewhere. I was in awe, I really was.

Frankie smiled and then I told her the only thing that was hard, really, was that I got the Xerox. I know that sounds petty, but Jen sent her father the original and she sent me the Xeroxed copy. And I never said anything, not even to Frankie, but I knew Ron hadn't kept the letter. I'd bet a million bucks. Ron's a smart guy, and he's done very well for himself, all in all. He even paid for Jen's college. He told her, If you get in, I'll pay, and he did. Ron's a decent guy, but he doesn't think about things like keeping a letter, or—I don't know what. Anyhow.

I told Frankie it didn't bother me if Jen was gay; that was her business. Besides, there were other gays in our family, and my cousin Karen is just the greatest lady in the world. Whenever she'd visit us, she always used to bring Jenna a bag of green grapes, no matter what time of year it was. Please, no one cared. And it wasn't like we didn't know Karen was gay from day one. But that's the thing: I never had any idea Jenna was gay. None.

Honestly, though, when I found out that my daughter was gay, I was relieved. I thought, Thank god, at least she's having sex with someone. I mean, I couldn't figure out where she'd developed this great love of women, but I figured that was probably naive. Because I certainly know men who don't like women, and that doesn't stop them from being heterosexual. So there were things I wanted to talk to her about after she told me, but it wasn't like, Oh, so what exactly do you *do* together, you know? Basically, I just wanted to know if she'd always known she was gay, and if so, why she waited so long to tell me.

But it didn't go very well the first time that I tried talking to her about it. I said, I got your letter, and Jenna said, Yeah? I said, Yeah. And all I want to say is I think you're brave. I said, I think you're courageous, or you have a lot of courage, I can't remember exactly how I put it. But then she winced. Courageous? she said. I just meant if it were me, I said, I don't think I'd have the courage you have to— But you act like it's a choice, Mom, she said, and I said, No, I don't mean it like that. Well, it's not a choice, and it's not a phase, she said. Okay, I said. Okay, okay.

Then she became so militant that I could hardly keep up. First, she moved into the Rainbow House, and then it was the bumper stickers and the I'm-here-I'm-queer-get-used-to-it buttons. I always found it strange, though, because when Jenna was in college, she used to go to all these rallies; she'd bus down to D.C. or wherever, and she got really political. But then she never mentioned anybody in her life. I kept wanting to say,

Jenna, are you seeing anybody? Is there anyone special? But we never talked about those sorts of things. Don't ask, don't tell, right? Well, there's one trend that wasn't late to reach the Midwest.

But our troubles hardly started when Jenna came out. I mean, we had problems way before that—about everything, you name it. Makeup, bras, anything remotely feminine, she didn't want my help with any of it. Once she hit her teens, she kept all her toiletries in her room, so I didn't know what she used, and when I offered, if…I don't know. Say I asked if she needed me to pick anything up for her at the store, she'd say, Can't think of anything. Then if I asked again, if I said, You don't need Tampax? Pads? Nothing? Jen would make this disgusted face and recoil. I mean, I don't even know when my daughter got her period, because she never told me. Thirteen? Fifteen? I have no idea.

What's funny is that I used to have all these ideas about how Jen'd have lots of friends and boyfriends, and how I'd be the cool mom, you know. I'd be the mother who was cool with her daughter drinking and having sex. I always imagined she'd talk to me, really tell me what was going on; and I'd take her to Planned Parenthood when the time came. Then we'd go out and splurge on a nice lunch…What a laugh. Honestly, every time I hear or read about these amazing mother-daughter relationships, I think, *Who are these people?*

But, no, I think the only time we ever talked about sex was…well, whenever she got on my case about it, I suppose. Because Jenna disapproved of every guy I ever dated. Honestly, the way Jen told it, it sounded like I dated Hells Angels or something. Please, Jim drove a Kawasaki: I wasn't a *biker chick*. And if they came to see me at work or stopped by for a drink, Jenna would just assume that's where I met them. She'd wrinkle her nose and say, Mom. Don't they have rules against *employees* sleeping with *customers*? Such a snotty voice, too: *Don't they have rules...?* So I said, Yes, they do, Jen—that's why I take them to the back room *before* instead of *after* they order. I mean, honestly.

But it was sad that she never had any real friends or boyfriends. No, it made me really sad that no one ever called her; she never went out on Friday night, the weekends. But Jen really didn't seem to care, so long as she had her books. Then in high school, she started wearing those clothes, the baggy army pants and black hooded sweatshirts and those canvas shoes that made her feet look ducky. And I'd always thought I'd take her and her friends shopping for new clothes, prom dresses, that sort of thing.

I remember one time when she was about fourteen, and I came home and found Jen in the big chair, curled up, reading, and I realized I couldn't remember the last time I'd seen her body naked. I mean, I couldn't tell if she'd gotten boobs or what she looked like under all those layers. So I said, Jen, why do you wear those clothes? Are you trying to make yourself look ugly? I just meant that maybe if she let people see her, they might actually want to know her. And I was about to say there was probably a very pretty girl underneath it all, but of course she got upset before I had a chance. You think *my* clothes are ugly...?

We—Ron and I—we divorced when she was three. So it was just the two of us all those years. But then we didn't know how to talk to each other. From the very beginning, when she used to have those fits — she'd storm into the room, all of three years old, and she'd say, Mom! What's the word? What's the word?! She'd grab on my shirt and try pulling herself up, like she could reach the answer by scaling my waist. So I'd grab her hands and say, What word? And she'd say, The word, the word! And I'd say, I don't know, honey, is it a color? No. Is it an animal? *No.* A toy? No! Food? No, no, no! So I'd say, Sorry, I don't know what word you mean; and she'd throw her head back, pleading. I couldn't deal with it. I'd just never felt that way about a word.

And the way insults came so naturally to her — it was like peeing or something. I mean she could be so nasty when she wanted to that there were many times I thought she was actually a gay man trapped in the body of a gay woman. Really, Jenna was so good at knocking me that I thought she must practice. I'm serious, for years, I honestly believed that part of the time Jen spent in her room wasn't reading, it was spent practicing insulting me. I mean, why else did she have a mirror in her room?

I think the last time...yes, the last time she came home for Christmas was her second year in California — that's right. I was really hoping that Frankie would be joining us again, but Jenna said Frankie had a serious girlfriend now, so. I tried not to show how disappointed I was, saying, That's great! We were in the kitchen, and Jenna said, I really like her, too — Sarah or something, I can't remember, but Jen said she's great. So Frankie's good? She's happy? I said, and Jenna nodded, Very happy. But it's he now, she said, and I stopped cold. You mean Frankie got a *sex change*? I couldn't believe it—she'd talked about it, but I didn't think she'd actually go through with it. Jenna said, *Mom.* I said, I'm sorry, but— She rolled her eyes, No, Mom. Frankie didn't get a sex change, but she's transitioning and now refers to herself as male. He, she said. Well, I thought Jen was kidding, because she does this sometimes. She baits me.

I said, Wait, I'm missing something here. So Frankie's transitioning—I still don't know what that entails, but anyway. I said, She's transitioning, and Jenna said, I told you: he. I said, Excuse me. *He,* I said. So Frankie's transitioning, but he's not getting a sex change? Jenna said, At some point, maybe, but not now, no. I said, Okay. So Frankie's not getting a sex change, but he's keeping his vagina? I wasn't trying to be a smart-ass, honestly. But that did it. Jenna bit her lip, nodded yes to herself, and then she stood up and walked out. And that's how it was, those last few visits.

Anyway, I wanted to have a proper sit-down dinner that Christmas, so I made turkey with all the trimmings. Then, once we sat down for dinner, I asked Jenna if she'd ever read Mary Karr's book *The Liars' Club.* I said one of the women at work was raving about it, and I tried to make it sound so, Oh, by the way, have you heard of this book...? But it wasn't really like that. No, I made a real effort with that one.

When I started, I knew what Jen would say if she could see me, buying the book. So I made sure to go to the college bookstore, even though it was a total pain in the ass, finding a place to park, but anyway. Then, once I bought the book, I made sure not to turn to the last page and count how many pages there were before I started reading, because I know that's one of her biggest pet peeves. Anyway, I had this fantasy that I'd read the book, then I'd *just happen* to mention this great book I'd read... and what do you know? Jenna would say, Oh, I love that book!

Then she said no, and for a split second there, I thought, Wow! I've actually read something she hasn't? I said, *Really?* She nodded: No, I've only read her poetry, she said in this monotone, picking at her food, not paying any attention. Talk about bursting my bubble. Then she started scraping the turkey to one side of her plate, and I knew what she was saying. That was her way of telling me I should've known she was a vegetarian, vegan, or whatever—and I did. I do. I know she's vegetarian, but I saw her eat a piece of barbecue chicken at a family reunion not two summers before, when she also said she was a strict vegetarian. So I thought there were allowances for special occasions. I mean, in our family, gay is a lot easier to take than vegetarian, but anyway.

When she said she'd only read her poetry, her voice just sounded so completely uninterested. Like the book would be a waste of her time or it was beneath her, I don't know what. But I'd read the damn thing just so that we'd have something to talk about at dinner for a change. That's all I wanted. I didn't *know* the woman wrote poetry, it never crossed my mind to ask. But, honestly, even if I had known, I wouldn't have read it. No, I wanted to read a book—I really did, but I'm sorry, no poetry. Anyway, after that, I didn't tell her I'd read the book.

There are a lot of things I never told her. Like that magazine—after Jen went back to school, I bought that magazine, the one with the kids from her school. Actually, I think I bought it the next day and just hid it until she left. Probably. Anyway, I paid like four bucks for pictures of all these kids, just hanging out in their dorm rooms, looking cool. Or this one, where this girl's sitting in this ratty old velvet chair, and there's all this stuffing coming out of the arms, but she's just sitting there, with one leg thrown over the arm of the chair. She's got a gold shoe dangling from her heel and she's wearing this dress that costs more than I make in a year...It was ridiculous, and Jen said it wasn't really like that, but I didn't care.

Anyway, then I ended up getting pissed off. That night at the table—I mean, first the book disaster, then the turkey, then I lost my appetite, watching her pick at her food, and then, on top of that, there was her posture again. So I told her to sit up. I said I was tired of watching her sulking over her plate like an overgrown child—like a hunchbacked child, I said. No, I'd really had it with her sulking and her terrible posture and her hair hanging in her face all the time. But I came down too hard and I knew it.

So I smiled and said, You know what your grandfather would say, don't you? I reached over and tucked a lock of her hair behind one ear, but then she shook her head, freeing the hair. Well, I said. He'd say, Unless you've gone and changed your name to Veronica Lake, *I suggest you get that goddamn hair out of your face, young lady!* I spoke in this deep voice, imitating my dad, hoping that would crack a smile, but no such luck. She listened, staring at her plate, and then she got up. She calmly scraped her turkey into the trash, rinsed her plate, and walked out of the room...I—I was stunned. The silent treatment was still new to me. That only started in college, really. So I sat there for about an hour before I got up to do the dishes and then I called it a night.

I went to visit her once. That summer, she invited me to visit for a week—well, almost, not quite a week. But after that last Christmas, she said she always came to see me, but I never went to see her where she lived. So I went out and I saw her apartment and met her roommates—all five of them, yes. I'd really hoped to see Frankie, too, but I guess she—he, sorry—he, he. Christ, I'm never going to get used to that, but anyway. I guess they were in Seattle visiting Frankie's girlfriend's family, and I guess Jenna hadn't thought to mention it. I wish she had, but what can you do?

So the afternoon I arrived, we went out for coffee. Jenna took me to this cute little coffeehouse in her neighborhood. It was a beautiful day, and I thought, This is so nice, the two of us sitting here, talking…then Jen told me she wanted me to go to therapy with her. I didn't even know she went to therapy, and before I could say anything, she said, Because there are some things we really need to discuss if our relationship is going to move forward. I thought, *Move forward?* What the hell does that mean? Talk about watching too much TV. I mean, personally—aside from my opinion of therapy—I thought it was sneaky to wait until I got there to ask.

So I said, Jen, why didn't you tell me this before I got here? And she said, What does it matter? I said, Well, I would've known why you wanted me to come, for one. She said, That's not the only reason I wanted you to come; and I said, At least I would've *known*— If you don't want to go, she said, say no. I'm not saying no, I said, I'm just saying— Sorry I asked, she said, clenching her jaw and looking away. I said, Jen— Please, she said. Let's just forget about it, Mom.

So I agreed. What else could I do? She'd already scheduled an appointment—I hadn't even agreed, and she'd gone ahead and scheduled it for the next day. Anyway, the whole thing stressed me out so much I could barely sleep the night before. So that day, I went out for a walk until it was about time for our appointment. I walked around Jenna's neighborhood a bit and then I sat in this little park. Well, no, it wasn't exactly a park. It was more like a grassy median in the middle of this two-lane road, but it was a gorgeous day, and there were lots of people lying in the grass, so I decided to join them.

Everybody was so young, and there were all these girls just walking with their arms around each other. Such pretty girls, too. I wasn't sure if they were gay or just the prettiest tomboys I'd ever seen, but I envied them, how comfortable they all seemed with themselves. I don't think I was ever that comfortable with myself, much less at their age. And it was nice imagining Jen was like that, too. I mean, that's why I'd come: because Jenna said I'd never seen her where she was most herself. And I hadn't seen that person yet, but it was nice to think that's how she was, too. So I stayed there as long as I could, people watching, and then it was time to go.

Therapy. Well, the first surprise was Jen's therapist, Susan. For one thing, she was younger than I expected; I thought she'd be about my age, but no. She wasn't at all California New Agey, like I'd feared—no wavy gray hair or turquoise jewelry or those flowy raw silk skirt-and-top ensembles, no. Her name was Susan, and she was about thirty-five, I'd say, and very attractive.

Well, more cute, really, with short red hair and this fifties dress. It was this deep green that reminded me of the wallpaper my grandma Flora had in her guest bedroom for twenty years, not that the woman ever let anyone sleep in there. So then Susan smiled, inviting me in, and her voice—I could swear she was a smoker. I'm positive. I didn't think anyone smoked in California, but anyway. She was very welcoming.

We sat down, and I smiled and folded my hands on my lap, wanting to make a good impression, but not trying so hard that Jenna'd think I was being phony. And then Susan started it off by saying that it was her understanding that there were some things Jenna needed to say to me. Things Jenna doesn't know how to say to you, she said, and I thought, Well, that would be a first. I almost smiled, but then Jen looked up and she must have seen the look on my face, because she glared before looking away. I mean, daggers.

That's what I was expecting, pretty much. So when Jenna opened her mouth and started sawing her jaw back and forth, I thought, Oh, here we go. Then she said, Mom, I want to apologize. I didn't think I'd heard her correctly. Apologize? For what? I said, and I laughed, because she'd caught me completely off guard. Jen frowned and covered her mouth with one hand, then she said, Because when I used to come home—, and I knew what she was going to say. I said, *Jenna, please.* I know I screwed up, okay? We've been over this a million— Susan interrupted: Peg, why don't you give Jenna a chance, and then you can respond? I got one of those bitter hot flashes in my chin and then my lower lip started quivering. I hadn't had that sensation since Sister Mary John.

I said, I'm sorry, I shouldn't have interrupted. Jenna

winced, and then she said, One time, I got home from school and I found you passed out on the couch. So I dropped my backpack next to you, hoping that would wake you, but it didn't. So then I poked you and I said, Wake up. Wake up, Mom, and I shook your shoulder, but you still didn't move. So then I got up and walked away. I just left you there. I didn't even turn you over to make sure you could breathe, in case you threw up, she said.

Because the first time I found you like that and I cleaned you up, I swore I wasn't going to do it ever again. You even promised me — the next day, you said you were sorry you were so out of it — that's how you put it. You said, Baby, I'm sorry I was so out of it yesterday, I was just having a really bad day. But it won't happen again — I promise, you said. Remember? she said, and I nodded yes. Then Susan said, Peg? and I said, *Yes*. Yes, I remember, I said. What I wanted to say was, Listen, I don't know who the hell you are, so back off, lady. I literally had to bite my tongue, listening.

So when it happened again, she said, I was so angry, I tried to think of the most spiteful thing I could do to get you back for lying to me. So then I went into the kitchen and I started making myself something to eat. I thought that would be the ultimate fuck-you, she said. You know: *Stupid bitch,* see if I care — Jenna, Susan said. *No,* she said, I thought, If you wanted to kill yourself, go on. Do it, just don't — *Jenna,* Susan said, and I thought, This is more like it. Now Jen's going to throw one of her fits and tell Susan what a terrible mother I was. But no, Jenna just sat there, and I thought, Come on. Let's have it —

I'm sorry, she said. Then she started sawing her chin again, staring at the ground. What I was trying to say was that I couldn't—I couldn't do it, she said, crossing her legs and kicking her foot. I ended up leaving the kitchen to check on you every few minutes. But then that only made it worse, she said. Because every time I checked and you were okay, I got that much angrier. So I left you once for almost ten minutes, and then I couldn't take it. I went in and I tried sitting you up, and I started shaking you, slapping your face, but I couldn't get you to wake up. Then I leaned over and your breathing was so shallow, I thought, Oh my god, she's not breathing...

I started panicking—I really thought she was going to die because of me, she said. Susan furrowed her brow, and Jenna said, Because I'd always thought that if something happened to her, I could go and live with my dad and start over, and so I almost wished something would happen, she said. I knew what she was saying, but Susan had to get in her two cents. She said, What do you mean by *if something happened*? Jen looked away, nodding no. She took a deep breath and sighed, and then she finally said, I meant if there was an accident or...she died, Jen said, chewing the skin on her thumb.

Susan furrowed her brow, staring and nodding like she really understood, right, and I thought, Oh, screw you. No, really, if you actually think— Then, Jen said, When I couldn't get you to wake up, I thought I was being punished—no, really, I thought God was punishing me for having such horrible thoughts, because I was a horrible person. I was eleven, you know. After that, I became convinced that if anything happened to you, it would be my fault, she said.

I knew she was looking at me, but I couldn't bring myself to look her in the eye. I don't know how long I'd been staring at my hands, my cuticles. But honestly, I couldn't look at her, because I didn't feel anything. I mean, aside from Susan scolding me, I didn't feel mad; I didn't feel guilty...I didn't know what I was supposed to feel, and I really had nothing to say for myself. So I sat there, like an idiot, listening. Maybe that's what I was supposed to do, I don't know.

For years, I had this fantasy that I was adopted or there'd been a mistake at the hospital, she said. Susan cocked her head, and she was about to speak, when Jen said, Because then I could find my *real mother*. Then Susan laughed—they both laughed, and then Susan looked at me. I tried to smile at her, but I was annoyed. I didn't think I'd ever be able to read Jenna like that, pick up on things, laugh—

I mean, we didn't *look* anything alike, she said. In school, I once heard this girl say, Oh, it must be really hard for Jenna, when her mother's so pretty, and she's so *not*...And so of course my response was like, Yeah, well, you should see her when she's so fucked up she bursts a blood vessel in her eye, puking over the toilet—now that's *really* attractive, she said, smiling, and that hurt. That really hurt. I thought you always said sarcasm was the lowest form of wit, I said. I think I actually surprised her, and then she said, You know how I love to be right, and I nodded my head, right, but I couldn't smile.

What can I say? she said. I wasn't you. I wasn't voted Life of the Party and Best-Looking or whatever, she said. I never told her that, though. I wanted to say, When were you looking through my yearbooks? I didn't even know where they were. Sometimes it really got to me, she said. I mean, I wanted to be popular; I wanted to be asked out. I was such a *loser*—it's true, she said, laughing at herself. Then I was about to tell her she shouldn't feel that way, because she was way ahead of the rest of us— *But,* she said, there were times I was relieved to be alone, relieved I was nothing like you, she said, and I closed my mouth.

Because I thought, What's the point of being beautiful if you have so little respect for yourself? If you let men treat you like shit, or even worse, you treat yourself like shit. What good is it, you know? It made me so angry, she said, and I thought, What is *wrong* with you? At that moment, I almost stood up and walked out the door—I was this close…I mean, maybe Susan was getting paid for this, but you couldn't *pay me* to listen to this.

Then Jenna turned to me and said, I'm sorry I was so mean to you. I didn't look at her, but I nodded and shrugged. I think I said something like, We all make mistakes, I don't remember exactly what I said, but I tried to tell her to forget it. No, Mom, she said, I enjoyed it—I *enjoyed* making you feel dumb. Because I knew you were listening and you'd remember. But that's no excuse, she said, I'm sorry. And I heard her, I heard every word, and I knew I should've told her how pretty she is and how smart and how much I'd always admired her, but all I was thinking was how soon I could leave and how I—

Peg, were you going to say something? Susan said, and I automatically said no. I've always been that way. Even in school, when I used to get called on, I'd just say I didn't know the answer, even when I did, sometimes. I don't know if it's shyness or what, but anyway. Susan said, What were you thinking, then? I said, Nothing, really, and I kept nodding, but Susan sat there, staring at me. She wasn't going to let it go.

Honestly? I said, and Susan nodded. But I was so sick of her nodding that I said, I was thinking how much I'd like a drink…I mean, it was true, but I was just being flip, you know, that's how I am sometimes. But as soon as the words came out of my mouth, I thought Jen would get angry. I really didn't think that Jenna'd understand it was just a reflex, but I was wrong again. Jenna looked up and smiled. Me, too, she said, sighing. *Me, too.*

I'm sorry, I said, that's not what I meant; and Jenna nodded no, still smiling. She took a deep breath and rolled back her eyes several times, but I still didn't know what to say. She stared at her hands in her lap, twisting a silver ring on her finger, and then tears started rolling down her cheeks. But she was so calm, so quiet, playing with her ring, it wasn't crying, exactly; it was more like…I don't know. I had no idea what was going on in her head.

And me—I mean, everything Jenna had said was true. There was no denying it. It wasn't always like that, but there were times, yes. I guess I expected Susan to say something like, Peg, how do you feel about what Jenna just said? But Susan didn't ask how I felt, and Jen didn't have anything more to say, so no one spoke. We just sat in silence. It was unbearable.

Finally, Jenna dried her eyes and looked at her watch. Oh— we're over, she said, I'm sorry. Susan waved her off. It's fine, Susan said, don't worry about it, but Jenna was already on her feet. I stood and followed her to the door. I'll see you next week, Susan said, and Jen said yes, and for a moment she almost seemed embarrassed. Then Susan turned to me and said, It was nice to meet you, and I said, You, too, and I expected her to say something else. I thought, Shouldn't there be some sort of resolution, something? But all Susan said was, Take care, and then she closed the door behind us.

After we left Susan's, Jen hailed us a cab. We got in, and she told the driver her address, and then we sat there, both of us staring out our own windows. She seems very nice, I said, Susan; and Jen said, Yes, she is. She's very nice. Then I said, Well... how about that drink? And I knew I shouldn't have said that, so I braced myself, but then Jen smiled and said, Another time, maybe. If anything, I thought she'd either go off or ignore me. Instead, she took my hand and gave my palm a kiss before returning my hand to my lap. She gave my hands a squeeze, then she returned to her window.

I felt more ashamed at that moment than I had the entire time in Susan's office. I was provoking her, and she didn't want to fight. I knew it, too, but I still couldn't stop. I mean, why? *Why* would I do that? Jen's right. I mean, what is *wrong* with me? I saw my reflection in the window, and I thought, What a sad woman you are...So I dropped Jen off, and then I went back to my room. I slept twelve hours that night, and I probably would've slept all day, if Jenna hadn't called at ten.

That afternoon, we went to the Japanese Tea Garden, which was torture. No, I mean, the gardens were beautiful, but we were so polite. It was like, How did you sleep? Out like a light. How did you sleep? Or, I like your ring; thank you, I like your sweater. No, we weren't ourselves at all—understandably, but still. I left the following day, and Jenna offered to take me to the airport, but I said it wasn't necessary. So she came to the hotel to say good-bye and she said, Call me when you get home, okay? I said I would, but it was probably a good idea for us both if I took some time, and she agreed. We said our good-byes, and that was it.

Jen's surprise party was last weekend, but I missed it. No — I knew I wasn't really going to go. Michael's left several messages, and I should call him. I mean, I was the one who called him this time. I called him on his cell last week, because I wanted to get Jen a gift. For a good week, I became obsessed with the idea of getting her a gift, but of course I didn't know what she'd want, so I called Michael. I wanted to talk to him about some other things, get a few things straight as well, but then he didn't answer. So I left a message, asking for suggestions. I said I was all set, but there was no way I could show up without a gift.

So Michael called back and left a message saying that the only thing I needed to bring was myself...No, what he said was, *You*—that's what you can bring, Peg. Other than that, I can't think of anything else Jen really wants, he said. I listened to that and...honestly, it made me sick. I mean it was such a sweet thing to say, but I felt completely disgusted with myself. I almost started crying, then I became furious and I started blaming Michael for this whole mess. I thought, Why are you doing this to me? Why can't you just *leave me alone*? And I knew then—I knew I wouldn't go.

I mean, forget Michael, it's amazing what I can make *myself* believe sometimes; and for a couple weeks, I truly believed I was going. I did. I'd even chosen an outfit—a nice pair of pants and a simple blue cotton sweater, no dresses or panty hose this time. And I got a sporty new haircut—no more perms for me. Seriously, though. I'd packed and set my alarm, the whole nine yards.

Friday morning, I lay awake in bed from four to six o'clock, feeling miserable because I couldn't pretend any longer. And part of it was my feeling sorry for myself, but part of it was frustration. Because there was a point where I wanted to call Michael and say, *Tell me*. Just tell me how to get on that goddamn plane, because I don't know how to do this—I really don't know *how*. I needed a little help, and I was willing to ask for it, I was, but then there was no way I could call him. I mean, it was like three in the morning there, and who knows, Jenna might have answered...There was no way.

I went back to sleep around the time I should've been arriving at the airport. When I woke, I thought, What are you *doing*? Get up, Peg. *Get up!* And I wanted to get my ass to the airport, but it was too late. I mean, I could have caught a later flight, but there was something in me that said no, no, and I couldn't get around it. Then I thought, Well, this is what you wanted; this is what you get. There's no turning back now.

On Saturday I was in such a funk; I couldn't stand myself. So around the time the party was supposed to start, I went out and bought her that book and this big bottle of champagne. I felt so much better that I changed my flight when I got home. I decided I'd take them to her, myself, and then we'd toast together...I was so hungover I barely made it to work on Tuesday morning. I haven't had a drink since, but it's only been eight days, give me a chance — sorry. Sorry.

I don't know what to do anymore. I'm thinking I should just forget about the book and send a card, instead. Or maybe write her a little note, and see what happens...I think that would probably be best. Now I just have to figure out what to say for myself.

Young
Professionals

The first attack occurred after I had forgotten to lock my front door. But the only problem then was that I *hadn't* forgotten to lock the front door—and *attack* is an exaggeration of what was nothing more than a shortness of breath, a momentary anxiety. Anyhow, it was easily remedied; I simply returned before even leaving my building. No, I was right, after all: I locked the door, and so I wrote the matter off to forgetfulness, distraction, general confusion first thing in the morning. But for a few days I returned and checked my door, just the same, before leaving my building, because I was increasingly forgetful, rushing out the door every morning, forgetting something—wallet, ATM card, cash, tokens, gloves— always something. Still, I then became increasingly worried about my forgetfulness, and I soon began experiencing pro- longed anxieties—cold sweats, palpitations, all the usual symp- toms of a panic attack, yes—but generally focused on my door; so, continuing exactly as before, I began double- and even triple-checking. Once, for the sake of security, and twice, second-guessing any irrational response, all before I reached the sidewalk.

Within a matter of days, I returned home, after walking a block or two, though I knew fully well that I had locked the door, double- and triple-checked, because I found my house keys in my coat pocket, as a quick reminder. When this key trick began, I don't remember exactly, but then, whenever I checked my pocket for the keys, I knew I had not forgotten to lock and check my front door at least twice. Although, a few days later, I somehow became convinced that I must have forgotten one lock, either the top lock or the dead bolt, so I immediately returned home, checked the top and the bottom locks, turning the doorknob, then shaking and shoving the door.

So then this pattern continued for a while, through the shaking-and-shoving bit, until one morning, when I basically body-slammed the door—not so that I was hurt, or ever risked hurting myself—just a quick body slam or two, and then I returned to the street, continuing about my business. I want to make it perfectly clear about this thing with body-slamming the door—which was kind of fun, really, and helped relieve a great deal of related stress—but it went no further than that—I never stomped one foot in place while nodding my head, like some talking horse—nothing out of the ordinary, and certainly nothing that could not be easily explained, were a neighbor to notice my actions. But in that case, if someone noticed or actually went so far as to ask if there was a problem, I would tell my neighbor the truth: No, I was simply checking my front door, true; and everything seemed fine, also true.

So this routine — returning, checking the top, then the bottom lock, shoving and body-slamming the door, thereby checking the security of the locks themselves — this continued for a while, and when this routine became insufficient, I returned, unlocked and relocked the door, thereby anticipating and compensating for my irrational response, not once, but twice, and doing so in one continuous, time-saving motion, usually before I ever reached the sidewalk. Then this new-and-improved routine, with all its built-in safeguards, continued for several days, a week or two at most, as I assumed it was only a temporary quirk, because everyone had their idiosyncrasies, and I had only just moved to New York and, really, nothing was strange in New York, or so they always say. I also felt greatly reassured by that saying, and often repeated it to myself during this period, however untrue it often seemed.

After moving, I lived with my best friend, Jessica, for several months, while I searched for my own apartment — also incredibly stressful, the stress of which I avoided through denial and procrastination — so it was actually her apartment I'm discussing, not mine, even though I felt completely at home there. Actually, I felt greater responsibility for her apartment, and most especially for her cats, precisely because the cats were not mine, and if anything happened to her cats, it would be all my fault, which would be worse than if something happened to my own cats. But I even mentioned this matter to my friend, explaining my constant anxieties about the door, returning, double-checking, and although I didn't mention the part about body-slamming her front door, she also felt reassured by my precautions and my concern, especially after I told her that she needed new locks, but which Jessica already knew and which she had already mentioned to the super several times herself, though he claimed that the locks seemed fine.

But after discussing this matter with Jessica, and the lack of results from the super, I somehow became convinced that I'd left an electrical appliance on high or soup cooking on the stove, no matter that I never cook—or almost never. But, nevertheless, anxiety required that I return, check the door, both locks, all appliances, and the stove, often removing any pot or pan from the stove top, or even removing the gas knobs and carrying them in my bag for safekeeping, in case I forgot—all this, before and/or after returning to the street. So again, either way, the drill went something like this: leave, return, check, leave, return, put keys in pocket, return, unlock door, check appliances and stove, remove knobs, lock and unlock the door, carefully body-slamming—so as not to chip the porcelain gas knobs—put knobs in pocket with keys, instead of bag…However, the problem then was that by the time I returned home, I was usually running late for work, only adding to my anxieties, because I hate to be late.

I truly envy those types of people who simply stroll into restaurants or their workplace with complete disregard for the time, or even note their tardiness, but simply laugh out loud and shrug their shoulders, even if their colleague or the person whom they have kept waiting seems perturbed, or angry even. I often wished that I was one of them, living amongst the happy-go-lucky habitually late, but I was not. No, I was barely arriving to work on time and increasingly agitated by my own tardiness, and I had to leave the house earlier every day, five and ten minutes, here and there, allowing enough time to turn around and check the locks and all the appliances as many times as needed. Sometimes I returned two or three times, even after reaching the street, depending on how far I had already walked, or the weather, or my workload on any given day. But other days, when I was simply too tired or too late to return home, instead I felt anxious throughout the day; unable to work, or concentrate; repeatedly checking the digital clock on my desk or my computer or my watch; synchronizing, then calling my answering machine to make sure the machine was still picking up, therefore there was no fire and I could make it home in time, just. All this occurred within a matter of a week or two, while I was working a great deal and sleeping very little — less and less, every day — so I figured it was only natural, a phase, as might be expected in times of high stress and sleep deprivation.

Then, after adjusting to this routine, the one through keys and knob, I arrived at work one day, having forgotten whether or not I checked the iron, because, removing my coat, I noticed that I had actually ironed my clothes that morning, and the iron fear led me to worry about the cats. Assuming I left the iron turned on high — because I didn't have the time or patience for low, and because all my clothes were heavily wrinkled — I easily imagined the cats chasing each other through the apartment, knocking over glasses and books and lamps, as they often did almost daily. So I easily imagined the cats somehow tipping the hot iron on to the old wooden floor and thereby starting a fire. Immediately, I imagined the cats burning in graphic detail, and, sickened, I had no choice but to leave work during my break, and just to make matters worse, in transit there were always sirens in my neighborhood, night and day, between the hospital and the fire station nearby. Never mind that the fire department was only three blocks away from my apartment—that was not close enough to save the cats from asphyxiation. So, returning home in time to save the cats required I taxi instead of taking the subway or bus, and spending more money on my commute than I had budgeted—yet another concern—but I actually enjoyed the taxi rides, and I treated myself—seemed perfectly healthy, now and then. And usually I returned to find the cats sound asleep on top of the duvet, mildly annoyed by my interruption, as I woke and petted them, reassured by their startled breathing.

Then, sometime around the beginning of December, I passed a fire on Fourteenth Street, between First and Second Avenue, walking home one night—a third-story apartment burning less than two blocks from my friend's apartment. Though there wasn't any smoke or flames, a crowd had already gathered around three fire trucks, and a fireman was climbing the truck's ladder to the third floor, wielding an ax, with which he broke the front window and then cut through the protective metal bars with some type of special saw I couldn't see, and I was thinking that must be kind of enjoyable in itself, breaking a window and cutting security bars in half. Fortunately, no one was home and no one was hurt or injured, so I left, returned home, and told Jessica about the fire. It was her sincere belief that my anxiety was more than mere coincidence—no, my fear was a *premonition* of this very fire, and I was willing to agree with her—guess I kind of I liked the idea.

So, for a while I felt relieved, further bolstered by my psychic abilities, until a few weeks later, mid-December, when our next-door neighbor knocked on our door. We were on friendly terms with this neighbor, Clarissa, but she only stopped by to ask if we had heard about the fire in *our* building, and Jessica gasped: No! What fire?! Last night, Clarissa said: I knocked on your door several times, and then, assuming neither one of us had been home, Clarissa began explaining how a fire started in the boiler room, located directly beneath our apartment— which came as no great surprise, really, considering the building and the slumlord and the inept super. Jessica hadn't been home the night before, and she immediately demanded to know where I was and why I hadn't told her about the fire, and I stammered: I didn't know—I was right here, sleeping, and so we continued listening to Clarissa, who said that she had no choice but to evacuate her own apartment due to the plastic fumes. I was worried about your cats, and I was going to break into the window (through our common garden), Clarissa continued, but I didn't know how I'd break through the security bars, so then I told one of the firemen instead, and they were planning on breaking down the door, to save the cats, but they put the fire out just in time. After the fire was put out, the firemen suggested that Clarissa pick up one of those safety stickers, IN CASE OF FIRE, SAVE CATS, for her cat, Dinah, and in turn, she suggested we also get one of those warning signs, and we all agreed, but I don't think Jessica ever picked one up—I know I didn't.

But the strange thing was that I never heard any knocking or pounding on the door, as she had claimed, and though I believed Clarissa was an extremely honest woman, I still doubted her little fire story. I was pounding and pounding, she insisted, nodding her head. You must have heard me! But I said, No, I didn't hear anything. You didn't smell anything? she asked, pulling her bangs aside, and looking around our apartment, and

I said no, and she sniffed the air, several times, then she agreed: That's so odd—my apartment reeks of plastic fumes…

Now, I've always been a deep sleeper, likely due to the fact that my father blew out stereo speakers throughout my childhood—I argue this was because my dad was cheap and rowdy, while my dad argues that it was because the *speakers* were cheap and *he* was rowdy—in any case, deep sleep has always been a gift, whatever the cost to my eardrums. Still, after Clarissa left and Jessica left for the night, shortly thereafter I doubted my ability to wake, in case of emergency—maybe I really could sleep through a burning fire and plastic fumes, like my dad always said—and then I wasn't able to sleep, not that night, nor the next, nor throughout the rest of the holidays. Never having suffered insomnia, I lived amongst those deep sleepers who imagine insomnia might be nice, once in a while, like I might get a few extra things done, put those extra hours to good use—catch up on some reading or watch some movies; it sounded pretty relaxing, actually—but needless to say, I quickly changed my mind.

Like after the first fire, when Jessica said: Don't you feel much better now? Yes, but on second thought, no, I did not feel better: my fear was of a fire burning in our house, not a house, or just any fire, and if I was to believe in my psychic abilities, there was still a big problem, like any day. I somehow managed to forget all this for roughly two weeks, and then there was that fire in her building, another stressful couple of weeks, Christmas and last-minute shopping, a visit with my folks, all before I found my own apartment, and then I moved, following New Year's. After I moved, I temporarily forgot about the cats, as well as the fact that I didn't own any cats anymore, and it was a week or two before I even remembered that I had no cats, after returning to my apartment several times just to check on them. So I had no cats anymore, but I had chosen a cat's name, a great name, for the time when I finally adopted my own cat, when my life was stable enough to care for a cat as well, and I decided to name my cat Roy, even if it was a girl. I'd like to name a female Roy, even though I don't want a female, because they're too high-strung. On the other hand, male cats tend to get fat once they're neutered, never mind their shorter life spans. Like Jessica's cat Curtis, whom I took to calling Curtis Mayfield because he sang a lot—more like the sound I imagine pterodactyls made, very strange. But maybe I shouldn't have called him that, maybe it was bad mojo somehow, even though I meant it in a soulful way. And, I mean, Jessica really liked that name, Curtis Mayfield, too, or at least she told me that she really liked that name, but then she started calling him Curt, and I really didn't like that name at all, because it reminded me of guys we knew in high school, all the Chads and Brads and Curts, whom I had almost forgotten, quite happily.

Anyway, one day, when I pointed out the fact that her little Curt had a big paunch, this comment really upset Jessica: How could you dare say that about my cat? she demanded, in utter seriousness. And in my own defense, I said: How could you not notice that your cat has a paunch? Just look at him, and we turned our attention to poor Curtis, running away—animal intuition—and sure enough, his paunch nearly touched the ground, flapping from side to side, and certain angles were to be avoided altogether. Then, in her own defense, Jessica swore: But I thought it was *fur!* And I reminded her that tabbies were generally a short-haired breed and, regardless, Curtis Mayfield was definitely short-haired, and we discussed the nature of her denial in some detail. But it was my sincere belief that the cat had grown to fit his new nickname, though I did not tell her this, because I figured there was nothing to be done and I would only further upset my best friend, which I did. Anyway, then I started calling Curtis "Poncho"—affectionately, of course, but which she said was *offensive*—that was, until she started calling him Poncho, too. But still, Jessica put both her cats on a low-fat, all-natural diet—Science Diet or Max Cat Lite, I can't remember—and she even bought this overpriced wooden stick, with bright turquoise-green feathers, attached to the end of a rubberized string, called a Johnny Cat Jumper, or something, and she exercised the cats when she had the time, or whenever she remembered, excitedly waving the stick and calling: Here, Curt! Jump, jump! Hey, Poncho, get over here— *come on, now*—we don't want any fat boys, do we? All this, in the hopes her cats would live longer, healthier lives.

But I felt bad for Curtis, who was the only male in the house, and he wasn't even all-male, and on the occasions when men were in the house, men who happened to be undressed, reclining on the bed, with one or both arms clasped behind their heads, Curtis sweetly nuzzled their armpits, as if longing for male companionship. Well, this was how stage one began, licking and nuzzling, but before too long, Curtis began kneading their armpits, softly, with one paw, then slowly digging in his claws. Then, having made it that far, Curtis immediately attempted nibbling, as if a little love bite, and chewing, as he advanced into stage two and, inevitably, ravenously biting any given man's sweaty armpits, never satisfied until he removed a clump of hair—and this all happened pretty quickly, from start to finish—which I always found pretty amusing, but often upset our company.

Sure, I laughed, or until this sort of behavior disrupted my sexual activity, and I had no choice but to lock both cats in the bathroom, just to be fair, before turning up the stereo, which kind of nauseated me—because I certainly didn't want anyone to think I was the type who needed mood music or something. But I also didn't want to be distracted, and, most of all, I didn't want to mention feeling distracted by Curtis and his ridiculous squawking. The problem was that the more I ignored the cats and their temporary incarceration, the more often and the louder they meowed, finally requiring I interrupt my guest, excuse myself, return to the stereo, and turn up the volume another decibel or two, as needed, all of which wrecked the mood, or at least my mood, anyway. But I also want to make it clear that I took no pleasure in the lockups; I only locked the cats in the bathroom for the duration, and I only did so, knowing Jessica, their owner, had locked them in for half the night sometimes, or however long, until she had to pee.

I feel sorry for men who don't like cats and who must undergo the rigors of being introduced to their partner's cat—well, somewhat sorry, and only sometimes, it all depends. For example: I loved those cats, and I was annoyed to hear Jessica's old flame—another exaggeration—when this guy she was sleeping with on a semiregular basis for two or three months called her cat *That fucking cat!* and actually kicked little Hattie—kicked her—I couldn't *believe* this. His bare ass was sleeping on Jessica's bed, and he had the nerve to kick her cat? Well, I was glad she got rid of that guy, anyway, but who, in all fairness to Jessica, was a good short-term decision, all in all.

Still, I felt badly, as I listened to the story about this guy kicking Hattie in the head, so I never told her that I, too, had kicked her cats, maybe one or two mornings, or a few times, when they clawed my feet and I desperately needed to sleep. But I said nothing, because I was not nearly as big as that guy, and I knew I hadn't harmed the cats, because they persisted at clawing my feet, even after kicking them several times. I mean, I never kicked them without provocation: first I tried cocooning my feet in the duvet, but they broke through every time. So, having slept with her cats, I understood his position—not to say that I condoned his actions, but I understood.

And I've since noticed that many young women who own cats experience conflicts with new partners, due to exactly these types of insults and abuses, but I still don't blame these men, because no one really likes to have their feet bit and clawed at five or six in the morning, due to the fact that in the throes of passion, their partner forgot to feed her cats—her own cat, who she will in turn defend, after the man kicks her cat in the head, however mistakenly, as is often the case. I mean to say that the vast majority enjoy sleeping, and at least most men I know don't like to have their feet bitten at five or six in the morning, but again, this is only the men I know, and perhaps a gross generalization. Anyway, now that I don't have any cats, I must walk over to Jessica's house to make sure that she did not forget the iron, as she had done several mornings while I lived with her. But these days I walk to her place, worrying about my place and if I will ever have a cat of my own.

Because, since September, I've also learned that it's increasingly difficult to adopt from a respectable agency, requiring an application and personal interview, and Jessica's interview was downright brutal. She actually cleaned her house, brushed Hattie, and carelessly threw a few new toys on the floors, but still, the Mighty Mutts volunteer almost denied her application on the sole basis of her backyard—the *garden,* as we call the common area, enclosed by six-story brick walls and a few dead ivy branches—more like an aired cell block with a grill, table, and four chairs, and you literally have to jump out the window, but it's private and we like it. Well, Jessica nearly lost Curtis, because the volunteer said it was quite possible that the cat might lick the same square inch of red brick where another, infected cat once licked, and thereby acquire feline leukemia and die a horrible, painful death, which he then described in grotesque detail, until Jessica begged him to stop. But the Mutts man wouldn't stop, because he'd seen it happen before, dozens of times, he said, angered beyond reason. So, dead serious, he made Jessica swear to God that she would never, never allow her adopted cat outside, and she wanted the cat so badly, she swore—she actually shook the man's hand.

Upon hearing this tale, I told her that I thought the whole thing was ridiculous, though I certainly appreciated the fact that it was her word we were discussing, and so I never told her the number of times I let Curtis play in the garden, back in the fall. To this day, every weekend when we pass the Mighty Mutts stand at Union Square, Jessica must point out that volunteer, who instilled the fear of God, before she glares at him openly. But aside from her behavior, I prefer to avoid the display altogether, not just because the animals depress me, even though Jessica says they're well taken care of, but also because she insists on asking me when I intend to adopt my own cat—save a life, share my love, all of that—but I'm just not ready yet, and then I feel guilty and selfish, which leads me to worry about Curtis and the iron, on and off, for the rest of the day, even if it's Saturday.

Then, during the height of the holidays, Jessica said that there was something urgent she needed to discuss with me, face-to-face, so we met for coffee one afternoon after work. We sat at a corner table, due in part to the gravity of the situation, I thought, but also due to the fact that my best friend has always been a freak magnet—always. But we were in the clear that day; for some reason, her reception was down, at least Leather Man wasn't on the prowl, as Jessica held her cup, warming her hands, paused for a moment, and then she said: There's something I need to know right now, and I need an honest answer, and of course I said yes on both counts. Then she paused again, staring into her cup, before she finally spoke: I need to know that if something happens to me…Her voice broke and she sounded tearful, and I almost reached for her hand, but she nodded, as though she could not continue if I were to touch her, so I allowed her to continue, feeling somewhat tearful myself. I just need to know that if something happens to me, and I die…She inhaled and exhaled a deep breath, If I die—will you take care of my cats? Yes, of course I will, I said, utterly relieved that she was not ill, but then I was afraid she might still be gravely ill but had not yet told me, which explained why she was asking this special favor before she told me the worst possible news.

But when I began laughing nervously, she snapped: This is *not* funny—this is serious, and it really bothers me at night. I cannot sleep, worrying about them! And because she was shaking, I immediately apologized. Although the fact of the matter was that her cats kept her awake, they're nocturnal cats, and they chased each other across her bed all night, which was probably why she worried in the first place, she just needed a good night's sleep. But I didn't want to belittle her feelings, so I agreed for her sake; it was indeed serious, and then I asked: Is there something else you need to tell me? Though she sighed and said: No. That's it—I just needed to know that you would take care of my cats if I die. Thank you, I feel much better now. She sighed again, then downed her coffee, before reclining in her chair and scanning the room.

But after I moved to my own apartment, I realized that if something happened to Jessica and she died, I would inherit her cats, and I just don't have enough room for her cats and my cat, when I finally adopt Roy, if I'm accepted as a responsible owner. Besides which, the cats might not get along, and because I gave Jessica my word, I would have no choice but to carry out her dying wishes. Really, I would have no choice but to move, after she died—although I wouldn't mind an extra room—like a one-bedroom with an actual bedroom would be nice. So I simply asked her, Will you provide for the care of your cats in your will so I can move to a larger apartment? And she said I would be the sole benefactor of her estate, on the condition that I cared for her cats, and then we agreed.

Another problem occurred to me, which was that I do not want to be one of those single women who owns a cat and behaves as if the cat were her child, or she even goes so far as to refer to herself as *Mommy*. But, on the other hand, it's quite possible that I will die single, and my only regret will be the fact that I never adopted a cat from Mighty Mutts and I suffered years of loneliness for no good reason. I decided that when I was stable, earning a regular income at least, I would be better equipped to make these sorts of decisions, and again I felt greatly relieved.

Yet another concern: and that was my original unspoken fear that my best friend had AIDS. I worried about this over coffee, before she said a word, and then I worried about my own health, because I had not taken a test in over six months and I had several partners in that time, no matter what precautions. Like they say, The only sure protection is abstinence. Perhaps, for some, but I never feel certain, even when I do abstain—and then, on top of that, I worry that I will never have another sexual partner—never, never again—and this concern overrides my fear of STDs, or worse, the possibility that I might not have sex ever again, even if it's only been a week, or a single day, for that matter. As I am in my mid-twenties and the women in my family live to be ninety, I am far too young to abstain—unless I so choose. All in all, I find abstinence unduly stressful, and it is this very concern that so often drives me to take another unsuitable partner, however temporarily suitable, and however many other precautions I take.

Because when I fear that I will never again have sex, I feel most vulnerable to selecting a sexual partner at random, more or less—certainly more randomly than when I have a regular partner—and so abstinence actually increases my risk of contracting the AIDS virus, all in all. Now, if I were consciously abstinent—rather, if I chose abstinence consciously—that would be a different matter, perhaps a healthy choice, just so long as the decision was mine. But there's a chance that if I consciously choose abstinence, then I might not be psychically available to the right person, so I think it's much better to remain sexually active until the day our paths cross, if ever.

And just in case I never meet that person, or if that person does not exist, it will have been much better that I remained sexually active and I did not wait another day, like a fool. But it's equally possible, in this day, that I might contract AIDS from this person of my dreams, not knowing they carry the AIDS virus. Or, equally probable, this dream person is not quite as conscientious as I am and contracts AIDS from another during one of my periods of psychic unavailability and/or abstinence, and I meet this person thereafter, only too late. Yet another possibility is that meeting the person of my dreams would prove lethal: I might die for love, which would all be terribly romantic, yes, but it's not really my bag—no big rush, there. In any case, I still need another test to allow for a grace period. But before I test again, I must first get health insurance, in case I already have AIDS, even an undetectable level, and even if my insurance company tries to cancel my policy upon detection. Health insurance and renter's insurance, and then I might feel more at ease, or at least that was what I decided, one sleepless, sexless night.

But that afternoon, over coffee, I took my best friend's hand and I asked: Jess, are you trying to tell me that you have AIDS? She had just been to her gynecologist and so, naturally,

I figured that she had taken another test. Why would you say that? she frowned, and I knew what she was thinking—she thought I was insinuating that she slept around. Because I love you, I said, avoiding argument, and she squeezed my hand, and then she smiled, answering: Well, no, I don't think so—but how can you be certain? We discussed our uncertainties for a while, and then we decided she best ask her little sister to care for her cats, as a precautionary measure, as my second. I've also learned, since then, that everyone in her family has planned for who will care for their animals if they should each die, with backups, seconds to family members, in case they all die together, in a car accident or something.

Then, last week, Jess called to tell me that her little sister, Dorie, had agreed to take the cats, but only after Dorie scolded her over Curtis and his apparent weight gain. She said she won't agree, not unless I quit feeding them so much, and that I'm *hurting* them, Jessica whined. But it's not free-range—I mean, you don't leave food in their bowl all the time, I argued, trying to defend Curtis Mayfield, no offense to her little sister, who was only thinking of his welfare, increased risk of heart disease, and so forth. Maybe there's something wrong with him, she said, like a tumor or a thyroid condition? Maybe, but a tumor? I laughed. *Seriously,* she warned me, when I touch his stomach, it feels like he's got a water bottle stuffed in there, and he's very sensitive around his stomach. Well, I asked, then why don't you take him to the vet, if you're still worried? I know, I *know*..., she agreed. But that seems silly. Besides, I don't have the money this week, she said. Next week, then, to put your mind at ease, I suggested. We'll see, she said: I have other things to worry about first.

Having known Jessica since we were eleven years old, I could not imagine my life without her; instead, I worried about my house, or her house, and our cats, who might be burning alive as we discussed their welfare. Maybe the cats tipped over the hot iron, or I'd been careless with the ashtray and cinders were burning through the plastic bag, lining the trash can—I might've dumped the ashtray while a butt was still burning, which supposedly causes numerous fires every year—and the cats were asphyxiating on plastic fumes as we spoke. I know that I must quit smoking this year, yet I worry what will become of me without a vice, and I don't know if that's healthy, and then I worry what vice will replace smoking, as we need our vices, at least one, and I'm happy with my vice, especially while drinking coffee. I dismissed these thoughts as sheer nonsense that afternoon, partly because I was too lazy to return to check, and, instead, I considered the possibility that my worries were the onset, the early stages, of agoraphobia.

Whether or not the crazy person knows they're crazy, I think the agoraphobic knows fully well they don't want to leave their house, whereas I didn't mind leaving my house, in itself, and I am not afraid of something terrible outside; it was only the process of leaving my house that upset me. So then I considered numerous possibilities, but with no magic number, no closing the kitchen cabinets ten or twenty times, no horse stomping—whatever the explanation, I could still nip this problem in the bud, if, in fact, there was any problem. And aside from the fact that I always thought agoraphobia was for plus-thirties, the condition would throw a real damper on further sexual activities, with or without a cat; causing further problems, inevitably leading to worse habits. I guess what I'm saying is that I have absolutely no intention of becoming one of those aging, agoraphobic, intimacy-fearful, porn junkies.

But finally, with Jessica's and Dorie's help, I found an apartment I could afford, though just barely, and I moved into a building, over one hundred years old, immediately after New Year's. Sometimes I worry about the possibility of faulty electricity, but, fortunately, several of the breakers are turned off, and I have almost no electricity in my new apartment, three outlets in total. And although I might overload the circuits one day, I have not reported this shortage to the super, figuring the previous tenant, a lovely older woman who lived in my apartment for five years, felt the same as I; also a great relief. And perhaps the same reason that my buzzer does not work, she wanted peace and quiet, too.

But this morning, when I heard a knock on my door, I was afraid someone had managed to slip into my building and chose my apartment for their horrible deeds, and though I was afraid of this intruder, resting my cigarette in the ashtray, I thought there was also a chance that it was Jessica's mother, who has never seen my new apartment and who doesn't know that I smoke. I certainly don't want her mother to know that I'm a smoker, and Jess gets on my case about that all the time, because Jessica herself used to smoke, in front of her mother, who always lamented: *Oh, you're breaking my heart!* My friend also asks why, if my parents know I smoke, I cannot tell her mother, further claiming that her mother will discover the truth sooner or later, and I agree, completely. But I would rather her mother discovered later, like after I quit; then I'll tell her

mother the truth myself. So this is why I've never exactly invited her mother over to see my new apartment—I haven't
been able to air out my place, due to the weather, and now I'm
afraid that her mother will think I'm avoiding her, which I am,
but not for any of the reasons she might think, simply because
I value her good impression, however uninformed.

Well, I only answered the door for fear that it was the super
and there was a serious problem, because we're due for a building inspection next week: Who is it? I yelled, and a man's voice
answered, Exterminator! in a thick Spanish accent. Still, I didn't
take any chances, leaving my door chain locked, opening
my door a crack. Yes, it was only the exterminator—an older,
smallish man, at that—but that was when I realized that I
must've been glaring, because he held out his spray can for me,
repeating himself: Exterminator! as he wiped his sweaty brow
beneath his dingy baseball cap. Then I felt bad about glaring at
a helpless old man, an immigrant simply trying to do his job
and earn an honest living, and this tired, little old man must
have been close to sixty, mid-sixties, older than my grandmother, and he was just trying to keep my house insect-free,
and then I felt really bad about my rude behavior, like I
had no manners. I mean, god, what a bitch I was, and I guess I
might've tried to recover, somehow, compensated, seeing as he
hadn't even lowered his arms, probably aching from the weight
of that rusty canister, but I really just wanted him to leave me
alone, because I was feeling bad.

Then the man repeated himself a third time, Exterminator!
Even though I had already opened the door, so I obviously
heard him the first time, and he shouted in my face, anyway.

Then I immediately felt angered by this grimy little man, because, really, why should I be made to feel bad in my own house? Besides which, I didn't know this guy from Adam—he might live alone, happily; he might very well make more money than I do, and he still might try something, prey upon my sympathies—even though I felt pretty sure I could take him if worse came to worse. Just the same, I quickly sent him away: No, thanks; closing the door in his face. Later this afternoon, when I found a dead roach on the bathroom tile, I cursed myself for my stupidity, fearing that next time he knocked, I would not be home and, soon, my apartment would be infested. Nevertheless, I thought it best not to worry for the time being.

Now it's mid-February, and I must check my appliances three or four times, even though, as of last week, when that number became insufficient, I began scribbling a checklist every morning, then I dated the list, so as not to confuse the numerous scraps of paper in my bag. And since then, every morning I quickly check off each appliance, including the gas stove, coffee machine, iron, and my hair dryer. I check off each item, sign my name at the bottom of the scrap of paper, and leave for work. Now, if I get nervous on my way to work, I can usually find the scrap of paper in my bag. Sometimes I cannot find my checklist, because there's way too much junk in my bag, as I said, and I must find an entranceway on the street, where I can thoroughly search my bag, then my person, searching every pocket, undisturbed by the rush-hour traffic. After this happened several times, I decided it would be wise to place the checklist somewhere I would not forget, though this is exactly what I had done before, so I would place the checklist in one pocket, the same pocket, every morning. I decided upon my right coat pocket, as before, and all I needed to do was put on the same coat, every day, before I checked my apartment.

But this morning, heading to work on the train, I noticed a woman, sitting across from me on the subway, eating a salad, situated on her lap. It was one of those nasty pasta salads from a deli, a typical cold salad, consisting of white pasta—rigatoni, I think, or spirali—spirali, I guess, with slices of black olive, carrots, and celery, which she was eating with a flimsy white plastic fork, and which only reminded me of the fire in my old building, and the fire before that fire, and then I quickly searched for my list, lowering my hand into my pocket but never taking my eyes off the woman. All this time, nearly five stops into my trip, the woman continued eating her salad, and each and every time she lowered her white plastic fork, she gouged one pasta spiral—if she gouged two pieces, she lowered her fork and removed both pieces, scraping the fork against the far side of the tray, then gouged again—only one spiral at a time, and only the pasta, never the olives or carrots, that seemed to be the rule.

Understanding something of irrational thought processes, I figured the woman bought the salad in order to eat something healthy, but, because it was a deli salad, exposed to the elements and all types of pollution, then, if the food did not touch her lips, she was somehow immune to various types of airborne germs, and she probably avoided the vegetables for fear of the insecticides, although she did not shove the veggies to one corner of the plastic tray, as I might in her position—no, she seemed to prefer the added difficulty, which probably made each bite that much more rewarding. Then she raised her fork, inspected the pasta, lowered her hand, raised her hand again, sniffed the pasta, lowered her hand, and raised her hand, one last time, before she placed the bite into her mouth, careful not to allow the pasta or fork to touch her lips. This required that she open her mouth fairly wide, straining her jaw a bit, but when the subway suddenly jostled, her lips mistakenly touched the pasta, she had no choice but to begin again, with a new piece, and she carefully wiped her lips, dabbing them on a Kleenex from her bag. Afterward, I noticed that she was clearly dissatisfied with the single piece of pasta that had touched her lips, and she pushed it to the side of the oily plastic container and chose a fresh bite. And honestly, I felt relieved, just watching her—*we're talking serious fucking outpatient, here*—I felt much better about my situation, as this ordeal continued for another three or four more stops, returning from Midtown on the F train.

Raise, lower, raise, sniff, lower, raise, bite, chew—I found her rhythm quite soothing, actually. Sniff, lower, raise, bite, chew...But the chewing—god, how could I forget the chewing? Truly obscene, this woman chewed each and every bite ten times, with her jaw rotating in a bovine, counterclockwise fashion; chew, chew, chew, four, five, six; awful, too painful to watch. Well, at first, I thought it was a woman, but then I wasn't so sure if it was a man or woman. I had thought it was a thin woman, legs swimming in her new fuzzy, dark blue 501s, a black V-neck sweater, and black boots, with long, dark hair covering her face—except when she looked up, that time the pasta touched her lips, I was no longer sure, because of the amount of facial hair, a slight mustache and darkened area, like a goatee. So I wasn't sure if it was a woman with heavy facial hair or an effeminate man with incredibly smooth skin. Well, all I knew for sure was either she wasn't very pretty, or he was—but not androgynous, she wasn't that self-conscious.

Nevertheless, I stuck with my first guess, my gut instinct, which they always say is the best bet, statistically—even though my first guess had become rather complicated, but anyhow—a woman, it was. Again: chew, chew, chew; five, six, seven, eight—then I heard a crash, and the far doors of the car blew open, as this big guy entered our car, carrying a boom box over his left shoulder, and this woman turned to look toward the sound; a deafening bass; *throbbing,* as they say, on the down-beat: *Boom*-chicka, *boom*-chicka, *boom, boom, boom*-chicka; *boom*-chicka, *boom*-chicka, *boom, boom, boom*...Relieved, the woman returned to her tray, raised her fork, and ate the spirali. Now, I'd been watching her the entire time, as the man passed through our car; I watched her as I searched my pocket for my list, and I knew she did not sniff the pasta—she inspected the pasta, lowered her fork, and raised her fork, but she didn't sniff it this time, which really disturbed me. I thought maybe I should warn her, and she could spit her bite into a fresh Kleenex, but then I decided that was ridiculous, however annoying and lax. But still, it was none of my business, and I wasn't about to incriminate myself. Instead, I got off the subway, and by the time I reached the street, I was already laughing.

So in the end, I turned around, heading home, knowing perfectly well that I owned no iron, and that I would be fifteen minutes late to work. But, once home, I would call my boss and tell him that I was running late, blame mass transit, and although I had never called in late before, I worried that he might say: I certainly hope this does not become a problem, as I heard

him say to several of my coworkers, because there was a defi-
nite possibility that my tardiness *would* become an ongoing
problem, just as I already knew that I would have no choice but
to consciously lie to my boss, and say no, as I feared and antic-
ipated—because I truly value honesty, and I am trying to be
more honest with people—but even more importantly, I really
needed to keep my job in order to pay rent for the apartment I
could barely afford.

Regardless, I would call my boss and lie, anyway, and then
I would call my best friend, to check on her and our cats, and I
would be five or ten minutes later than I was already. Because I
was not late to begin with, no, I was early, in fact, which explained why I took the interminable F train, thinking I would
have to find something to do for twenty minutes in Midtown,
of all places—window-shop, smoke a cigarette, something—
anything, instead of arriving early and working an extra unpaid
half hour. Then I began laughing—I was laughing so hard that
it was difficult to run or breathe, and I narrowly avoided an oncoming taxi, then I missed my street altogether, and for a moment, I completely forgot where I was going in the first place.
No matter, because I had since realized that the woman on the
subway would eventually realize her mistake as well; so I
laughed, doubled over, holding my stomach, because by the
time she realized, it would be too late—*man, what an amateur.*

The Former World Record Holder Settles Down

I'm walking down the street and I see this guy I recognize. This was a couple weeks ago, on my way to Chelsea Lanes, over on Twenty-second, between Ninth and Tenth, or right around there somewhere, and the guy, he was across the street from me, up a ways, you know. So I stopped and I stood there a second. Because I was like, I know this guy, I know this guy...I *know* I know this guy...What, did I go to high school with that guy? Is he a friend of a friend or something? Where the hell do I know this guy from...? I'm totally racking my brain, you know, because I know I know this guy from somewhere, and it's really bugging the shit outta me. So I'm just standing there, you know, trying to think, and by the time he's right across from me, I remembered—and I'm like, I know where I know this guy from! I was like, *Oh my god...I had sex with that guy once!* That's where from!

I mean, it was more than one time. We kinda went out for a while, but he was never my boyfriend or anything like that, it wasn't anything serious between us. So I raised my hand, I was going to say hello to him, like flag him down, because he was this super-nice guy, and I hadn't seen him in years and years. So I raised my arm to wave at him and I opened my mouth to call out to him and I started to speak and—I couldn't remember his name. I was just standing there with my arm in the air and my mouth wide open, and I couldn't remember his name, and I'm like choking, you know. I'm being totally serious, *I could not remember his name for the life of me*... Well, good thing he hadn't seen me or anything, so I was like, Oh well. *C'est la vie,* you know. You win some, you lose some, or whatever. I was late, anyway, so I kept on walking.

The thing is that this happens to me a lot, like seeing someone on the street or I'll see some guy out of the corner of my eye, and I'll get this funny feeling, and that'll be my very first thought, you know. Like, where do I know that guy from, did I ever have sex with that guy before? But then, that time, with that guy, I wasn't thinking about sex because I was thinking about my husband, and so of course the *one time* I was dead certain I knew the guy, sex totally didn't occur to me at all. Like, doesn't it just figure, the one time? So I kept walking, trying to hurry up, because it was League Night, Tuesday nights at eight. There are all kinds of leagues, there's like a gay league and a league for people in the rap industry, and those brothers *get down,* they have some *serious* bowlers in their league. Our league isn't as good as theirs, but that's all right, we've met some nice people, anyway. So then, like by the time I got to the bowling alley, I thought the whole thing was pretty hilarious. Can you just see me standing there, with my arm up in the air, and I'm like waving, waving, all excited to run into an old friend or

whatever, starting to say, you know, like, Hey, Ja—, or Bo—...
Hey, sorry I forgot your name, but didn't we have sex? God,
how *embarrassing* is that.

So I was going to tell my husband about it, because I
thought it would make him laugh, because he's got such a sick
sense of humor, but then I decided that that was a bad idea.
Like *really* bad idea. But Joel saw me enter the alley, laughing,
and he was like, What's so funny? And I just shook my head
and gave him a kiss. What's so funny? he said again. And I was
like, Nothing, just some kids outside. Then I put it out of my
mind, but I only bowled a high of 136 and a low of 97 in eight
games—totally pathetic—I sucked so bad that I forgot all
about the guy on the street by the time we left. I don't know
what my problem was, but I was so *upset* because I let the team
down. I'm being totally serious here. I don't bowl for fun. And
people always think I'm kidding, pulling their leg, when I tell
them I've joined a league. But I'm not, it's no joke. Some of my
old friends, when they call me and I tell them, they're like,
What's *happened* to you? And I'm like, I got married, you know,
and this's what happens, so be careful out there.

It's true though, because my husband was the one who got
me into bowling in the first place. He took me bowling on our
first date. We met on a blind date, a mutual friend set us up. My
friend Laurie, she was my maid of honor. And Laurie knew Joel
from her job; they used his company for all their special printing jobs. Because Joel owns a printing company, he's in ad
specialties; they print like mugs, book bags, mouse pads, or
whatever. They can print just about anything. They have these
special UV-cured dyes, and they could print condoms if someone wanted them to. She was always raving about Joel, how

good-looking and successful he was, how much everyone loved him, and what a great guy he was, so finally I caved, just to get her off my back.

So as far as our date, well, he picks me up, right, and I was like, What are we going to do tonight? And he goes, I thought we'd get something to eat and then bowl a few, if you're up for it. How's that sound? And I was like, *What?* I totally started laughing, because I thought he was kidding, you know. *Bowl a few?* Like what's up with that, you know, I wasn't expecting dancing, but bowling? For real? I tried to stop laughing, because he was just looking at me, and then I didn't know what to say about it, so I go, Well, okay, you know. It's one date, what can it hurt? Why not, let's bowl a few. I go, Sounds great.

And then, after I said okay, I was like totally reminded of this friend of mine, Maxine, from L.A. who went out on a blind date, and he took her—this is so funny, he, her blind date, he was this CPA—oh my god, I can barely tell this without laughing. This CPA guy took Max to like Ren Fair because she told him that she worked in *theater,* okay, and he thought that would be something she'd enjoy. So when she told me, I was like, What's Ren Fair? And she was like, a Renaissance fair, you know, where like everyone gets all dressed up like it's the Middle Ages or whatever, they all play like they're lords and ladies, jesters or whatever. They joust and drink ale and shit. It was like out in the middle of nowhere, in BFE, like a two-hour drive out of the city, and it was like a million degrees, and she had no way of getting back into the city, she was *so* bummed. I just thought that was so damn funny, I couldn't stop laughing when she told me. Like how when they got there, she just sat in the car for a minute, feeling like her life had just ended…

So at first, I thought I'd call Maxine like as soon as I got home and tell her about this guy who took me bowling on our blind date, even though there was really no comparison. I mean, Joel wasn't a CPA, and I wasn't stuck out in the sticks, I could always leave, if I needed to. And the other thing was that I thought he was handsome, you know, really hot. And I was so totally shocked that my blind date was hot, like my friend Laurie swore, that I was willing to give it a go just to spend time with him. I was like, Well, least there's some good visuals...Because I'd certainly never dated a bowler before. Honestly, he was totally serious about it, too, even that first night, and I didn't realize that, when he told me. I mean, I'm competitive, but Joel's a fanatic. I'm being totally serious, he's a fiend. Like if he bowls badly, he barely talks for the rest of the night. I'm getting there, but I'm nowhere near as bad as he is. Or like we'll be having a perfectly nice conversation about something that happened at one of our jobs that day, and out of the blue, he'll interrupt and say: If it weren't for the split in the third frame — that's where it all fell apart for me...Or, I failed to convert on a couple crucial splits and left frames open in the ninth and the tenth. But I bowled sixty-four points above average, so that's pretty good...

When we started living together, like my friends would call and they'd say, Where's Joel? And I'd say, He's bowling, and they'd say, Oh, that's nice. Like, Oh, that sounds like fun. Like it was putt-putt golf or IMAX or something. I understood, because that's how I thought of it, too, at first. I had no idea that he rented a locker and had his own shoes and not one, not two, but three balls of his own. And this handgrip thingy. It's like a brace or something. Oh my god, I was *so* embarrassed the first time I saw him put that brace thing on, I totally hid my face. I was like, Would you take that thing off, you look like such a *geek*! But of course I didn't say anything, you know, I just bit my tongue. And he goes, You certainly laugh a lot, huh? And I was like, Yeah, just naturally happy, that's me.

But I had a really good time, that night we went out. Course I didn't feel very sexy in the shoes, but he made me laugh at myself, and that was almost as good. Then, like when we started going out, he started picking me up, coming straight from the alley, and like he'd be in this nasty-assed mood, and I'd say, What's wrong? What happened? He'd cross his arms and run his tongue across his teeth, and he'd say, One-fifty-seven. Average of 157...What is *that*? And I still thought he was just kidding.

I'm sorry. Do you need to be alone? I'd ask, resting my hand on his biceps.

Ah, no, he'd sigh, taking my hand. I'll be all right, he'd say, shrugging. I'll feel better, once we get something to eat. Are you hungry?

Oh no, he wasn't, he wasn't kidding at all. He was dead serious about it. I was just kidding about him needing to be alone, but I didn't tell him that. But then, over dinner, this was like on one of our first few dates, and he'd start talking about his game. The first time it came up, I was like, What game? And he'd snap, Bowling. My game. I'm talking about *my game*. And I was like, *Sorr-ry,* you know. So then he'd go on and on, detailing each frame, how he'd opened with a strike; how he struck in the first, second, third, and fourth frames...I was thinking, He's really, really hot, but this guy's not right in the head. It's kinda sad, really, I'd be thinking, trying to pay attention while he went on and on about how he'd tried changing balls, his approach, on and on, maybe it was his release, something not right with his hook, *bawk bawk bawk*...

Am I boring you? he finally asked.

No-no-no...

He goes, Really. Tell me. I am, aren't I? You can tell me.

And I go, You know that saying about if you like have to ask the price, then you probably can't afford the item?

What I was saying was like, Buddy, chances are pretty good that if you have to ask a woman if you're boring her, you're probably long past due. But he totally got what I was saying. He always gets what I'm saying. Like sometimes even when *I'm* not sure what I'm saying.

In other words, yes. Why don't you just say so? he snaps, and then he goes and gets his nose all bent out of shape.

In my experience, men get really bent out of shape if you tell them they're boring you. They'll ask, sure, they'll suspect, or they'll even know they're boring you, but like they'll still ask. They might even be boring themselves, but if *you* say so —

Well, I don't want to *bore* you. Sorry about that, he says, giving me the cold shoulder.

Come on, you aren't boring me. I just don't know anything about the game. I'm not really into the sports thing, you know. So tell me. Go on...

No, forget about it. Sorry I ever mentioned it. It's probably not interesting enough for you...

But I could always coax him back into the subject. Sure, it might take a little more coaxing sometimes, and he might have even known that I was just pretending to be interested, but he still couldn't help himself. I guess that was what interested me at first. I don't really know how to explain it, but there was just something so…I don't know what, like there's something so genuine about it. I'd never met anyone that genuine before, or that unconcerned with what other people thought. Anyway, he never tried to get me to go after that first date. Like when I told him I thought it was so funny he took me bowling that I was going to call my old friend, Maxie Priestess, who went on the date with the CPA to Ren Fair. But when I told him that, he didn't seem to think it was like as funny as I did. No, he just wanted to know how she got her nickname.

Another thing that I immediately liked about him was that he was so handsome and so awkward, all at the same time. Not like clutzy awkward, just sort of oblivious. Because Joel's one of those guys who only became really handsome in his early thirties. Like about the time when all his friends who'd been handsome all their lives started losing all their hair and gaining weight and they were gripping that image of themselves as the total twenty-year-old studs they had been for dear life, that's when Joel came out. *You blossomed,* I like to say, teasing him, but he just rolls his eyes, doesn't make a big deal out of it. So it wasn't until he was like thirty-two when women started calling him up, and before they'd get a chance to ask him out, he'd reach for his hankie, you know, assuming they were calling because they needed a shoulder to cry on. Because by then he'd become so used to not being good-looking, like not ever being the one who got noticed, that most of the time he still operates that way. He acts like he fits right in at the alley, and other people are like, Wow, what's that really good-looking guy doing bowling?

I see people do this all the time, double take or whatever, when they see him walk past. I see the looks on their faces, like they don't get it. And I think if Joel were to overhear what they must be thinking, he'd just like look around and wonder who the handsome guy was. No, no, no—I can totally tell you what he'd do, he'd probably look around, wanting to know what the guy looked like first, but most of all, he'd want to know if Mr. Handsome could bowl, like for real, you know. Joel'd just assume the guy was a total poseur before he even got a look at him. Like, Oh, some pretty model-boy came to the bowling alley, thinking it'd be a kick. Yeah, prove it... He always goes off on that. Like people who think bowling's hip or retro or whatever, like how it's a joke to most people. But no, he'd never know who people were talking about, even if you told him he was the handsome one.

The good thing about it is that having always assumed that no one was looking, that no one was noticing him, he kind of developed this, like... It's like grace. Like how some adolescents are so afraid of being watched, they're stunted, or the other extreme, they're like always posing for the camera, you know, but that wasn't Joel—he just assumed no one would ever bother watching him one way or the other that he sort of developed focus. And the really good thing about it is that he isn't one of those guys who like covet the myth or whatever that their life would've been forever changed, like how their life would be so much better today, had they gotten laid in high school. I'm not sure where men come up with this shit, like how if they'd gotten laid at fourteen, what, it really would've changed the course of their lives or something? *Please.* Like there aren't complete losers out there that got laid back then, and what difference does it make now? Besides, everyone knows it's the guys who didn't get any that become the most successful.

So what I liked about Joel was that he didn't share this hang-up, it didn't drive him into compensating in any one of like a thousand different ways, the way some guys get so damn compulsive about making up for lost time. Yeah, like those great three years they missed out on…No, he's way too practical for that. He's a total Virgo, way too down-to-earth. It's like somehow he always knew his life wouldn't be any better today, had he gotten laid at fifteen, but his attitude is like, damn, he sure wished he had. Sure woulda been nice, migh-ty nice… He's like that about it. I think he said that once even, and I just had to laugh. That's the other thing I really liked, right away, because he never has to do anything to make me laugh. It's just who he is.

But of course he's always interested in hearing about what other kids were doing back then, how much action they were getting, what it was like, how it felt, what kind of sex…I'm like, Honey, it wasn't that great, okay. Really. It was clumsy and kinda stupid and it was over pretty quick, that's about all I remember. Fifteen-year-old boys are bullets, so like which second do you want to hear about? *Come on,* I don't even think about it.

How can you not think about it?

Easy.

You're saying it's the luxury of having had sex young?

Yeah, whatever.

The first time we slept together, like the first time we had sex, I mean, I told him, straight out. It was on our first date. After bowling. But I'd never been on a blind date before, and I'd never slept with a blind date—I'd never slept with anyone on the first date. I'm being totally honest here. It's like I know how when someone says like, It's not about the sex, or, It's not about the money, nine times out of ten, it really *is* about the sex, and it really *is* about the money. But honestly, I'd never slept with a guy on a first date before. Because for one thing, I almost never dated. I wasn't even sure what a date was, you know. Seriously, I couldn't even remember the last time I'd been asked out like that, Great, so I'll pick you up at such-and-such a time, how's that? This was arranged and formal, my blind date with Joel. He wore a jacket and everything. Like he picked me up at eight at my apartment, and he'd even made reservations—everything. I was like, Wow. A real date.

I had such a good time with him, too. I never felt nervous or worried about my voice or how I spoke or what to say with him. We weren't anything alike, but he made me feel so comfortable, totally at ease. And like I really wanted to see him again…So I thought he should know. It's a terrible thing to drop on somebody on the first date or any date ever. But like I told him because I wanted to see him again, and if it was going to cause problems, I thought he should know right away and—like, Okay, there's the door or whatever, *later.*

We were just lying in his bed, and I said, There's something you need to know about me, putting a pillow behind me and sitting up in bed.

Yes? he said, propping his head up with his hand.

There are some things in my past, skeletons or whatever. I used to lead a very different life.

We all have a past.

Yeah, but I think I have more past than most.

You did hard time?

Yes.

You did time, really?

No.

You never killed anyone, did you?

No.

You don't hurt animals or small children?

No.

Then how bad could it be?

Pretty bad.

How bad?

It's like this bad: I used to hold the world record.

A world record.

Yes.

A world record *in*...?

Sex.

Sex, he said, and started laughing like I was kidding or something.

How does one hold the World Record in Sex?

Because...Well, because I had sex with more men at one time than any other woman in recorded history.

I don't understand.

One hundred and ninety-seven. At one time. One hundred and ninety-seven men.

Wait. Back up. There was a record before that?

He was resting on his elbow now, looking at me in the strangest way.

One hundred and seventy-three, officially. Before me. Before my record.

Officially.

Yep, it was all organized, but that's not important. It's not something I want to talk about. But the thing is that I really like you, so like I thought you should know.

Because you like me so much.

Yeah, now as opposed to later. Like when I really, *really* like you. Because I don't want to lie to you or hide anything, you know. I don't think that's the way to start something if it's going to work. I mean, not like we have to get serious or anything, I just wanted to be honest, you know. However long…

He looked at me a long time. Didn't speak a word, he just like — he just looked.

What…? What, already? Say something.

Okay, he said.

Okay?

Okay.

That's all you have to say about it?

Are you still at it? Do you intend to break your own record?

No. I told you, that was then.

Is there more?

Yes, but I think that's enough for now.

Okay, he nodded, kissing my cheek. No rush.

Now I know that's funny, him saying, No rush, it's like dry or droll or whatever, but I don't come from dry. No pun. I just mean that I didn't grow up around dry people. It's not a natural thing for me, you know, it's not my nature. It takes me awhile, I usually have to remember back before I get it, and then I think, that was really funny, what he said. So, anyway, then he went back to like the staring thing, in bed. It drove me crazy. I was like enough with the staring already, *What? What's your problem?*

I don't know what I expected, but something — some reaction. I mean, we'd used a condom, so I knew he wasn't going to be too worried about that, but still, something. But no, not a twitch. Well, I decided then and there he was like a way bigger freak than me. That or I just hadn't made myself clear. Then I thought maybe he didn't really get what I'd told him, so I wrote it off to shock. I just kept waiting for him to come to or whatever, but he never did. No, that's just how he is — nothing ever really fazes him. That's what I realized.

But I was scared there, for a moment, I really was. I was like, There's something seriously wrong with this guy, between the bowling and being so calm about what I just told him. Maybe he's some sort of freak himself, seriously. Or psycho. Like he's got something worse up his sleeve, or he's going to chop me into pieces, and then I thought about hightailing it out of there myself. Seriously. Or I thought that he was just pretending he was cool, but the next day, it'd be like, This isn't really going to work…But no. He always says, I'm not a very complicated man, but it's not true at all. Because I don't think there's anything simple about kindness.

But it's true, he's a pretty satisfied person, I'd say. He's happy with his lot in life. And he's had a good life. He came from a good family, with lots of kids and solid parents, a really strong marriage. His parents are just the greatest people in the world, they're so damn cool. They've been really, really good to me, too. I wouldn't say it was all white-picket, his life, but it was sane, you know, like warm and loving. His parents were really supportive. And Joel likes to say that's why he's always been interested in freaks. Take you, for example, he likes to joke. He says that all the time, Freaks — like you, for example.

Oh, ha-ha-ha, aren't you funny. But it's true, he's into freaks big-time. Not just like real circus freaks, he's also really interested in, you know, congenital birth defects, Siamese twins, midgets, and weird groups, like the Masons, the Mafia, Hasidic Jews, you name it.

He'll search the *TV Guide* for the week, just looking for surgery specials. I mean, like Joel was surfing the Web this one night, and I'm like, Oooh, that's so *disgusting*! Because he's watching this operation of I don't even know what the thing was, but it was just beating, like pulsing, and blood everywhere, and he goes: You want to hear something interesting? And I was like, Yeah, what? And he goes on to tell me that the same people who are responsible for this surgery shit are also one of the biggest porn dealers on the Web. Sponsored by Viagra, of course. Isn't that interesting? he says. And I'm like, Sure is, baby. Sure is, looking over his shoulder, reading the ads. *Complimentary cosmetic procedures,* wait—go back…

But like at the alley—no, I'm serious. This is his latest thing. Because Thursday night is like the big date night for Orthodox Jews at Chelsea Lanes. I'm not sure if they're Orthodox or Hasidic or what. And I don't know if Thursday night's like their Friday night or what the story is, like why Thursday, but you're sure to see them then. At least it gives us something else to talk about, if we're bowling badly, which has been happening a lot lately. And Joel has so many questions he's dying to ask the kids. Like how to pronounce their names, for one thing, because most of the time they can't even fit their names into the spaces allowed on the computer screen, you know.

I'll see him staring at their screen, trying to pronounce their names to himself, like trying to mouth the syllables. He's just dying to ask them questions about the dating rules, but of course we never speak to them. We try to be respectful, you know. But like you can't imagine how excited he gets when a chaperone appears. It's kind of perverse, really, but nothing makes Joel happier than a chaperone sighting, like some old man who just sits there with the kids, and no one says anything at all.

What I like about bowling is that I don't think about anything else. I stand, pick up the ball, and I focus on my approach, bending my knees, finding my spot. I look at the pins, and if I miss, I try again. It's so simple. Well, it's not simple at all, but it's straightforward, you know. I don't have to think about work or bills or anything. And I've never really had anything like that before, just like watching what's going on ahead of me, not worrying about anything else. It keeps you in the moment, you know, every frame. You're like always looking ahead of you, and I like that a lot. But I still don't tell many people I bowl regularly, because I remember how strange it seemed to me before I got into it. And boring, too, it seemed so damn boring. Now I think it's so relaxing.

I've learned the rules, how to score and everything. I even bought my own shoes...Well, Joel bought them for me, and my own ball, too. Course I didn't tell my friends it was part of my Christmas gift last year, because they would've thought he was an asshole, but anyway. I drew the line at a carrying case for my ball, but that's just a technicality, I know. And like when it got so damn hot, this last summer, we bowled almost every day. Chelsea Lanes has got to be the most expensive bowling on earth, but we have league cards, so we can play half-price any-time. Which was money well spent until we got a new AC. And on the weekends, especially, the place was totally packed for three months straight, kids running everywhere, the smell of gluey nachos and pizza. Then on Thursday nights, you know—can't miss date night.

Sometimes I'd feel a little self-conscious, depending on what I was wearing, like even shorts or a short skirt. Not that I'm ever like falling out or anything, just in the way that I won-der about their hair, and they stare for why ever they're wonder-ing. Well, we bowled almost every night. But only until eight, and then it's this disco thing, Extreme Bowling they call it when they turn out the lights, crank the music. Backstreet Boys or whoever. You can't even see the lane. Joel thinks it's a disgrace. He takes it personally, no kidding. And he gets really angry when people don't know protocol or etiquette or whatever, like if two people approach at the same time, the person to your right has the right of way. And these people, they run up just as you're about to release, and they can totally throw your game.

Joel was all over me about this, from the start, like the sec-ond time I went to the alley with him. We get there, right, and right away he sits me down, and he goes: Now, in bowling, the person on the right goes first. But that's assuming two bowlers are at the ready simultaneously. More relevant is the importance of acknowledging the bowlers to one's left and right, and not rushing past them. Courtesy, in other words—not thinking you can do whatever you care to within the confines of your own rented forty inches…I'm sitting there, my hands folded in my lap, and I'm thinking to myself, *More relevant? Seriously, what planet are you from*…? Then he goes, Are you listening?

I'm like, *Yes, I'm listening,* but can we just bowl now? I under-stood why it was important later, sure, but at the time, I was like, I'm not asking to borrow the car on Saturday night, I just want to throw the damn ball, you know.

So one night last summer, Joel came home and he was *so* excited. I'm telling you, the man was glowing, and he goes, You're never going to believe this! Guess what the big thing is now? I didn't know what he was talking about, I was like, The big thing with like what are you talking about? And he said, The Orthodox dating scene! I'm like, Oh, right, what? And he goes, Rollerblading! Isn't that *excellent!* I have to admit I kinda wished I'd seen it, too. I go, Nooo! Yes, he nodded, grinning from ear to ear, opening a beer. I don't know if they wore hel-mets over their yarmulkes or what, I forgot to ask. But what about the girls? Did the girls Rollerblade, too? I asked. He said they did, but mostly just sat on the benches in their skates and watched the guys fall over.

And I don't mean to sound judgmental, but sometimes I just wish those girls would participate a little more. Like get in there once in a while. Because that's how it usually is at the alley, the Orthodox girls, they don't really bowl more than one game. Sometimes the girls will quit in the middle of a game, and the guy will bowl her games for her, and she'll just sit and watch him. *Damn,* I said. I really missed out. And it's true, I've be-come sort of fascinated myself. Like I wonder what's the deal with the hair, because I thought they shaved their heads when they got married, but sometimes they look like they've shaved, and it's obvious they aren't married yet. So I don't know.

And this one time, when I was like just starting to really get into bowling, Orel Hershiser was there at the lanes with his wife. She was really pretty, too, his wife, not like a trophy wife, but she was lovely, you know. And she seemed very sweet, genuinely nice, nothing like what I'd have expected of a baseball wife. Joel totally agreed with me about her, too. Course I didn't know who Orel Hershiser was until after he left, because Joel had to whisper, and I kept saying, What? What? *Like what are you whispering about, Joel?* I don't know if he heard or not, Orel, but he was bowling right next to us. If he noticed, he didn't say anything about it. His son was there, too, and his son's friend. Really good kids, too. They were fourteen, maybe, that age when boys can be absolute nightmares, and I thought we might have to change lanes, but not at all. They even clapped when I struck. And I struck like three or four times, and they were really encouraging. Kind of made a case for a Christian upbringing, those two, but when I found all this out, I had to wonder what the man would've thought if he knew he'd left his son with me.

When Orel stepped away, I go: Enough, already, what are you whispering about?

That's *Orel Hershiser,* I said.

Yeah, so? Who's Orel Hershiser?

He's a Cy Young winner.

A what winner?

Cy Young.

Okay, but you're like not ringing any bells here.

Cy Young... *Cy Young,* like Greg Maddux.

Oh, Greg Maddux is *so sexy.*

You see him once on TV, and suddenly he's a sex symbol.

He makes me laugh, all right, that's what's so sexy about him.

Uh-huh.

How do you spell that, anyway? Like heavy sigh, or—

Cy, he said, *C-Y*.

Don't get all huffy, *Jesus Christ*.

Watch your mouth, he growls at me.

And I was like, God, what's up your ass, already?

Then Joel pulled me aside—I didn't know what was going on, I was like, Mellow the fuck out, Joel! I'm serious, he like nearly ripped my arm off, too, pulling me over to the concession stand. So, anyway, that's how I came to find out the man who was teasing me about my approach—because I was just starting to understand the game, then I started screwing up my approach, taking one too many steps, overthinking it, you know. Well, that's how I learned that the guy in the lane next to ours was a famous Christian baseball player.

Joel couldn't get over it, either. He called everyone he knew that night when we got home. Joel's friend Tom came over for pizza and beer, and Tom's a hardcore Mets fan. He *hates* the Yankees. Tom just loves to hear himself say that rooting for the Yankees is like rooting for Bill Gates. I have a sneaky feeling that Tom heard that Gates comment on talk radio and he thought it sounded smart, so he took it for his own. But I'm like, I have *my own reasons* for rooting for the Yankees, Tom, the World Series is just the cherry…Or two, or three, or…And he's like, Yeah, what? What reasons? Let's hear *one*…And I'm like, Look, we can't all be born losers, okay? Just because *some teams* fill the quota.

So Joel was telling Tom all about it, like how Orel Hershiser bowled like a 110 or something, first game, and second game he bowled like just over 200, then he left with his lovely wife and left the kids behind. If he'd stayed, I know he would've scored well over 200, he kept saying, Joel.

And I go, He seems like a very nice guy. Super nice.

That's his reputation, Tom said.

Well, he was very nice to *me*.

They both just looked at me, so I took my glass and walked into the other room. I mean, Joel insisted on telling the story even though *I* was the one who had words with the man. Because of my approach. I'd just started to understand the mechanics, and I was overthinking everything. I kept fumbling, taking too many steps. I was just totally Knoblauching, you know. We were down by the Chairman's Lane, and Orel was teasing me about my approach being a dance step or whatever, like doing this little cha-cha-cha, with his hand on his stomach and his other arm turned up, you know. So I mean, shouldn't *I* have been telling the story? He wouldn't of even *noticed* Joel if it weren't for me. I was totally his connection.

Anyway, it was like on and on. Fifteen minutes later, I could still hear him from the living room, saying: You could tell what an amazing athlete he was, how well he knew his body by how he corrected himself, made the necessary adjustments, found his stroke...I got to admit, Orel *was* a little buffer than Maddux. I just mean that Orel Hershiser looked like a real Cy Young winner, you know.

But they were still talking about it during *SportsCenter,* Joel was still talking about Orel's strike and his spare. Talking in that way like he does when we're watching a game, and he'll go, Hey, did you see that? Did you see that? Patting me on the arm. And I'm like, I'm right *here,* Joel. What do you think I'm seeing? So I was just watching the report, not even sharing what Orel said to me, let them talk all they want…I just don't know why they have to bark at me like that—the *SportsCenter* announcers, I mean. It's like on one side, I got my husband treating me like I'm blind, and in front of me, I got these guys treating me like I'm deaf. I guess that's the style these days, but it drives Joel completely nuts.

Anyway, I think they should give me a shot at announcing—at least I'd bring a little life to the party. Not like that Hannah Storm and her little pastel sweater sets and rhinestone bobby pins. Tom thinks she's sexy, and I'm like, *Hannah Storm? Are you on crack?* You wouldn't know sexy if it bit your ass off, Tom. And Tom goes, Jealous? I'm like, *Please,* you couldn't pay me a million bucks to get my hair cut like that. But maybe in my next life that's what I'll do, show her how it's done…Well, the real reason I wasn't joining the conversation was because by then I'd found out about the kids and their being Christians and I just felt really crummy. Like thinking about their eternal souls, like osmosis or breathing in secondhand smoke or something, like polluted just by standing next to me. The boys even congratulated me, patted my arm after I struck twice in a row. But I swear I didn't know they were good Christians when I high-fived them back. I don't know, maybe we should've changed lanes or something. But I mean, Joel *knew* they were Christians, and he didn't think to move. Next time, definitely, I swear.

But it's not just bowling, Joel loves almost all sports, really, but especially baseball. Joel loves the game, and I used to think, Baseball: like, *yawn.* I used to dismiss the sport completely, baseball. All sports, really, I couldn't stand to watch sports, and now I'm really starting to get into it. But with baseball, I just thought it was a bunch of guys with fat asses, scratching themselves and snorting and spitting. I didn't understand anything about the strategy of a pitch, how mathematical it was, timing, nothing. I never woulda believed how meditative it was, but I've totally come around. Joel knows all the stats, the history of teams and players and stadiums, everything, so I've learned a lot about baseball since we met. And he explained all about Irabu and Steinbrenner's fat pussy toad comment, how like in the papers, they didn't know whether to spell it *puss'y* or *pussy*. I have to admit, I thought that was pretty funny.

I just had no idea it could be so relaxing just to read the paper with the game on. Now I can barely read the Sunday *Times* without a game playing, it's just too stressful and too depressing without a game on. I didn't even know what to do with myself when the season ended, I wasn't ready for basketball. And like these days, Joel says I'm brutal, but that's not true. Thing is, if a pitcher's not performing, I say he's out. Second inning, I don't care, pull him. Pull him! Perform or get the hell off the mound! I'll yell. Joel always looks at me like he's horrified or something because I'm so quick to pull 'em. But I'm like, Look, I just call it like I see it, baby. And all I'm saying is that if he doesn't want to play like a major league pitcher, there are plenty of places for him to go.

So the first time I saw that commercial, I thought Greg Maddux was an actor, he was so perfect as the dorky guy, and so the whole Cy Young thing, it didn't really occur to me at all, it just went in one ear, out the other. I figured if it was a couple of actors, then the whole Cy Young thing, that was made up, too. I totally didn't know Maddux was a real somebody—I mean, I couldn't tell just by looking at him. Come on, it's a commercial, what was I supposed to think? What, like I'm supposed to believe he's really been doing sit-ups, too? Oh, right.

Course then Maddux totally choked against the Yankees, pulled in like the fourth, but what do you expect? It's a psychological game, and he couldn't hack it, playing in New York, and that's okay. Happens all the time. But I still think the eye surgery was a big, *big* mistake. The glasses were really sexy, kind of bookish and vulnerable, you know. But now that he can see, forget it. I'm totally over Maddux. *So over.* Now my heart belongs to just one man, and only one: and that's number fifty, the great Don Zimmer, bench coach of the Team of the Century. And I can tell you that there are exactly 204 entries on Don Zimmer on the Web, and I've read every last one of them. The very first entry is a Zim quote, *What you lack in talent can be made up with desire, hustle and giving 110 percent all the time.* What a man. Donald William Zimmer, born January 17, 1931: he's a Capricorn, which totally makes sense; same day Muhammad Ali was born. So you know they're ladies' men.

I even printed out a picture of him from when he was with the Red Sox, and he's like leaning on one knee, with one foot out of the dugout, wearing this little red hat, and he just looks so precious, I could *die.* So after Knoblauch clocked him with that foul liner in the fifth inning, and Torre was all freaked out and almost crying, I was like, Don't cry, Joe. Because I knew Zim was hit with a ball in 1953. He was unconscious for almost two weeks, so I didn't get myself too upset, because I *knew* he'd pull through. Because he's a fighter—played second base for the Dodgers, the very next year, after not being able to *speak* for six weeks, okay. He's like totally my hero. I put my hand on my heart, just thinking about him, like I pledge of allegiance to Don Zimmer. Baseball is a form of intelligence and Don Zimmer is a genius. I'm being totally serious.

And when I see him on TV, I'm like, Ohhh, there's Zim! I just get all choked up every time I see him, and if they'd leave the camera on Zim all night, my life would truly be complete. But then I got really worried, there, when he was in the hospital. I think he had some sort of heart problem, I don't know what it was. And so I kept asking Joel, Where's Zim? What's going on with Zim? Like why aren't they *telling* us anything?

Well, finally Zim returned, just as I was about to write and ask, he came back just in time. But then there was that fight— I think it was like the Mariners or something. I'm telling you, I don't care about what the players do, fisticuffs, or whatever. Doesn't matter to me if they want to look like the Stooges, bitch-slapping each other—it's such a joke when baseball players fight—but it broke my heart, to see this great, great man pushed on the ground like that during the fight. Right flat on his ass in the dirt, and after everything with his heart, what the fuck is that? I mean, talk about *that's not baseball*. Pushing Don Zimmer on the ground is *totally not baseball*. That's a goddamn travesty, is what that was. I just kept thinking of his arms flying up in the air when he lost his balance. To this day, I hope whoever it was that pushed him down, I hope they feel like total shit for the rest of their lives because that's exactly what they deserve. And they will never be forgiven in my book. *Never*.

But every time I see him, my chest wells up, and all I can do is wave my fists and quiet this screechy feeling I get in the back of my throat. And I have this fantasy—Joel knows about this, too, I tell him all the time—and it's not as bad as it sounds. I mean, *fantasy* might not be the right word for it. *Dream of dreams* might be more like it. And so my dream is of sitting on Zim's lap. That's all. Just sitting. Or maybe just sitting there and giving him a little hug and asking about his day or telling him about my day. Or we could talk about the old days, and I could ask him questions about his career…And all those times that Torre can't be cajoled, when Zim's telling jokes, I think, Me! Tell *me* that joke, I'll laugh for you, Zim! I love to laugh! I'm being totally serious here. And it's nothing more than that. Joel gives me a hard time, jabbing me in the ribs, and that's fine. I'm just like, *Get your mind out of the gutter, Joel.* Because I know I would never let it go any further than that, sitting on his lap. Just even thinking about going any further makes me sick.

This is kind of funny, too, but the very hardest thing, like when we first started living together, the hardest thing was sleeping together. Because the thing is that Joel has sports dreams, you know, dreams where he's playing in a game. Like this one time, I rolled over and put my arm around him, trying to cuddle or whatever, and then he *shoved* me. Really hard, too. And good thing I was on the inside, or he would've knocked me right out of bed, like right onto the floor. I'm not kidding, that's like exactly what he did, I swear. I hugged the man, and he shoved me, and I'm like, What the hell, Joel? So I shoved him back, not as hard, but still, and then—then he shoved me *again,* even harder than before, and he's got like seventy-five pounds on me, and I'm like—I totally yelled at him, I go: Hey! What is the matter with you? And then he woke right up and caught himself, and he was like, I'm sorry, baby, I'm sorry, I'm sorry, I was having a dream…, patting me and shit, trying to cuddle back. I still didn't know what was going on, so I was like, Get the hell away from me. *I knew you must be psycho...*

I don't know, I guess he was having a basketball dream, and he said I was *boxing him in,* okay, like how I was wrapping my arms around him. Well, I don't know if I was boxing him in or he was boxing me out, exactly, but whatever—all I know is that I became like the opponent on the court and I took an elbow in the boob, and it really hurt, and that's when I lost it. He was just lucky he woke up, I was about to pop him one. And sometimes he'll have dreams about playing baseball or whatever, and you can tell because he's like running to catch the ball, he's like probably in the outfield and it's the eleventh inning or whatever that he's dreaming. You can always tell because his knees and his feet will be kicking and everything, and he'll sort of lunge and twitch his arm... It's like sleeping with a dog sometimes, I swear.

Oh, and another thing, Joel's big thing lately is donkey shows, okay. But that was totally my mistake. Because we were talking about some friends of his who went to Tijuana in college, and he was telling me one of those old college buddy stories, and I interrupted and I go, What, let me guess, they went to Tijuana to catch a donkey show? And Joel—he's so innocent, he's like a little kid who manages to catch the one dirty word spoken in an entire conversation—he lights up, and he goes, What's a *donkey show*? Like radar or something. If I hadn't known what an innocent he was, I'd have thought he was fucking with me. Maybe he was, I can never tell.

Come on, what's a donkey show, I want to know.

A show with a woman and a donkey, okay.

What do they show?

Joel.

What?

A woman and a donkey, *okay*.

I get that much, but are they screwing or does she blow the donkey?

Joel.

She couldn't actually take a donkey all the way—

See this fork? I'm trying to eat here, okay.

I just need to know.

No, you really don't need to know.

All right, then, I really want to know.

No answer. I returned to reading my magazine, ignoring him.

Sweetheart… tell me this…

I was like, *I'm ignoring you, see? Ignoring you, leave me alone now…*

And he goes: Honey, you never—

Hey!

Just asking.

You might think that's some funny shit, but it's not. Joel, that's not funny, I said, getting up to rinse my bowl and leave the room.

I'm sorry. I am, I was just kidding, he said, grabbing my arm and pulling me to him.

The answer is no, I've never blown a donkey. There. Happy now?

So it's fellatio, not—

Stop, okay? I mean it.

Have you ever seen one, a donkey show?

Yes.

Yes?

Afraid to say I have.

Where?!

Tijuana, what do you think?

What were you doing in Tijuana?

I told you.

No, you never told me about Tijuana.

I was sightseeing, what do you think?

With one of your boyfriends?

No answer. I'm serious, leave me alone now…

You must have been a hellion…God, I don't even want to think, he says, wrapping his arms around me.

Me, neither, so let's drop it, I said, knocking my forehead against his chest.

For a while we watched *Loveline,* like all the time. Like a ball game would end at eleven, and we'd just stay up until *Loveline* was on. I thought Dr. Drew—he's *Loveline*'s board-certified internist, you know. Well, I thought he was pretty good at first, even though you always knew what he was going to say—he's so predictable. And then all the questions got to be the same, over and over again, same damn question, so I quit watching. I mean, sometimes they'll get a real doozy, like this one chick who called in—a sorority girl, naturally. She goes, I usually pass out before I get a good buzz, I don't have a very high tolerance for alcohol, you know, and one of my sorority sisters told me that if I douche with Everclear, then I'll be able to get drunk without blacking out. What do you think, Dr. Drew…? I was like, *And I'm ashamed?* Anyway.

I got really fed up with Dr. Drew always calling people *chaos creators* or whatever. I mean, get real, that's like anyone practically, chaos creators, *please*. But guys would call up and say, My girlfriend wants to get another girl to join us in sex, she wants to have a threesome. What do you think of that? I'm like, Don't you ever watch this show, pal? Don't you know that Dr. Drew's going to like tell you that your girlfriend obviously has deep, deep emotional problems, and she's trying to create chaos in your relationship, and that you shouldn't do it if you really care about her? So do you care about her or not? I mean, come on. And I was right, that's exactly what he always told them, too. And Adam, Dr. Drew's sidekick, Adam Carolla, he could be relied on to supply a lame joke or two, like a one-liner about *I wish I had your problems,* or whatever, oh, yuck yuck yuck, but then another guy would call and ask the same damn question. *Unbelievable.*

The other thing that really started to annoy me was how Dr. Drew always thinks people have been sexually abused, if they're like promiscuous or adventurous or they just want to try something different. If you aren't into like milquetoast sex, then you must have been molested. And I wasn't. There really are people who weren't molested and still get into shit in their lives. Like there are rich kids who've never known any hardship and they become drug addicts or whatever, why? What, because they feel guilty about their millions? Everyone has a story; anyone's infinitely capable of fucking up without any good reason other than the fact that they're human, and that doesn't mean you had to have been molested. I got so angry after a while. Joel even asked me if that's what happened to me, and I was like, No! No, that never happened to me.

This one time, I got really upset because this twenty-four-year-old woman called and she had like a really young voice, she sounded like a little girl, and Dr. Drew said, Susan, or whatever her name was, how old are you? She goes, I'm twenty-four, and he said, You don't sound twenty-four, you sound about nine, Susan. Did something happen to you when you were a child? And she was like, No. I don't think so. He was looking into the camera, and he was like, Are you sure? Then he went on to say how that people with young voices, childish voices like hers, they've often experienced some sort of abuse or trauma or something. And I'm really self-conscious about my voice, you know. It's like really hard for me to hear my voice or look at my handwriting. But what am I supposed to do, go to a voice therapist? I can't help it.

I've never really wanted to talk about it, but I try to tell him things, Joel. I try to put it all together for him, so he can understand. But it never quite adds up for him. It just never seems enough for him. Like I told him how I never knew my father, and that has a lot to do with it, I think.

He took off like before I was born. He left when my mom was like eight-and-a-half months pregnant. He just went to work one day and never came home again. I never understood how he could live with himself. Not like even guilt or shame, just the curiosity. Like didn't he even want to know if I looked like him? Didn't he even want to know if I was a boy or girl? Or what my name was? When I was a kid, I used to think he'd come back. I'd step out the front door and I'd try to look as pretty as I could, pretending he was sitting in a car across the street, watching me. Because I thought if he saw how pretty I was, then he'd want to come back for good. Never happened, of course. I have some pictures of him, but I have no idea where he is.

But the truth always comes out, no matter how much I didn't want him to know. I didn't want to feel pitiful. I didn't want to feel like a number, a statistic, even if I was one. Mostly, I just didn't want Joel to look at me differently. But I've never ever lied to him, and when he asked how old I was the first time I had sex, I said young.

How young?

Too young, okay.

Afraid I can't take it? I'm not that insecure, you know.

Eleven.

He stopped for a second, and it was like you could feel something around him drop to the ground or evaporate.

I'm sorry—

You had nothing to do with it.

I know, but I'm still sorry.

He turned off the TV and sat on the coffee table, taking ahold of my hands.

Don't be, he's gone.

Did they send him up the river?

No, Mom sent him to the convenience store to pick up cigarettes and Tampax.

Do you want to talk about it?

Not really. The only thing, the hard part was that she didn't believe me when I told her. I'd been suspended from school for being drunk in class, and we got into it, and I got so pissed off I told her everything. I didn't tell her because I wanted her to know, but just to hurt her. He wasn't even around anymore, and she still didn't believe me. His name was Wayne, and he used to sit on our couch and drink beer and watch games every night until he came into my room. He'd say, Are you awake…? I'd pretend I wasn't, even when he started touching me. The whole time I'd keep my eyes closed, try to breathe heavily. Like I could just sleep through it. I'd be trying to pretend I was asleep, and he'd keep trying to put my arms around his neck…That's what I remember most of all, my arms flopping all over, wishing more than anything that I could hit him back, knock him out. So that's why I reach my arms behind me when we're having sex, like when I'm on my back, you know—it's not that I'm afraid you're going to ram my head into the wall and I need to brace myself. It's just that that's how I used to be sure. Straight-arming was one way I could be sure it was my choice, and that it wasn't Wayne. You're always teasing me, saying I do that just to make my tits look better, but that's not why…Anyway, sports always kinda reminded me of him.

I wish you'd told me.

You said no rush. Now you know, it's done. It's just hard when people ask, Like when was the first time you had sex? you know. It's a simple question, but I have to think about it, and I'm like, Well, you mean the first time *I* chose, or…? I don't know what to say, because I'm not sure which time is true. But I've gone through it enough times now, I can talk about it. It's fine.

I told him how my mom was a nurse; she used to work graveyard, so I never had to be home at any certain time. She met Wayne at the hospital, he'd cut his hand on the job or something, probably on purpose, a workmen's comp scam, knowing Wayne. So when he asked her to move in with him, we did, and then we moved to Cranston, Rhode Island, when he got a transfer. And I thought Cranston would be way cooler than Des Moines, but it wasn't. Cranston sucked. We haven't really talked that much since I moved out, my mom and me. I know she always blamed me for Wayne leaving her, because we totally didn't get along, I wouldn't even speak to him or answer him. And when she'd say, *Chrissy, answer your father,* I'd just about heave. It seemed so unfair to me that my real dad left, but this loser stuck around. I know she thought I drove a wedge between them or whatever. And I was like, Whatever, you are so delusional, lady. After I told her the truth, she threatened to kick me out, she said I was lying to try to get out of being punished for the drinking, and I was like, Fuck you, I was drinking to try to get Wayne out of me, and she raised her hand, hit the roof. I can't say why, but somehow I think my dad taking off screwed with my head way more than Wayne ever could have.

That night I told Joel, he tried to hold me when we got in bed, not like sex, he wanted to like do something more than that, make love or whatever, and I couldn't—I couldn't stand it. I thought I was going to be sick. Anyway, that was like our third date. First date, I told Joel about gang banging, and third date, I told him about Wayne. He stuck around, anyway.

I once asked him what he saw in me, like why he didn't go out with someone who was more like he was, from a good family. Like someone who'd gone to good schools and lived a clean life, and he didn't even need to think about it: Because you're so wise, he said. It was the very nicest thing anyone had ever said to me, but I felt like I was being stabbed.

I guess those were the big things, but there were little things, too. Like I told Joel how I knew this girl once. This was in middle school, junior high, in Cranston. Her name was Sunny. Sunshine Morris. Sunny was a year ahead of me, an eighth grader—I guess she must've been like thirteen, then. We never spoke or anything. I didn't know her, I just knew *of* her. Everyone knew who Sunny Morris was, because she bleached her hair and wore hot pink skintight jeans, like stretch jeans, but other than that, I don't remember what she ever did to earn a reputation. I was small for my age, and Sunny seemed like *statuesque,* you know. She always kinda reminded me of a Skipper Doll whose eyes and lips had been colored with Magic Marker by some kid. But she wasn't mean or anything. She just never talked, and no one talked to her.

At lunchtime the eighth-grade boys, this group of like popular boys, used to push these mats together. They were huge, these mats, used for track, for high jumping or pole vaulting. They were for pole vaulting, I think. And the mats, they looked like enormous blocks, like these rectangular blocks with a semicircle cut out of one side. The boys used to push two of those mats together, with the semicircles facing, creating this full circle in the middle of the mats. The circles were large enough for four or five boys to fit, and then the boys would act like they were drowning.

Let me out! Help! they'd yell, acting like they were struggling to get out, trying to save themselves from drowning.

They called it the Sunny Hole. Help, help, I'm drowning in the Sunny Hole! and they'd gurgle and shit.

For a good month, during the winter, when we couldn't go outside, they couldn't get enough of that game. And everyone would hang out in the gym, because we weren't allowed to play in the halls. So everyone would watch and laugh, you know,

everyone got such a kick out of it. And I remember the day
Sunny walked in and saw them at it. I didn't notice her at first,
because I was talking with my friends, and then I heard one of
the guys yell, There she is! Help! *Help...!* I think she must've
been standing there for a while, just watching them. If you
could've seen her face—I thought she was the most beautiful
girl I'd ever seen at that moment, like just standing there, holding her head up high. She had real dignity. Didn't matter what
she was wearing, she had so much class, she just rose above
them, everyone gawking at her. Like the whole time it was
going on, that whole month, I thought they should've been saying that about me, but they said it about her, and she probably
hadn't done anything wrong at all. People just talk shit. I don't
think I'd ever seen anyone so brave in my life and from then on,
I wanted to be just like Sunshine Morris.

By the time I was fourteen, I'd completely developed. Like
tits and ass, just add water. For once, I looked older than I was,
and then I started drinking a lot, doing a lot of drugs after
school, on the weekends. I didn't hang out with my old friends
anymore. I'd just get really fucked up, party with this group of
older high school kids. I thought I might see Sunny around, like
hanging out with those kids, but I never did. I don't remember
what happened to her after junior high, what happened to her
in high school. I think she moved or something, I don't know.

So like my sixteenth birthday I spent in a frat house in
Providence. We sneaked in behind a group of freshman girls. It
made the papers later, the fraternity taping sex with unknowing
coeds and everything. It was like a BIG TO-DO. Total scandal,
everyone wanting to know who was on the tape. You can just
imagine, like every girl who ever had sex in that house was

sweating it. Of course I always wondered what would've happened if they'd found out that one of the girls was underage. I wasn't tempted to squeal or anything, but it would've been interesting. Ginny Spinelli and I, drinking a couple of Big Gulp cups full of like gin and tonic before slamming tequila shots. I remember walking upstairs, into one of the bedrooms, and this guy had built like pillars around his bed, like it was a temple or something. God, I just laughed my ass off, like, Yeah, buddy, you're a real Ivy League stud muffin… That's all I remembered, laughing hysterically about the word *muffin,* calling him *Prince Muffin,* before I totally passed out, beneath his Greek coliseum. Didn't feel a thing. Ginny didn't remember anything, either, like after I took my shirt off and stood on the table. Next day, I took three packets of birth control pills, and I got my period like the very next day. Lucky.

See, I once saw this movie where it'd killed a woman, it was like this war movie or something, and this woman *died* from having sex with so many men at once. I don't know, it was from that or maybe she just like killed herself after that happened to her, but I think she just died from it, just from like the number of men she fucked at once. It might've punctured her internal organs or I don't know what, but I saw this as a kid, and I totally believed it could really happen. And when it didn't happen, when I didn't really die, I thought, Well, I was never a good person, anyway, and now this just proves it. I thought if I'd been a good person, and if I'd been pretty enough, my real dad would never have left, but he did leave, so I wasn't. I don't know who'd understand it, but I always felt better, afterward, like after parties, I'd almost feel relieved. Things would make sense to me, you know. Like there were reasons why bad things happened.

My first serious boyfriend was Damon Grady, he was like the very first guy I ever had sex with sober. I'd known him since I moved to Cranston, because we rode the same bus. I always felt close to him in this weird way, even though he was always so mean to me, just because he was adopted. I felt like he knew what it was not to be wanted. Also, because he totally didn't get along with his old man at all. So when we first started going out, like the first month or two, before we'd ever even had sex, Damon would borrow his dad's truck. This one time, his mother found a box of Trojans in the glove compartment, and she blamed me. I mean, it wasn't any secret that she thought I was a tramp, you know. So we walked in the door, one day after school, and she was sitting at the table. She was so angry with us that she took half a day off work, and she goes, Sit down, you two. Then she launched in on how we didn't have the *decency,* on and on, and Damon let her. He gave her just enough rope, and then he was like, Look, sorry, but you're accusing the wrong person. Why don't you ask Dad who they belong to? It's his truck, after all…She was crushed. God, her face…I felt so bad for her I almost wished he'd lied.

I didn't tell Damon about the frat house until we were like halfway to California. We left the day after graduation and drove across country in his Tercel. Of course it kept breaking down, like the entire way. And so we didn't have any money. We got this great place on Los Feliz, like right beneath the Observatory, before that area became hipster central. We both took jobs at this restaurant, and one of the guys saw us going at it once, in the back, and then he mentioned something to Damon about these people he knew who did videos, you know. They wanted sexy, good-looking young couples who liked to have a good time. They wanted it to be natural. No one professional. We were always at it, why not make some dough? At least that way someone would tell me if the tape was rolling, you know. I wasn't even eighteen. Twenty-one didn't seem possible. So one thing led to another. It wasn't true at all, but for a while I really played up the whole nymphomaniac thing. I played it like I just couldn't get enough. Even with other women, I never let my guard down. Only with Damon, but then he knew everything.

Then, after a while, it was like we had to decide about doing videos with other people, group stuff, like Seymour Butts, that sort of thing, and we decided it would be okay for the videos, but nothing more. We weren't going to have an open relationship. The lowest point was like right after we broke up, four years later. I stayed in bed and watched TV for six or seven weeks straight. I didn't go outside. I didn't see anyone. I didn't even check my mailbox for like two months, and when I did, there was an eviction notice. Then I got this call, like about a week later, from this guy who heard that Damon and I split, and he asked if I needed work. I said I didn't want to do videos anymore, and he said, You wouldn't be the one on video. He said they were organizing an event, and it'd be some good exposure for me...By then I'd heard Damon'd been fucking around on me for months, and I wanted to hurt him. I don't know why I thought it would hurt him, but it kept me going.

My most vivid memory? He asked me that one time, Joel. I said I'd have to think about it, and then I never told him. Because I have the article that was written about me, and my record and everything. There's this one picture of me, and another picture of these two guys, up in the bleachers, they were pretty decent-looking guys, that's what I remember. Some of them wanted to break into the industry, so it was a good opportunity for them to get recognized. I sort of remember them, those two, but I remember the picture as if I'd see them when it was taken, the one guy looking down, zipping his pants, and the other guy just getting his shirt over his head, pulling one arm through the armhole, while looking over his shoulder at me. It's like I could swear I saw them, at that moment. So I guess I sort of made up my most vivid memory.

There was also this one guy, one time, a sex reporter or something, and he said, Are you having a good time? Enjoying yourself? It was like he knew I wasn't, but he really wanted to believe that I was, you know. I felt like he could tell, but I appreciated him asking, even if we both knew that I wasn't going to tell him the truth. I mean, come on, I'm working here, and you're going to review me, critique me or whatever, so what do you think I'm going to say? I said, Thanks for asking, that's really nice, that's all I said, though. Most people never even think to ask.

I still think of Damon all the time. Just like how he's doing, what he's up to. Then I figure if he's not dead yet, he's still giving it his best shot. Because when we left for California, you know, I really thought we'd get married and I'd spend the rest of my life with him. I was so in love with him. And I think of everything, Joel has the hardest time understanding how it was okay in the videos, having sex with other people, but not outside. Because Joel's not someone who really understands turning on and off, like flipping switches.

But so then, the next morning, after I told him, of course Joel had some questions. Like after he had some time to think about what I'd told him. But I just kept putting him off, because it was never comfortable when we talked about it. I'd just as soon behave as if it never happened, so I did. What's the point of going into detail? I'd put it this way, like, Do you need to tell me the intimate details of every woman you've had sex with? I mean, I've never asked him how many women he's had sex with. I wouldn't do that to him. To tell you the truth, I don't want to know, and I don't think it's really any of my business. Because that's my attitude about it, honestly. He tried to be respectful, but it'd come up again and again, and I would get pissed off, and then we'd get into it, and I think a time came that we just agreed to disagree. He feels he needs to know; I don't feel that way. I know I have problems with intimacy, I've known that for a while now. I'm not stupid. But what's the point in knowing if it doesn't change a thing?

So the night Dr. Drew said that thing about the woman's voice sounding like a child, I woke up on the wrong side of the bed the next morning. It was overcast outside, and I just felt so foul, you know. Course Joel noticed right away. I walked into the kitchen, and he goes: What's wrong?

I had a really bad dream.

You want to tell me about it?

Yes, but only if you promise not to get angry, I said, collapsing into one of the dining-room chairs.

Why would I get angry?

I can't say until you promise.

I'll try, how's that?

You promise to try really hard?

Yes, I promise to try not to get angry, now what is it?

Well...I had this dream that I cheated.

You had an affair.

Yes.

With whom?

Derek Jeter.

This doesn't sound like what I'd call a bad dream.

No, the thing was that you were there.

Oh, I'm sorry, I hope I didn't interrupt anything, he said, turning off the gas on the stove.

No. Well, kinda. It was like you were there, before anything happened, and you said, It's okay, honey.

I told you it was okay to have sex with Derek Jeter? Go on, babe, have fun?

Yes, that's what you said.

Well, that was pretty big of me. So what's the problem?

The problem is that afterward, I didn't want to come home, because I realized it was a test. You seemed so sincere when you gave me your blessing, but then, like afterward, I realized that you were testing me. It was a dirty trick, see.

Why would I do that?

Because! You wanted to see if I was a good person or a bad person, like if I was true, and I failed the test. I was untrue to you.

He leaned against the sink, crossing his arms and his legs, and he said, But I thought Bernie Williams was your man, I thought you said Jeter wasn't such hot stuff.

Batting .339 with twenty-nine home runs and ninety-seven RBIs in 1998, Bernie *is* my man. But he's a *married* man.

Yes…?

He's a *family man,* Joel.

And because you're a good person, your conscience chose Jeter, the bachelor.

I think so, yes. I'm no home breaker.

You wouldn't break Bernie's home but you'd break ours?

See! That's exactly what I mean. *You set me up.*

Want some coffee?

Please. You wouldn't do that to me, would you? I said, walking over to the stove. You wouldn't test me like that, would you? Because I thought that was sneaky and totally unfair. That's why I woke up so angry, I said, taking the coffee cup from him.

You were angry with me for having an affair in your dream, but you don't want me to be angry?

Yes. Please don't ever do that to me. Don't say it's okay if it's not.

Okay.

You promise?

I promise. Okay?

Okay. Thank you.

So…—he sipped his coffee, leaning against the sink and looking up—was he worth $189 million?

Every last red cent, he was. *Oh my god,* I can't even tell you, he was like so unbelievable, *you have no idea…*

He just looked at me, set down his cup, ruffled my hair, and walked to the bathroom. I followed him into the shower.

You want to give details? he asked, stepping out of his boxers.

Not really. But the thing was—I mean other than the sex, the most amazing thing was his *skin.*

His skin?

Yes! Joel, he had the smoothest skin I'd ever felt in my life. It was like rubbing your cheek across a baby butt from head to toe.

He started the water, testing it with his hand. Feel better now? he asked.

Yes, thank you, I sighed.

It was true, I felt so much better after getting that off my chest that I thought to get in the shower with him and have sex, but then I didn't. I just patted his butt and closed the shower curtain.

I guess the reason I kept watching *Loveline* was that I sort of hoped someone would ask my question. I mean, I was scared to death that it would come up, and it'd be totally awkward between us, but at the same time, I wanted someone to ask. Because the thing is that I haven't been too into sex lately. Like I've just kinda lost all interest, so that day that I saw that guy, the one on the street, that's why it didn't seem the time to mention it to Joel. I mean, like I don't even know when it started, like when I started losing interest, but it must've been like sometime right after our first anniversary.

Well, that's when I knew for sure, so I guess it was like awhile before that, but I thought it was just the stress of the wedding. There was so much uncertainty, you know. And it might seem silly, but I was afraid there wouldn't be anyone sitting on my side, you know, on the bride's side of the aisle. And then there was no one to walk me down the aisle, and I didn't know who to ask. I mean, the only man I could think of was Ray, because he always treated me like a daughter, but I didn't think Joel'd appreciate that. So I walked down the aisle alone, and the whole time, I just wanted the service to be over. I couldn't help thinking people must be feeling sorry for me. So I thought the wedding was just stressing me out, you know. And there were a few points during the honeymoon that things seemed back to normal, but it never really changed. It just started to grow.

I mean, before all of that, like the first year we went out, we were having sex all the time, all night. But then there was just this one day that I didn't want to, and then I didn't want to the next day, either, you know. Then like a week went by. And it just got to the point that like I realized I wasn't that interested, and I felt bad, and I'd tell myself, Okay, like tonight, we'll have sex tonight, we'll get back on track or whatever and everything will be fine…But then that night would come, and I just felt too worn out to deal with it. So I told myself, Okay, tomorrow, before work. I'll set the alarm and wake up early and we'll have plenty of time. So then, the next morning, I'd be like, This morning, definitely this morning, but then I wouldn't. Or sometimes I'd try, but it wouldn't be natural, it'd be like watching myself, wondering how much longer, just wanting to get it over with, you know. Like I'd have to force myself, and that didn't help any, either. I don't know why I just can't seem to get with the program.

We have sex here and there, but afterward, I'll be like, Thank god, it's done, I can take a break now. And it wasn't that I didn't come or that I didn't feel desire or love or whatever, but it was more like the desire just didn't lead to my wanting to have sex again. It just kinda stopped there. Like no matter how much I enjoyed it—and I really did—but it still didn't lead to more desire or sex. Then Joel'd think things were back on track, and he'd want to have sex the next day, all over again, and I'd be like, We just had sex, you know, how about tonight or tomorrow...? It just started snowballing, and I'd try to make excuses, but now—I don't know. I don't know what else to say about it.

I just feel so bad about it, but that only seems to make it that much worse. Like I just feel like so much *pressure*. Then I think like maybe I shouldn't worry about it, make a fuss or whatever, because it's just sex, really, but it's like kinda important to the longevity of a relationship. It's not exactly a good sign, you know. I mean, it's me—it's totally me—I'm the problem.

So that's what I was trying to figure out like why me? Why me, of all people, and that's why I'd decided to walk the hour from work to the alley, so I'd have some time to think about whatever the hell's my problem. Really, like cut the bullshit, and what the fuck is my problem, you know. Because I can tell you one thing, this has never ever, ever happened to me. I've never lost interest before.

Here's the other weird thing. On League night I usually get to the alley before Joel does, because I get off work at six. I have a job as an executive assistant at this real estate firm, and that's how we scored our apartment, because I get the listings first. And it's not what I want to do with the rest of my life, but it's okay. I'm totally organized when it comes to other people's shit, just not my own. So, anyway, I always get to the alley in plenty of time, but Joel has to come straight from work, and it's always close. And so the weird thing is that sometimes I'll just be talking to someone or whatever, and Joel'll come through the doors running, barely making it on time, and I'll just catch his figure out of the corner of my eye, and I'll think, Who is that? Like, *Whoa,* who is that guy?

Of all the surprises of our marriage, the one that surprised me the most was that I fantasized about the man I was sleeping with. Like *after* I was already sleeping with him, you know. I'd daydream about him at work, how we'd do it that night, positions, all the places in the world or even just his apartment where we hadn't had sex, and I'd almost have to take a break and run to the bathroom to masturbate. Then I'd just want to call him and tell him about masturbating in the bathroom. And I even fantasized about him *while* I was having sex with him. During the act, like as if he was another man, but it was *Joel* in my fantasy, and *Joel* I was having sex with, all at the same time, if that makes any sense. It was really confusing for me, at first I couldn't get my bearings.

Well, that's never happened to me before, and that was how I knew, from the start, you know. I mean, *no,* that wasn't the only reason I knew, of course. But it was just totally inconceivable to me before we met that somebody could actually fantasize about the person they were already sleeping with, like without even forcing themselves to. I didn't get it, how I used to hear about chicks who fantasized about their boyfriends, and I'd think, Now why would I fantasize about some guy if I'm already screwing him? What's the point in that? But that was the old me.

But now the thing I don't understand is like I love my husband, and I'm totally in love with my husband, and he's really sexy—I mean, my husband's hot, and he's a really great lover or whatever. I mean, I feel kinda funny saying that about my husband for some reason, but it's true, he's the best. Well, he's no Derek Jeter, but who is? It's not like a matter of performance at all, and so I don't know what the hell to tell him. Saying, It's not you, baby, it's me, that shit only goes so far, you know. I used to hear about people losing interest, like you hear that all the time, and I always used to be like, *Bummer,* because I totally didn't understand.

And this one time, Laurie told me about this friend or coworker of hers who hasn't had sex with her husband in ten months, and I was like, *Ten months?* Oh my god, that's so sad, but now, like three or four months, it's not so hard to imagine...There are times I think, Oh my god, am I *frigid*? Like how could that happen to me? I'm so not the frigid type. And that's what I was thinking about while I was walking to the alley, and then I saw this guy from my past, and that's when it dawned on me that I've never really been with someone long enough to lose interest. I was like, No wonder. Because I've just never hung around long enough to lose interest, so of course it's never been a problem before.

I was at my locker, taking out my ball, thinking that it really sucks, my not being into it right now, how it's so unfair to Joel, and my not being able to explain, but it's sort of a natural thing, isn't it? I mean, doesn't everybody lose interest once in a while? Then it comes back, and I think that's how it must work. But I don't know, because it hasn't come back yet. And if you think about it, maybe it's like a good thing, in a way, because at least I'm sticking around this time. So I'm laughing, you know, shaking my head, like that's so damn crude, forgetting that guy's name, Joel's really going to love this one, and then I think about it a second, and I'm like, Oh, no. Like, uh, not today, he won't. He's been trying to be really patient, but I know it's getting old fast. He's not one to come out and say something like, Why aren't we having sex? It comes out in other ways, though, jabs.

I guess it's because I've said no so many times now that he's stopped touching me. He's just not that affectionate anymore. And I can see what's happening, how he's touching me less, and so I'm touching him less…One night, I rolled over and hugged him, and he goes: What are you doing? *We don't touch in bed.* That really hurt my feelings. I know he meant to, but I don't know if he knew how bad it hurt. But when he gets mean or says something cruel, I know that's why. I know he must feel rejected, because I probably would, if it were the other way around. Maybe not right now, it might be good for us if he turned me down, like a little child psychology or whatever, that might kick-start things, who knows. But I also think he probably feels totally gypped, too, like the last problem he ever thought he'd have with me was lack of sex.

Sometimes I—I just wish he'd get angry with me, yell or something. There are times I wish he'd just say like, You know what, I was wrong about you. I was wrong. I think that's what he's going to say sometimes, when we have fights, which is happening more and more, and I'm just waiting for it to come out. I don't think he's ever felt ashamed, really, just that sometimes, I figure he must've really thought about it and what it means and maybe for like a split second he could truly imagine what I'd done. And sometimes I think maybe he'll decide that I'm not really the person he tries to see. I mean, he always tries to see the best in people, but what if he doesn't see the best in me anymore. Like what if his parents or his brothers or sisters or one of his friends finds out what I used to do, and he'll be ashamed of me. Maybe he doesn't now, but what if he was to start feeling ashamed of me. What then?

I think most couples go through this, it's just like a heavy adjustment period. But I catch myself speaking these days, and I can't believe how domestic I've become. I wake up in the morning and start thinking about dinner, and I think about the laundry and the shopping and the mortgage. And there are the dry-cleaning receipts on our refrigerator beside the postcard my dentist sends every six months. And like, What do you want for dinner tonight, honey? You know what I mean, it's like how did this happen to me?

We watch a lot of games at night, and I'll be watching and then suddenly I won't get it. I'll think, Is this what other people do? Is there something else we should be doing? Because I never really knew anyone who was married. It's not like I have any complaints, though. I'm perfectly happy with our life. I like watching games and falling asleep to *SportsCenter*. I just wonder sometimes. Like I hear my mother's voice out of nowhere, and it'll totally freak me out. Then sometimes I feel ashamed for nothing at all, really, it'll be just something I've said. Like, Hon, you want milk or no? Or, You want pasta for dinner? I'll ask, and I'll catch myself. I'll stop cold and think, What's *happened* to me? I'll hear myself saying this stuff, and I'll think, *Tortellini or ravioli?* What am I saying? Who *is* this person? You know, like who have I become? It's just that the whole little wifey thing creeps me out sometimes, and then, in my head, I'll repeat myself. Any given phrase. What time will you be home?

Hon, that's the *recycling,* not the *trash.* You. Want. Milk. Or. No. You want. Hon. Milk or no? I say it over and over in my head like I might start to understand, but I don't.

I've been thinking maybe I need to make some changes, get out and try some new things. Like my job, I've been working there two and a half years, and I've gotten promoted twice, but I don't like real estate. It kind of grosses me out, and I just don't think that's what I want to be doing with my life. I mean, I'm good at my job, I get along with everyone, my boss loves me, I never lose my cool, and that makes me feel really good. And I'm great with people, you know. It's like I feel for them, I really do. They come in and they need a place to live, and they're desperate and they're vulnerable. But the thing is, when people are vulnerable, sometimes they can behave like such assholes, you know? Well, I've just been thinking that maybe there's something else I could do.

So awhile back, I wrote the New School and City College for course catalogs or whatever. I was thinking I might take a few classes. Like anthropology always sounded interesting to me. No idea what the hell it is, I think it has to do with people's hands or something like that. Or maybe a sociology class, I think I know a little about that, at least. I don't know, it's just something I've been thinking about for a while now, and this is kind of strange, but I've been carrying the books around with me, in my bag, everywhere I go. I like to sneak a peak at the catalogs during my lunch break, read about all the courses you can take, their descriptions. It's kind of my little secret, you know. Like Joel's really into stereo equipment, and he carries his magazines around, coveting *Stereophile* or whatever, and so I call it his porn. Seriously, you can't believe the way the man salivates over like *speakers*. Well, these catalogs are sort of my porn, I guess.

So I mentioned it to Joel, and he got all excited. Do it! Babe, that's great, he said, but then I got scared. I wished I'd kept my mouth shut, kept it to myself. I don't know, I said. You don't know what? he asked. We'll see, I said. Because it kind of scares me, you know. I haven't sat in a classroom since like third quarter of my senior year. I can't even remember the last time I wrote a paper. Maybe I could just take a class pass/fail, see if I can manage that much before I get too carried away with the idea of quitting my job and going back to school. I have lots of computer skills, maybe I should just take a computer class or something basic like that, but that doesn't really interest me, it just seems like more of the same, you know. Laurie wants me to take a cooking class with her or maybe kickboxing, something just for fun, so maybe I'll start there. Joel has his basketball league once a week, things he likes to do, so like I think I need some things of my own, too.

We've been together for almost three years, married for over one year now, but sometimes I'm like still afraid to meet his old friends. Joel has a lot of old friends from like all over the place. So I'll ask to see pictures of them, before we go out to dinner, if he has any. He'll ask, once in a while, but I just tell him that I'm curious to put a name with a face. I never forget a face. Of course I might not remember right away, but I never forget. Sometimes Joel thinks he like sees someone on the street that he recognizes from the gym or the basketball courts, and I know what he means, but I don't tell him that's because sometimes if I'm slumped in a chair or whatever…I guess it's just the position. I should tell him the truth, but I don't want to

worry him. Or like, I don't know, maybe it'd sound like an ac-
cusation and he'd get all defensive. It's not like that's what I
think of his friends, it's just—you never know, you know. You
just never know about people.

The other night, Joel came into the alley, he was late and he
hadn't changed yet, and he stopped by our lane, and I could tell
something was bothering him, but all he said was, Your record's
been broken. I didn't know what he was talking about, and I
forgot all about it by the time he returned. I just wanted to
warm up, check the lane conditions, in case it was too dry or
too oily. Then I remembered what he said once we got into
bed; Joel was rubbing my hip, and I remembered. I guess I was
sort of putting him off, too, but I wanted to know. What were
you talking about when you said my record had been broken? I
asked him. He sighed and turned on his back, staring at the ceiling, with his arms behind his head.

I read in a magazine about some porn star who broke your
record.

Don't you have *work* to do at work? Must be nice, just sitting around watching porn all day…

It was a regular magazine.

What magazine, like *People*?

No, but mainstream, right beside *People*. You going to let
me finish?

Sorry, go on.

I read that this woman had sex with 250 men.

No.

Yes.

Where?

In L.A., I think.

Did you catch her name?

No.

What did she look like?

Beautiful Asian with implants.

Could you be more specific, that could be half of L.A. What did she look like?

I don't know.

You said she was beautiful.

They didn't show her face.

Then how do you know if she was beautiful…? *Never mind.* What else did it say about her?

Something about her next projects.

Like what *projects*? What do you mean by projects?

I don't remember. Just that there was a documentary about her.

She got a *documentary* out of it? A documentary? What, like it's a work of art or something?

Why does that bother you?

What bothers me is I didn't get jack, that's what. It's all about timing. Everything…Honestly, this was like a regular old magazine?

Like I said.

I just can't believe this is happening to me.

What's wrong?

Nothing's wrong.

What?

Nothing. It's just that these days, women build entire careers out of it, you know. Was her name Angel, or Coral maybe?

I don't remember.

Was it Jasmin St. Claire? No, she's not Asian. I heard about her, anyway, after I moved to New York, but that was totally different—she got paid, for one thing.

You didn't get paid?

No. It got my name out, but it wasn't about the money. And it wasn't like all this trash-talking, beating their chests stuff that I hear about these days. It was just a handful of girls who wanted to go further than anyone else could. Least that's all I wanted to do, I just wanted to go further, and I did. I did. So maybe it didn't last that long, but there was a time I'd done something no other woman had done. Maybe in the whole world. But now people are probably going to think she was the first, and she wasn't, *I* was...And I chose. It was my choice. Two hundred men.

Now you're rounding up?

Oh, like three men make a *big* difference, Joel...When I heard Jasmin got paid for it, too, I was like, Oh, yeah, well if you'd paid me ten thousand dollars, I would've blown her away...Because I didn't have a sponsor or anything. I flew solo... Well, I'll tell you one thing, at least my tits are real—least my nipples don't look like the parasols stuck in a piña colada.

That's the spirit.

And you know what, someone will blow her record away, too, one day, that's all I have to say. Twelve- to fifteen-hour events, a thousand men, $59.95 on Pay Per View. It's only a matter of time, you know.

What can you do?

I don't know...It's just like they branch out into talk shows and advice columns these days.

What else would they do?

Oh, probably become housewives and glorified secretaries, I guess.

Regretting your decision again?

What do you mean by *again*?

Nothing.

Say what you mean.

The only reason I mentioned it at all was that I thought you might realize that no one cares anymore, that's my only point. Soon enough, no one will remember what you did back then.

I will, and you will.

You got me there.

Maybe *I* should write a sex advice column.

No.

Why not?

I had a friend who wrote an advice column.

Don't you think I'd be good at it?

That's not my point.

What's your point, then?

It was depressing; she found it very, very depressing.

Why?

Because the letters were always the same, *How can I get my girlfriend to have anal sex with me?*

Really?

Ninety-five, 96 percent of the time.

Oh, come on, there had to be more questions about sex than that. Look at *Loveline.*

You're the first to say the questions are always the same.

But there has to be more than anal sex that men want to know about.

No. Letter after letter, *I want to have anal sex, but my girl-friend says no, what do you recommend?* You think you could answer that?

They're saying that the girlfriend refused, like she's already said no once before, or they've never asked, or what?

Let's say she refused, what do you tell them?

I don't know. I'd have to think about it. Sounds like they're out of luck.

Well, then, you'd probably have a hard time getting hired as a sex columnist.

They have time — they don't have to answer their husbands on the spot. You don't have any faith in me, do you?

Not true.

Well, I could do it if I wanted to. You don't think I can, but I'll prove you wrong.

I think it would upset you, that's all I'm saying. If it's something you really want to pursue, then do it.

Maybe…I guess I'm just jealous because these girls seem so much smarter about it, and I just kinda stumbled into it. No clue what was going on. Not thinking about the next day, or next week, or next year. Like no concept of time. They're such businesswomen these days, working all the angles. I didn't make contacts and do the party circuit and talk shows. I didn't work it. It's totally different these days.

Why? So you could be on *Howard Stern*. What would you like to share?

I don't know.

Do you want to go see the documentary?

No! No, I don't want to go see it, what are you *thinking*? You think it's going to like tell me something I don't know? I just want to know why she should get a documentary, people admire her for it, and what do I get?

I don't know that anyone's saying they admire her.

Yes, they are. What's a documentary then, if not admiration?

I didn't know it would upset you so much.

Yes, you did. Don't even give me that—you knew perfectly well.

I suppose you could challenge her to a showdown. Just let me know when—we'll make it a date.

Well, unfortunately for us both, I'm retired. Good night, I said, turning over, doubling my pillow beneath my head.

Hey, if George Foreman can come out of retirement—

That's *so mean,* Joel. You know that makes me sad, every time I think about it—he was not a lean, mean fighting machine. He's shouldn't have even been in the ring. Why'd you have to remind me of that? I said, smacking his chest.

I love George Foreman, and he knows it, too. I mean, I don't love him like I love Zim, of course, nowhere even close, but Foreman's up there. I even bought the grill just because I love him so much. The swirly *G* of his signature is starting to wear off the plastic, I use it so much. And I've watched his infomercial so many times now, but it tears me up when George's like hamming it up with that super-white couple, the man and woman. God, they give us all a bad name when they go, Why don't you tell us how the grill works, George? You plug it in, and then what? Then there's that part where George goes, *Oh, I loves to eat seafood! I see the food and I loves to eat it!* I don't know why it upsets me so much, but it really does.

I'm just saying, he said.

Some fights are easier to fix than others.

Well, I'm going.

What?

I want to see the documentary.

No.

I'm not asking you to go, but I want to see it.

I said *no*.

I wasn't asking for your permission.

He's not even looking at me; he's talking to the ceiling.

Please don't, Joel. Please. Look at me, I said, tucking my feet under me and kneeling, leaning over his waist.

Why shouldn't I see what it's all about? You never want to talk about it.

That's not why, you're just going to spite me.

Maybe, but I'm still going.

I don't want you to go. I'm asking you not to go, please?

I would go even if I didn't know you.

But you do—you do know me! So why are you doing this?

Why are you so angry?

I'm not angry.

What did you want out of it that you didn't get?

Nothing, you wouldn't understand.

That's always your excuse.

What do you want to know, Joel? Tell me what you want to know, then.

Never mind. Good night, and he rolled over.

I'll tell you if you promise not to go—what do you want to know, Joel? What? No answer, he didn't move. There were bleachers, okay?

Bleachers?

At first, I was just what they call a fluffer, that's just like a professional cock tease, to keep the guys hard while they were waiting. The rules are that fluffers aren't supposed to have sex with the guys, you know, get them off, because then the guys will take longer, you know, they might take forever, and that makes it that much harder on the woman…Eventually we hired out this gym, it was like a small gym for boxing, with bleachers, you know. We needed somewhere private, where we'd have time and enough room. It takes awhile, like seven hours—it can take all day. And it was sort of a crummy gym, not in the best part of town. They brought in one of those hot dog stands, like push-carts, so the guys could stay inside, get something to eat. That was smart thinking. I mean, the guys still had to pay for their own food, of course, but at least someone thought of it. There were fifty guys, that first time; they each went twice. They were told the rules: Be polite, don't come in her face, don't cut in line, enjoy. Those were the rules, first time. Then word started getting around that gang banging was where it was at, the next big thing, you know. I met Ray a few months later…I'd smile. I'd just keep smiling and smiling. And if a guy was like really nervous but polite, I'd always try to pat his head and look him in the eye, like he wasn't just another number.

I—yeah…And they'd start by rows, or what?

No. Well, not exactly. I mean, they'd stand in line, of course, but after it got started, I sort of lost track. Ray was in charge of crowd control. It was more of a first-come, first-served—on a first-come, first-come basis. That was Ray's favorite joke. He'd do sort of a stand-up routine before things got started, and he was funnier than most of the guys who do it. But that night, after, I'd have to keep like a ten-pound bag of ice between my legs all night. Ray swore by ice. He used to say ice was like more effective than morphine for the pain, and I'm sure he knew from experience, he'd been in and out of so many hospitals, but I always told him that I'd rather have the morphine, you know. Like give me the good stuff...

Who was Ray?

Oh—Ray was my manager.

You had a manager?

And a trainer, of course.

A physical trainer?

Kind of, Ray's friend Mickey. He'd come down for the fight. He'd watch for bruising. Take my temperature. Make sure there were no cuts or tearing, wipe off my forehead. Keep buckets of ice around to keep the swelling down. Mickey'd pace things, keep an eye on the guys. You can use stirrups to keep your thighs from cramping. Your back cramps after a couple hours. You get charley horses in places you never knew existed. And your pelvic bone takes such a beating...Day after, your lips swell, for one thing. Fingers—fingers can do some of the worst damage, you know, nails. You swell from like the inside out. It feels like someone's just taken ahold of each of your labia and like pulled them all the way over each of your shoulders and tucked them behind your ears or something.

What do you mean by fight?

Please, Joel? I sighed.

Don't get impatient with me, I just want to know the logistics.

A trainer for the fight. Someone to look out for you while everything's going on. Make sure you don't get too dehydrated, make sure you have enough rest, someone to be there if something goes wrong...Mickey was great, really knew his business. And you would've liked Ray, too. I mean, he never touched me or anything, it wasn't like that between us. I don't know how he got into the business, if he'd done movies or what, but he'd been really handsome once. Kinda like Rock Hudson, but straight, you know? And Ray'd seen just about everything you could imagine. People said he once woke up with a dead woman in his bed, that she'd OD'd sometime after he fell asleep. I don't think that's why he cleaned up, but I don't know, I never asked. He would've told me if he'd wanted me to know...And my *favorite* thing about Ray was he really knew how to hug, like he was all there, not like both his arms were casted, and it's all lame, you know. I trusted Ray. I still send cards at Christmas, but I can't seem to bring myself to call. So, anyway, that's why. Because when we talked about it, we'd talk like it was a fight that I had to prepare for. There's a lot of adrenaline to it, too. It wasn't like sex at all.

I understand that, but who were you *fighting*?

I don't know.

I think you do.

Drop it, okay. Can we drop it now?

All right.

I mean, what do you want? You wanted some details, you kept badgering me, I told you. You say no one's going to remember, then you keep reminding me.

I won't ask again.

Don't do me any favors, I said.

Then he just rolled over again, not a sound.

Joel? I mean, like what's she going to tell me, that it's *liberating*? Sure, tell me what's liberating about not being able to walk for three days afterward. Tell me what's liberating about not being able to sit up in bed or find a position comfortable enough so you can fall asleep. I used to wake in a puddle of water, after all the ice melted, and I could barely even squirm down to the end of my bed, find a dry place to sleep. I started sleeping on an air mattress after that. Just hung it up in the shower to dry the next morning. Try sleeping with a ten-pound bag of ice between your legs, it's not liberating. Please don't go...

Go to sleep now.

I know he takes it personally because I don't like to talk about the past. But I'm like, Give me a break, what woman wants to talk to her husband about the thousands of other men she's slept with? Really, think about it. It's not about him. At least I didn't become one of those aging porn stars, like some forty-year-old woman who still shows up at the parties, and you hear people say, *Psst,* like who brought their mother? And the old men? Totally pathetic, I would've felt sorry for them, if they hadn't been hitting on me, with like HAS-BEEN stamped across their foreheads, saying shit like, Hey-hey, you know who I am, sugar? I used to be famous...I was just like, *Hit the road, Daddy-o...* I got out. I made a clean break, started over. But Joel doesn't understand that it's more than that, like talking about other men, it's like asking me to go back. And it hurts. It didn't used to hurt, I didn't used to feel anything, really, but it does now. I don't want to go back. And I don't want to talk about it. I'm not even sure I really want him to understand.

Because what I always admired about him was that he didn't know anything about that world, or the things people do to each other in this world, that he was separate, clean. That's how I think about my husband. Like when we're watching the Discovery Channel—it's his favorite, you know—and they show healthy lungs and cancerous lungs, and the healthy lungs look like a pink sponge and the cancer lungs look like rusted pipes, that's kinda how I feel about his soul compared to mine. He's a—he's a really good, fine man. He has the biggest heart you could ever know. And I know he just wants to understand, but no matter how much I tell him, it's not ever going to be enough. Besides, that's not who I am anymore, so I don't know what to say.

We went to a bowling tournament last weekend. The tournament was on Saturday and Sunday. There were two sessions and you could bowl in both the morning and afternoon sessions, both days, if you wanted, but the deal was the highest score from both days won ten thousand dollars. They had professional bowlers there to hand over the check and give a speech and everything. And the way a tournament works, you bowl one game on one lane, then you move to a different lane for the next game, so it's like always moving. You don't really get settled in any one place, and after a while, you find out who to watch, like who the best bowlers are. At first, everyone will be throwing strikes pretty much, but after a few games, people started to fall apart.

We had some friends competing, a few guys we knew from our league, and we were going to cheer them on. But we'd had a fight that morning, because it was Saturday morning, and I was still making excuses, saying that we'd have sex when we got home, I didn't want to be late. And then Joel said something mean, and then I ignored him, and then he just didn't speak to me. So we didn't have much to say on the way to the alley, and Joel didn't even take my hand on the way, and then I was like, Forget it, then. I'm not going to have sex with him if he's not even going to talk to me. Then I said that I wasn't going to spend more than a half hour there, just to check it out, because I'd never been to a tournament before, and he said, Do as you please.

So we got there, and it was so interesting, because there were all these people I'd never seen before who showed up, and I don't know where they came from. I mean, they looked like they drove in from the Midwest. Like tons of aging men, with their slicked-back hair and their pompadours and stuff. I swear, all those brown and gray polyester slacks gave me this midwestern flashback, I felt like I was about ten again. But everyone was really nice, high-fived after each person threw. There was really a good vibe, so I just sort of strolled around, watching different people, and there were some amazing bowlers there, like I couldn't even believe how good some of these guys were. And then, out of nowhere, I saw this man who reminded me so much of my father, I stopped cold. At first, I thought it was really him, and then I was like, No, it can't be him. But I still followed him around for almost two hours. I couldn't take my eyes off him, I was afraid he might disappear again. Then Joel brought over a diet Coke to share.

Thanks, I said, handing the cup back to him. Hey, see that man? Bright red pants, matching striped Lacoste shirt, the very handsome older man, there? I asked, pointing my chin at his lane.

Yeah.

Isn't he sweet? Don't you think he's *so* handsome?

I suppose, he said, not even looking very hard.

God, he reminds me of my father. Exactly, I said, shaking my head.

What? he asked. He wasn't even paying attention to me.

I said that's exactly what my father would look like today. *Exactly*. It's almost creepy…

Chrissy, for one thing, you've never seen your father.

I've seen him in pictures, my mom had tons of pictures.

Okay, well, for another thing, he's black.

But everything else about him looks just like my father! And my dad had really, really dark skin, too. That's why everyone called him Buck—short for Buckwheat, you know. That's where I get my dark skin and curly hair, from my dad's side. I couldn't remember if I'd told Joel all this before or not.

And he also had the classy James Earl Jones thing going, my dad, he always looked like really handsome and imposing in pictures. I wondered what his voice was like…I just wanted to hear his voice once, then I started tearing up. I kept trying to swallow and roll my eyes back, but I couldn't help it. Because he was losing, the man who looked exactly like my old man, he started with like a 237, but then he slipped lower and lower. By the time Joel came over, you could tell he didn't have a chance of winning the tournament. I just felt so bad. I wanted to help him or do something, you know. Then his game got worse and worse, and no one was high-fiving him anymore, like they didn't even want to touch a loser. He'd lost his concentration or something.

When they were switching lanes, I walked over to speak to him, cheer him up or whatever. I asked him if he'd mind my sitting with him, and he said he could use the support, and then tears started running down my cheeks. Joel walks over from where he was talking to one of our friends, and he goes, Honey? And I don't know what came over me, but I go, You did great! I'm so proud of you. The man said thanks a lot and reached for the chammy to polish his ball. And I don't know what came over me, but I go, Don't you *recognize* me...? It's me, *Christine*. My name is Christine. Mom said you liked that name, I said. She said you thought it was pretty. And I wanted to ask him how he could do it. I wasn't angry, I just wanted to know how you walk away and live the rest of your life, not knowing—anything, you know. Nothing about me. I wanted to know why and how he could do that when I couldn't. I always thought he just didn't think about it, because how else could you live your life knowing you have a kid out there, and it's growing up, and you don't know it? You don't even know if— And I tried. I really did. I tried so hard to do the same thing back, but it never worked. And I thought, Why should it work for him if it didn't work for me? What am I doing wrong? I was sure there was some secret or a trick no one had told me. I'd waited thirty years to ask, and I just wanted him to tell me what it was.

The tears started rolling down my cheeks, and I couldn't even hide that I was crying, and some of the men are starting to look at me. And the man who looks like my father just looked so confused, and then Joel says, Excuse us, and he takes my hand, and he says, Come over here. Come outside with me, and he's pulling me by my hand, and then I finally remembered: Rich, I said, after we got outside, standing on the handicapped ramp, and he said, What's going on?

Rich, I said. His name was *Rich*...! That old boyfriend I saw on the street, the one who I didn't tell you about because I

was afraid you wouldn't think it was funny, that was his name…
He was the first guy I went out with after I broke up with
Damon, and I didn't tell him at first, Rich. And then when I did
tell him, because I thought he deserved to know the truth, and
he said he was fine with it, but then a couple weeks later, he
didn't return my calls, and he never said why, so I think it like
freaked him out after a while. And I felt so stupid, you know,
because I thought he really, really liked me, too. He even said he
loved me, but I never held it to him afterward, because I figured
he realized he really didn't and couldn't really love me after all
the things I'd done, so I just had to block him out. And I didn't
tell you about seeing him because I was afraid you'd be angry
with me. Because sometimes I *don't know,* and I think I see
people that I remember from before, but that wasn't what I was
thinking that time, because I was thinking about *you,* and like
what's wrong with me. I'm not trying to create any chaos, I'm
just trying to hold on, Joel, that's all. And I didn't know how to
tell you that I haven't been very interested because I've just
never been with someone this long, and it's not that I don't
love you or love having sex with you, but that's the problem,
see what I mean?

Chris…

And that time you asked me how many men I thought I'd
had sex with, and you got mad at me when I wouldn't tell you,
well, it's because I couldn't tell you if I wanted to — I don't even
know, that's how many! I don't want you to go, because no
one's ever looked at me like you do, and you won't look at me
like that anymore… You won't, Joel! You don't know it yet, but
I'm telling you. I know what's going to happen! And what's
wrong with Howard Stern, I don't understand, because you

used to like Howard Stern! You said you used to listen to him all the time. Oh, what, when you don't know the woman, then it's funny, right, is that it? You think I want to be a secretary for the rest of my life? You think that's what I dreamed of doing when I grew up? Well, it *wasn't,* Joel, that's not all I want!

Sweetheart, tell me what's going on...

And he lost, that's what. That's what's going on, Joel. He lost, he lost!

Who lost? Honey, tell me who lost?

The man who looks like my father, he lost. And he's not going to win the ten thousand dollars!

Well, he had a great hook, but he didn't have enough power behind it, and zero consistency. Zilch. It's all about consistency, you know that.

Don't say that! Is that all you *care* about? Is that all that matters to you? So what, even if he wasn't very good, so what! I know he didn't have a chance of winning, but he was trying so hard, he was giving it his all, 110 percent. And I was rooting for him, too, giving him my biggest smile so he would know it was me, and then he started choking, and he didn't even have a chance of winning. But it's just like Zim said, It could've gone either way, you know, so I didn't give up on him. I never gave up!

Chris, tell me what this is about.

I am, Joel! I am telling you. Don't tell me I'm not telling you, listen!

Okay, okay, slow down—

Jesus Christ, I used to smile every damn day, you know, heading out the front door, because I figured if he saw what a pretty smile I had, he'd want to return. Like if—god, if he just *saw* me, he'd want to come back, you know? But he didn't want to see me, and I was too dumb to figure that out. You know what it's like to smile when you step out the front door on your way to school every goddamn day, because it's like if you don't smile, oh, well, maybe that's the *one* day he's watching and then he won't want to come back? All because you fucked up? I didn't quit. And what kills me is that I tried, Joel. I tried to quit and I couldn't...God, I even know his birthday's January 17, you see, the same day Don Zimmer was born is the same day my father was born, and the same day James Earl Jones was born, can't you see the *connection,* Joel? Don't you wonder how he can live with himself, not even knowing the day I was born when I know *his* birthday...? I started sobbing. I don't think he understood a word I said.

Chris, you want to go home now?

No. I want to talk to him. I want to know how he could do that to me—I didn't do anything wrong, it wasn't my fault. So why didn't—why couldn't he have even give me a *chance...*?

I started turning around, and I was going to find the man, but Joel held my arm, and he wouldn't let me go back inside.

Let's go home. You can tell me what's bothering you when we get home. We'll have some lunch, huh? Let's just go home and you can lie down, okay?

No, I don't want to lie down, I said I want to talk to him, Joel, *no...*!

We have this picture on the wall, it's like the first thing you see when you walk into our apartment, hanging in the entry, across from the coat closet. It's from our first wedding anniversary. Because we got our picture in the paper. We went to a game to celebrate, and the Yankees won, of course, but the best thing was that Bernie Williams hit a homer, and Joel caught the ball. He'd been going to games since he was a little kid, and he'd never ever caught a ball before. And he wasn't holding it like showing off, grandstanding—god, he hates how people do that, like turning to the crowd and fanning praise on themselves. Like, Look at me! Look at me, everyone! when they catch balls, acting like *they're* the ones who hit the homer or something, even just with fly balls, like get real. Well, Joel thinks that's just so totally obnoxious, that's what he says is really the worst part about there being so many home runs in the game today, *it's precisely that sort of behavior.* Joel always says, The problem is not *the game,* it's *the fans.*

But so, anyway, that's why we got our picture taken, because Joel just held up his hand and caught the ball—didn't even flinch, he just reached up and tore it out of the air. It was so beautiful; it must've been like a minute before I realized my hands were holding my heart. I just couldn't believe it.

And I can remember the exact moment that picture was taken, and in the picture, Joel has like one arm around me, hugging me, and he's knuckling the ball in the other, and I'm wearing my Yankees cap and my first anniversary present. It's this white T-shirt that Joel had screen-printed in big red letters. It says, I ❤ Zim. Joel contacted the photographer and he got a copy of the negative and he had the photo framed and hung it up last month. But sometimes I'm like so out of it when I get home from work that I forget all about the picture and it takes me a few seconds to remember who the people are. Because I look so happy, you'd hardly know it was me. Then I'll remember, and I'll think, Tonight, *definitely tonight…*